D0064489

Fiction from Modern China

This series is intended to showcase new and exciting works by China's finest contemporary novelists in fresh, authoritative translations. It represents innovative recent fiction by some of the boldest new voices in China today as well as classic works of this century by internationally acclaimed novelists. Bringing together writers from several geographical areas and from a range of cultural and political milieus, the series opens new doors to twentieth-century China.

Howard Goldblatt

General Editor

General Editor, Howard Goldblatt

Zhang Henshui

SHANGHAI EXPRESS

Translated from
the Chinese by
William A. Lyell

University of Hawai'i Press
Honolulu

Chinese version originally serialized in
Lüxing zazhi in 1935.

English translation © 1997
University of Hawai'i Press
All rights reserved
Printed in the United States of America
02 01 00 99 98 97   5 4 3 2 1

Library of Congress Cataloging-in-Publication Data

Chang, Hen-shui, 1895–
    [P'ing Hu t'ung ch'e. English]
    Shanghai Express : a thirties novel /
  Zhang Henshui : translated from the
Chinese by William A. Lyell.
        p.   cm. — (Fiction from modern China)
    ISBN 0–8248–1825–3 (alk. paper). —
    ISBN 0–8248–1830–X (pbk.: alk. paper)
    I. Lyell, William A. II. Title. III. Series.
  PL2740.H413 1997
  895.1'351—DC21   96–40374
                           CIP

Illustrations by Li Ji

University of Hawai'i Press books are printed
on acid-free paper and meet the guidelines for
permanence and durability of the Council on
Library Resources

Designed by Barbara Pope Book Design
based on the series design by Richard Hendel

Contents

SHANGHAI
EXPRESS

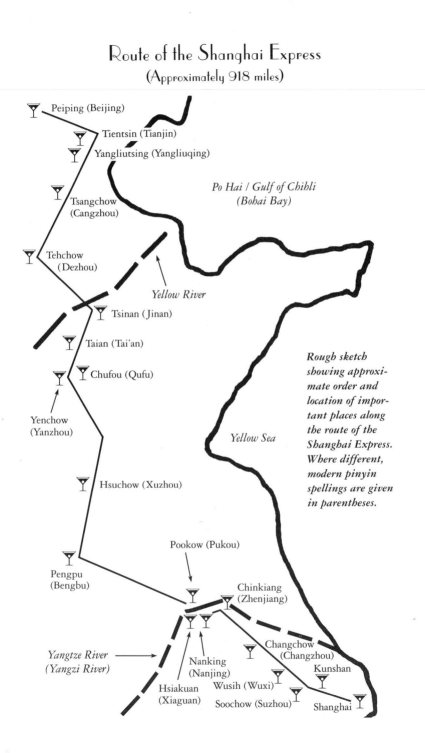

Route of the Shanghai Express
(Approximately 918 miles)

Peiping (Beijing)

Tientsin (Tianjin)

Yangliutsing (Yangliuqing)

Po Hai / Gulf of Chihli
(Bohai Bay)

Tsangchow
(Cangzhou)

Tehchow
(Dezhou)

Yellow River

Tsinan (Jinan)

Taian (Tai'an)

Chufou (Qufu)

Yenchow
(Yanzhou)

Yellow Sea

Rough sketch
showing approxi-
mate order and
location of impor-
tant places along
the route of the
Shanghai Express.
Where different,
modern pinyin
spellings are given
in parentheses.

Hsuchow (Xuzhou)

Pookow (Pukou)

Pengpu
(Bengbu)

Chinkiang
(Zhenjiang)

Changchow
(Changzhou)

Kunshan

Yangtze River
(Yangzi River)

Nanking
(Nanjing)

Hsiakuan
(Xiaguan)

Wusih (Wuxi)

Soochow (Suzhou)

Shanghai

1

Off in a Corner All Alone

If you were ever to work in a train station and had a bit of slack time, then when you saw a train pull into the station, you'd be bound to wonder, "Where are all these people coming from?" And if you saw one packed with passengers leave the station, you'd wonder, "Where are all these people going to?" What's more, there never seems to be any end to the coming and going of the trains and no end to the stream of passengers crowding in and out of them either.

Now, this is a curious state of affairs because if you think back to the days when there *were* no trains, weren't there just as many people who wanted to go on long trips? This isn't just some off-the-wall idea that I came up with out of the blue either, for even as I speak there are some people out there on the platform discussing this very issue!

It is 3 January 1935, 2:40 P.M.—twenty-five minutes before the scheduled departure of the Shanghai Express. We are in Peiping.[1] This is the East Station. You know, the one

1. After the Republican Revolution of 1911, the government was established at Nanking (lit. "southern capital"; now Nanjing) and then moved to Peking (lit. "northern capital"; now Beijing) the next year. Peking was China's capital from 1912 until 1928, when Chiang Kai-shek moved the capital back to Nanking. The Nationalist government, under Chiang Kai-shek,

by the Chengyang[2] City Gate. Passengers are pouring in. From the shish-shish and chish-chish made by every imaginable kind of shoe and boot scraping against the station platform, you can tell what a great swarm of people must be there. Yet even all the din raised by so much hustle and bustle doesn't lessen the overwhelming feeling of cold that hangs in the air. There isn't much snow—there is only whatever hasn't been swept clean from the tracks, plus the little that still nestles in the cracks between the bricks of the city wall just to the north of the station. Be that as it may, in the eyes of those passengers who look at it, it's more than enough to magnify the general impression of cold. It's a clear day, too. But once the sun is no longer directly overhead, it hides itself away in the afternoon sky, leaving the world below all the more drab and dreary.

With a great whoosh, a cold wind rises up, grabs the dry snow from the cracks in the city wall, and hurls it like so much sand against the faces of the people on the platform. Even wealthy passengers in bulky overcoats with fur collars turtle their necks in and wrap their collars tight. Even so, their noses turn red as turnips in the frigid air. Hot white vapor spews from the great steam pistons on the locomotive, while moisture condenses on the axles and drips down into thick icicles. In similar fashion, the hot breath of the porters steams from their mouths into the cold air, while clear mucus drips nonstop from their crimson noses. People in short jackets slip their hands underneath them to keep their fingers warm; they protect their ears by pulling the flaps of their rabbit-fur caps down over them, but their unprotected faces turn blue in the cold.

---

had its capital at Nanking from 1928 until the Japanese invasion of 1937. Since we are told that our trip takes place in 1935, this places the novel in the Nanking period.

2. Pinyin: Zhengyang.

Yes, it's cold out there on the platform, but on the train itself, in the first-class section, things were far different. Three men who had come to see off one of the passengers were crowded together with him in a small compartment. Although they had all taken off their fur overcoats and fur hats, they were still sweating.

Hu Ziyun, whose compartment this was, was a second- or perhaps third-rate figure in government circles. Clear-complected, round face; small moustache. Add a pair of horn-rim glasses to complete the effect, and you end up with something resembling an official. He wore a camel-hair gown lined with fine blue silk. The sleeves were rolled up, revealing a white silk shirt underneath. Mr. Hu held the bowl of a pipe in one hand and gesticulated with the stem as he spoke. As the three companions who came to see him off spoke, there was not a single serious comment in anything they said. Their coming to see him off was a formality, pure and simple. Besides, if you've got anything serious to say, you say it long before getting on a train. Mr. Hu stopped speaking now and, other than smoking, seemed to do nothing but smile. Since *three* people had come to see him off, he couldn't decide which one to speak to first and so simply smiled at them all.

"Porter, don't you have even *one* empty berth?" It was a woman's voice, gentle and feminine.

"No, not a single one," replied the porter. "Now, if you were a man, I might be able to work something out on the way, but I certainly can't arrange anything for a woman. Go to the dining car, if you please, and take a seat there."

"How can you be so unreasonable? How is it that you can work something out for a man but not for a woman? You're quite obviously bent on insulting me to my face!"

"Now don't get upset, Miss," replied the porter. "Listen while I explain. According to railroad regulations, we are only permitted to put men into compartments with other men and women into compartments with other women. At this moment, all the compartments in this coach are full. Every one of our compartments has two berths. If there was a woman in one of the compartments and the other berth was empty, I could let you have it. But if there's a man in a compartment with an empty berth, I can't very well put you in with him."

These negotiations between the female passenger and the porter had long since disquieted the entire coach. Even Hu Ziyun stuck his head out of his compartment door to see what the commotion was all about. He saw a young woman of about twenty wearing a fur coat with a high collar. In the midst of that collar there appeared a pretty, powdered face. A pair of jade earrings dangling from her lobes swung continuously back and forth with the movements of her head. Those flashing, deep black eyes and fluffy black hair were enough to captivate any man. As she raised her hand to smooth her hair, one could see a diamond ring as large as a good-sized bean on her ring finger. But how could a young woman so *à la moderne* fail to be familiar with railroad regulations?

Conscious of so many people staring at her, the young woman said, "In that case, for the time being I'll go sit in the dining car, but if a vacancy does occur, make sure to let me know." As she said this, she picked up two suitcases and, with a walk well calculated to show her figure to full advantage, made her way to the dining car.

Talking to himself as much as anyone else, the porter said, "If you get on the train without a berth reservation, you ought to take it up with the trainmaster. What good does it do to talk with the likes of us porters? Do you mean to tell me that a young woman as modern as all that has never been on a *train* before?" Just as Hu Ziyun was on the verge of asking the porter something or other, an electric bell started to ding-ding-ding: the train was about to get under way. In a great flurry of activity, those who had come to see people off got down from the train, while the passengers remaining aboard went to the windows to wave their good-byes.

In the course of so much activity, all that had previously transpired was quickly forgotten. Hu Ziyun was now alone in his compartment. He had reserved the lower berth; the top one remained empty. After the train got under way, he drew the door closed and quickly found that the compartment was even more unbearably hot than before. At this point, he took off even his robe and sat there wearing only a pair of shorts and a shirt. Looking outside, he enjoyed the passing scenery.

Hu Ziyun hadn't set foot outside of Peiping since arriving two years ago. Glad to be on the move again after such a long period of physical inertia, he was just in the mood for such sight-seeing. As soon as the train got past the Yungting[3] City Gate and into the countryside, everywhere you looked you could see the accumulation of several days of snowfall. Against all that white, peasant homes with a few bare trees around them seemed to have shrunk in size. No one was to be seen walking in the fields. This, of course, presented a desolate prospect, but at least it was one that you would not be able to enjoy within the confines of the city. How pleasant it was to sit there wearing only shorts and a shirt while enjoying this panorama of white, a panorama he continued to enjoy until the train pulled into the station at Fengt'ai.[4]

Peddlers rushed back and forth on the platform outside the train. Two things were worth noting: the hawkers of

3. Pinyin: Yongding.
4. Pinyin: Fengtai.

winter plum blossoms who held bouquets on high and the vendors of cucumbers that were thin as your finger and tied with dried reeds into little bundles of four each and arranged in flat baskets. Just as Hu Ziyun opened the window and stuck his head out, ready to ask the price, a man with two bunches of these minicumbers in his hand nodded in his direction. Ziyun said, "Well I'll be! If it isn't Mr. Li! So you're on this train too. Hurry up and come aboard so we can visit. You're just in the nick of time. I was so lonely in here all by myself that I couldn't take it much longer." Mr. Li was also all by himself and felt just as lonely as Mr. Hu and so, on running into this old acquaintance, quite readily hopped up on the train and hurried to Ziyun's compartment. The latter shook his hand and said, "Chengfu, how did you manage to get away from work at this time of year?"

Chengfu smiled and put the minicumbers down on the tea stand in front of the window. "Have some fresh vegetables. These minicumbers are a specialty along this stretch of track. They raise them in underground hothouses." Only after he had sat down did he answer Mr. Hu's question. "The school wants to make a few purchases in Shanghai, and they're sending me to take care of it."

"What number is your compartment?" Ziyun asked.

Chengfu laughed and replied, "Pauper professors like me can't be compared to a man of substance like yourself. I'm in the second-class coach."

Ziyun objected, "You must be using public funds, so what's the point in saving such a little bit of money?"

Chengfu said, "Well, that's the regulation. It's not permitted for me to make up the difference myself and go first class either. The compartment I'm in has four berths, but since I'm the only one in it, my situation isn't too different from yours up here in first class." He frowned and continued, "It certainly is *hot* enough up here in first class."

"The equipment that we Chinese use in our daily lives isn't scientificized yet," explained Ziyun. "We have steam heat, but once the steam arrives it's free to get as hot as it wants to, with no limitation whatsoever. If we were abroad, it wouldn't be that way. There you just set the temperature for whatever you want." At this juncture the porter came in with a pot of tea. You could tell from the thin uniform he wore that he too found the overheating very annoying. Ziyun queried him, "Since you are obviously aware of the overheating problem, why don't you make some improvements in the steam pipes?"

The porter smiled and answered in a thick Tientsin accent, "You're something else! Let me tell you how things are for other people. In a westward-bound uncovered car two people froze to death at T'angku.[5] To be sure, it's uncomfortably hot in here, but we ought to make the best of it."

Nodding in agreement, Chengfu smiled cheerfully and said, "He's got a point there. We really ought to make the best of it."

"Make the best of it—that reminds me of something that happened when the train started out from Peiping," said Ziyun. "A young woman got on and couldn't find a first-class compartment. Had to go sit in the dining car. But according to you the second-class coach is not at all crowded. Why didn't she go there? She'd have a place to sleep and save a little money in the bargain."

"But a lot of people getting on in Tientsin have reserved second-class berths," replied Chengfu. "Probably sold out. My good brother, Ziyun, has always had a strong chivalric streak in him that makes him look out for the welfare of pretty young women," he continued lightheartedly.

5. T'angku (pinyin: Tanggu) is a port city about thirty miles east of downtown Tientsin (pinyin: Tianjin).

"No, that's not it. It's just that what you said rang a bell with what happened in Peiping. After all, Chengfu, I already have three wives; why would I keep an eye out for another?"

Chengfu smiled and observed, "But a bigwig in the Tax Bureau like yourself has money to burn. You could easily afford four or even five for that matter."

"Well, I suppose *I* could afford it, but I wonder whether my *body* could?" Ziyun guffawed at his own humor. Chengfu picked up the teapot from the stand in front of the window, poured himself a cup, and was just about to put it to his lips when Ziyun stopped him with a wave of his hand. "Train tea is awful. Let's go to the dining car and have a cup of coffee." While saying this he stood up and donned his gown.

Also bothered by the overheating in the compartment, Chengfu stepped out into the corridor to wait for his friend. He hadn't noticed that the door of the compartment next to Ziyun's was half open. Suddenly he felt something soft and cool against his hand. He looked down. Seeing the head of a grey Russian wolfhound protruding from the partially closed door, Ziyun stepped back in alarm. Glancing into the compartment, Chengfu saw two young men dressed in Western suits. One of them was dark complected and fat, and it was he who was holding the leash. "You have to buy a half ticket to take your dog on the train," Chengfu reflected to himself. Anyone who could afford to take his dog in a first-class sleeper must have a lot of money. Initially, Chengfu had thought of telling the man to keep his dog on a tighter leash, but then he thought that since he wasn't staying in that particular compartment anyway, it really had nothing to do with him. What's more, since rich people like to get up on their high horses at the drop of a hat, Chengfu didn't feel like giving the dark fat man an excuse to jump down his throat over something that really *wasn't* any of his business to begin with. With this thought in mind, he drew back yet another step.

As Ziyun came out, he saw his friend draw back but didn't ask why he had done so. Seeing that he had gotten away with it the first time, the wolfhound stepped even further into the passageway, thrust his pointed muzzle in the direction of Ziyun, and began sniffing him all over with that strange-looking snout of his. Just as Chengfu had done, Ziyun stepped back with a start. Now, this passageway was no more than two feet wide to begin with, and so as Ziyun and Chengfu maneuvered in it they couldn't avoid bumping into each other. Not only did that fat, dark-complected young man not leash in his dog, he even squinted his chubby little eyes into an amused smile. Ziyun didn't say anything, but he did give him a dirty look before turning around and making his way into the dining car, which was right next to the first-class sleeper. Since it was much too early to eat, most of the tables were empty. A foreigner sat at one of the middle tables whiling away the time by dealing himself poker hands; a bottle of beer and a glass were set on the table before him. At the far end of the car, a group of dining-car stewards in white uniforms, some standing and some sitting, were passing their time in idle chatter.

As Ziyun entered the dining car, he put the tin of cigarettes he was carrying down on the first table. It wasn't until he turned to sit down that he noticed that a young woman was already seated at that table by the window, the same one who had earlier been looking for an empty berth. A foreign book in her hand, she was scrunched up in the corner chair by the window reading. Disturbed by the clang of the cigarette tin on the table, she looked up to find the source of the disturbance and found herself face to face with Ziyun. From his point of view, Ziyun thought he had been somewhat rash and impolite in tossing the can down without first looking, and so he couldn't help but blush. She, on the other hand, didn't seem to mind in the least and simply went back to her reading. "Excuse me," said Ziyun in a low voice as he backed down the car to the next table and sat down facing in her direction. Chengfu took the seat across from him. A steward came over, and as Ziyun ordered two cups of coffee he couldn't help but glance in the direction of the young woman.

By now she had taken off the dark fur coat with the high collar and sat there wearing a purplish red cheongsam. The sleeve openings and borders were decorated with white trim, the sleeves were cut high, the waist was formfitting, and beneath the front one could make out the clear outlines of full breasts. Although this cheongsam wasn't in the latest style, its color and the feminine figure it enclosed combined to lend it a provocative air. Holding that foreign book in her pale, smooth hands, the young woman sat there in the most artless of poses and continued to read. Ziyun wondered to himself, "What kind of woman is she exactly? She's a little too old for a student, and that kind of clothing is a bit extravagant for someone who's still in school. Could she be a social butterfly of the kind who's someone's concubine? No, that doesn't make any sense either. If you just look at the refined impression she gives sitting there reading—a foreign book at that—you can tell she's got some education behind her. Can't be a concubine." As these thoughts went through his head, he sat there with his eyes fixed steadily on this young woman.

When the steward set the coffee cups down on the table, Ziyun dragged his over to him with his left hand, all the while continuing to stare at the young woman; with his right hand he felt for a spoon, picked it up, and started stirring. "Don't you take sugar in it?" asked Chengfu. It would seem that Ziyun didn't hear him for he simply kept on stirring his coffee and staring. Though she was seated somewhat farther away, the young woman heard Chengfu's words very clearly. Slowly she lowered the foreign book and looked out over top of it in the direction of the two men; even if you didn't see her lips, from the expression in those lively eyes alone you could tell that she was highly amused. It was only for a second or so that she looked before raising the book again to eye level to resume her reading.

At this point, Ziyun took a spoonful of the coffee and put it in his mouth. It was so bitter that it curled his tongue. As he lowered his head, he discovered that the sugar bowl was still in the middle of the table. So that was it! It was bitter because he hadn't put any sugar in it yet! Noticing that Chengfu was also observing him with an amused eye, he couldn't help but feel embarrassed. He smiled and said, "I like strong tea too. That's why the bitterness of coffee doesn't bother me in the least. Ordinarily, I never put sugar into normally brewed coffee, but this stuff is so strong that I'll just have to add a little sugar. Coffee isn't like tea. When you drink tea, all that you ask is that it be hot and fragrant. You're not concerned with flavor. You know, *this* is really wicked!" He put two lumps of sugar into his cup. Just then, Chengfu bent his head down to light a cigarette. As Chengfu struck a match, Ziyun took advantage of the opportunity afforded to toss a third cube into his cup. Ziyun began to feel that he wasn't quite himself today and now no longer dared stare at the young woman all that much. Had she noticed his odd behavior? He had no way of telling.

But now it was the young woman who was talking. "Steward, is the coffee freshly brewed?"

"Yes, it is."

"All right, I'll take a cup as well." As the steward brought her coffee to her, he picked up the sugar bowl from Ziyun's

◀ Off in a corner all alone. ▶

table on the way and moved it over to her table. She took a small spoon and, stirring the coffee as she spoke, said to the steward, "Coffee has to be piping hot to be good."

"We'd never serve anything second rate in this dining car," the steward responded. "Our coffee has aroma."

"It's aroma that makes coffee enjoyable." Overhearing this, Ziyun couldn't help but be struck by the fact that the tenor of the young woman's observation was the same as his own. How could such a thing be entirely a matter of chance? And so he raised his head and looked in her direction again. Putting her book down, she held it open with her right hand, placed her left elbow next to it, and cupped her chin in her hand. She seemed to be looking half at the book and half in the direction of Ziyun's table.

As Ziyun saw it, you could say that she was so modern and uninhibited that she acted this way because she didn't care about appearances, or you could say that she actually was peeking at him. How Ziyun longed to peek right back at her! She was so modern and sophisticated, however, that he didn't dare. A woman as modern as all that wouldn't be intimidated by anyone. Who's to say she wouldn't come straight out and ask him what he thought he was looking at? On the other hand, how could a young woman who kept glancing about so boldly be annoyed by his attention? And so it was that as Ziyun conversed with Chengfu, from time to time he also looked in her direction. Furthermore, he made so bold as to talk in a good, loud voice.

"Even though we're in a recession right now," he told Chengfu, "you still see crowds of people traveling back and forth from north to south. Why just this morning I saw someone with a first-class ticket who couldn't find an empty berth in the first-class sleeper. Now wouldn't you call that strange?" At this point, the young woman was looking straight at their table and seemed on the verge of speaking. Initially, Chengfu had wondered why his friend was behaving so absentmindedly, but hearing Ziyun say this he now began to realize what was going on. How could Ziyun be talking about anyone else save the young woman sitting over there in the corner? This must be the person he was talking about when he had earlier told Chengfu that there was someone in the dining car who couldn't get a sleeper in first class. Chengfu couldn't resist turning around in his seat to take a look. She held a teaspoon in her right hand and was stirring her coffee. She held the spoon between her thumb and first two fingers and had her pinky and ring finger cocked up in the air. Her ring finger sported a sparkling diamond. Since she quite obviously came from a wealthy family, why was she traveling alone? Now that really was strange. Chengfu couldn't very well continue to stare at her indefinitely, and so after a glance or two he turned back and faced Ziyun, who suggested, "Why don't you move in with me? It only amounts to thirty or forty dollars more anyway."

Chengfu laughed and replied, "Didn't you just say we're in a recession? In that case, we ought to cut back on expenses, right? Besides, as I said before, people like me who make our living on blackboards and chalk can't be compared to important people like yourself."

Ziyun gave a cold smile. "You think too much of me. How can I be counted as a bigwig? I've got enough to get by on, to be sure, but that's about it. My monthly expenses alone must run to fourteen or fifteen hundred dollars. Just thinking about it scares even me."

"You spend *that* much every month?" asked Chengfu in surprise.

"Sure do. Can't figure it out myself. How can I possibly manage to run through all that money every month? And that's just household expenses—doesn't even include what I spend on social activities outside the home."

Just as Ziyun was hitting his stride in this exchange with Chengfu, the young woman called loudly for the steward.

When he arrived at her table, she asked, "I'd like some cigarettes. Do you have Garricks?"

"We only have Three Castles."

The young woman pursed her lips in the direction of Ziyun's table and said, "Aren't those Garricks they're smoking over there?"

The steward gave her a slight bow and replied, "They brought them with them when they boarded in Peiping. We don't carry Garricks on the train."

"You people in the dining car are stick-in-the-muds, every one of you! Never want to try anything even slightly different. All right then, go!" The steward had no choice but to smile and walk away. Now, since Ziyun was not deaf, how could he have failed to hear all this, especially since he had his eye on that young woman to begin with? Each and every word she said bored deep into his ears.

As the steward passed his table, Ziyun stopped him and asked in a low voice, "Did that young lady say she wanted Garricks?"

"Sure did, but we don't carry them on the train. Apparently, she thought you'd bought this tin after boarding."

Ziyun smiled and quoted an old saw, *"Tobacco and tea belong neither to you nor to me*—they're the kind of thing you can offer to share with anyone.[6] Why not just take this tin of mine and give it to her? All alone on a train ride, she's got to have something to relieve the boredom, right?" Saying this, he handed the tin of cigarettes to the steward.

The steward felt that Ziyun was making a bit too free in offering his cigarettes to a young woman he didn't know. Chengfu, too, was anxious about the reception such an offer would meet. After all, according to commonly accepted

6. *Tobacco and wine are neither yours nor mine (yanjiu bufenjia)* is the more commonly heard expression to the effect that such trifles are really public property.

rules of propriety, when two people meet by chance, they must rigorously respect the division that properly exists between the sexes. How then does it do to offer cigarettes to an absolute stranger of the opposite sex? However, cigarettes in hand, the steward took a distant peek at the young woman and discovered that she was still wearing a pleased expression, even though she must have heard Ziyun's comments. Since she *had* heard and didn't seem to mind, that meant she wouldn't refuse. And so the steward deliberately raised the tin on high, marched over to her table, and set them down.

He smiled and said, "These belong to the passenger there at the next table. He says that since *tobacco and tea belong neither to you nor to me,* he'd like you to have these. The young woman first looked at the tin of cigarettes and then, laughing lightly, stood up, nodded politely at Ziyun, and said, "Thank you."

"Think nothing of it." Ziyun also stood as he spoke. "Since they don't carry this brand on the train, take as many as you please."

"In that case, thank you again." Smiling, she fished out four or five cigarettes, gave the tin back to the steward, and told him to return it to Ziyun.

Ziyun, who was still standing, saw what was going on and waved his hand vigorously back and forth in her direction. "Doesn't matter. Keep the whole tin. I've got lots more in my traveling bag back in the compartment."

She smiled at him again. "In that case then, I'll just hold on to these. Thanks again." Having said this, she sat down quite naturally, lit a cigarette, and went back to her reading. Ziyun thought to himself, "You could say she's fairly uninhibited. A slightly more proper woman would never accept a gift from a stranger. Wonder if she could be a dance-hall girl? No, you'd never catch a dance-hall girl sitting there well behaved as all that and reading."

Just as he had decided that that riddle wasn't all that easy to solve, the young woman hailed the steward again. "When does this train get to Tientsin?"

"Six o'clock," answered the steward. "Are you getting off at Tientsin?"

"Well, what do you expect? Do you think I'm going to sit here in the *dining* car for two days and two nights until we get to Shanghai? I'll have to get off in Tientsin and work it out with the stationmaster so that I can change to another train."

"As long as you have a round-trip ticket, there's no problem," explained the steward. "There's no need to take it up with the stationmaster. Peiping-Shanghai round-trip tickets are good for forty days. The only requirement is that you get back to your starting point within forty days. Along the way you can get off anywhere you want to, doesn't matter a bit."

"There are a number of stations in Tientsin. If I want to find a good hotel, which one should I get off at?" she asked.

"Get off at the old station."

"Which is the *old* station?"

"It's the main station."

The young woman put one hand across the cover of her book and, lifting her head, turned her eyes away for a moment in thought. "Oh, you mean *Central Station,*" she said with a smile, giving the name of the station in English.

In general, people who don't have all that good a command of English like to say one or two words in it to show off. People who really know the language well consider that sort of thing tacky, but it's usually enough to fool the average person. And so when Ziyun heard her use two English words, he immediately decided that his latest guess as to her background—dance-hall girl—was also mistaken.

As she spoke, she opened the small purse at her side, took out a five-dollar bill, handed it to the steward, and said, "I'll pay whatever bill those two gentlemen have incurred. Just take it out of this." In his wildest dreams, Ziyun had never expected this young woman to be so generous. He immediately stood up and politely declined her offer; even Li Chengfu got up and said there was no need for her to pay. She smiled at the two men and replied, "Didn't I just hear this gentleman quote the old saw that *tobacco and tea belong neither to you nor to me?*" It was such an apt comment that Ziyun could find no comeback to it and simply let her pay the bill.

2

Relatives Met by Chance

When a man and woman eat, drink, or go sight-seeing together, it's always the man who pays the bill. This seems to have become a basic and unalterable principle. If it's reversed and the woman offers to pay, then the man will be in one of those binds expressed in the saying, *Refuse and you'll be downright rude; accept and you'll be in a guilty mood.* And so it was that when the young woman insisted on paying the bill for Ziyun and his friend's coffee, Ziyun didn't know what to do. Ordinarily, of course, he could have repaid the favor and relieved that "guilty mood" by inviting *her* to dinner. The trouble was that she had just said that since there were no berths in the first-class sleeping car, there was no way she was going to sit there in the dining car for two days and two nights until the train arrived in Shanghai. She had decided to get off the train when it reached Tientsin. That would be six, a full hour before the dining car opened for dinner. Ziyun sat lost in thought as he tried to work things out.

When the steward brought three dollars in change back to the young woman, she asked him if there were ever any no-shows among the people who had reserved berths from Tientsin to Shanghai. He smiled and responded, "Whether they show up or not is up to them; how are we supposed to know?"

"This couldn't have happened at a worse time," she said somewhat hesitantly. "If I get off and waste a day in Tientsin, I'm afraid that'll botch up what I have to do in Shanghai. On the other hand, if I stay on the train waiting for a vacant berth, it could well turn out that there just won't be one."

"If the young miss," began Ziyun rather boldly, "is willing to put up with the dining car until dawn, then the problem will solve itself because somewhere along the way —maybe in Tsinan or Taian—someone's bound to get off and free up a berth."

"Well, I do have two books that make excellent traveling companions," she said smiling, "and with a little coffee to keep me alert, I think I ought to be able to cope for a night. I still haven't had the honor of hearing the gentleman's name."

Ziyun had been itching to introduce himself to the young woman, and now she had asked him to do precisely that— just what the doctor ordered! "It's no particular honor for you to know it, but my humble surname is Hu." As he spoke, he stood and made a slight bow in her direction. At the same time, he drew his business card from his pocket and, holding it respectfully between the thumbs and first fingers of both hands, approached her. He intended to place it on her table, thus avoiding any unseemly direct contact between a man and a woman. Unexpectedly, however, she stood, walked toward him, and, inclining her body in a slight bow, smiled and received his card respectfully in both hands.

"Oh my!" she said in obvious surprise when she saw his name. Still holding the card in both hands, she raised it in front of her lips and gently laughed. Then she took another step toward him and gave him a deeper bow. "So it's Uncle Hu!"[1]

Ziyun was somewhat shocked to hear her suddenly start calling him "Uncle," but he was after all a man widely experienced in all manner of social situations, and so he calmly returned her bow and said, "I'm flattered that you should so address me. Flattered. But exactly how is it that the young lady calls me 'Uncle'?"

"Well, my own uncle," she replied, "is Yang Zilin."

"Oh!" exclaimed Ziyun. "So you're Zilin's niece."

"No, not *exactly*," she replied. "I married his nephew. I'm his niece by marriage. My own surname is Liu."

"Oh, now I get it. But Yang Zilin has *four* brothers. Which of them is your father-in-law?"

"I believe he's the eldest. You know him fairly well, too, don't you?"

"Ten years ago we were together quite a bit, but then he went back down south, and we lost track of each other after that. Didn't even correspond. But occasionally I get some news of him from Yang Zilin. How is he anyway?"

"Still hale and hearty; thanks for your kind concern." As she spoke, she made her way over to Ziyun's table. Ziyun sat next to Li Chengfu and invited the young woman to sit down across from them.

Ziyun smiled at her. "Aren't all your people down south now?" he inquired. "What was the young Mrs. Yang doing up in Peiping?"

She put her small purse down on the table and placed both hands over it. Blushing, she lowered her head and gazed down into the gap formed by her arms and bosom.

---

1. "Elder Uncle" *(laobo)*—which I have taken the liberty of translating simply as "Uncle"—is a term of respect for friends of one's father and does not necessarily signal an actual family relationship.

She said with a forced smile, "I'll be frank with you, Uncle. It makes me feel ashamed to hear anyone call me 'the young Mrs. Yang.'"

Admiring the two lush and fair-skinned hands resting on her purse, Ziyun was excited to begin with, and now he was even more intrigued by her words. There must be something to what she said; otherwise, she wouldn't object to being called "the young missus." Without thinking, he looked directly at her eyes. Though not looking at him, she seemed conscious of his stare and defensively drew her purse in closer to her bosom.

She heaved a long sigh and said, "I'm ashamed to even talk about it. In sum, in this transitional age we live in, many are sacrificed." Hearing her say this, Ziyun began to understand her a bit more. Something had probably gone amiss with her marriage. Of course, he couldn't very well come straight out and ask her if that were the case, so he decided to feel out her attitude cautiously from the flank. "Where is young Mr. Yang working these days?"

"*Working?* How could such a word possibly be associated with him? If you're talking about *play,* on the other hand, he's thoroughly at home there—ice skating, swimming, dancing, the opera, you name it. He has lots of other pastimes as well, but since there are strangers around us, it won't do to name them all." Her eyes stopped moving for a moment as she said this and filled with tears. She lowered her head, opened her purse, and drew forth a prettily designed silk handkerchief. Rolling it up into a small ball, she gently dabbed the corners of her eyes. When she was done, she returned the handkerchief to her purse. It was a simple action, but she performed it so slowly that it gave her ten seconds or so to compose herself before she had to raise her head.

Ziyun had previously heard that among Yang Zilin's nephews there was one who didn't amount to much, but since it had nothing to do with him he hadn't bothered to ask *which* one it was. From the looks of things, however, it was this young woman's husband. Since this was the first time that he had met her, Ziyun was in no position to offer her any comfort even though he realized that she was depressed. And so in order to keep the conversation going and simultaneously save her any embarrassment, he changed the subject. "Young Mrs. Yang hasn't, I daresay, been south for quite some time."

This was a question that caused her no embarrassment at all, and so she answered with a smile, "I thought I'd already announced that I really don't deserve that term of address." She took the fountain pen clipped above the top button where her dress came together, flipped over the card that Ziyun had given her, and wrote down three words: *Liu Xi Chun.*[2] The rapid calligraphy was both practiced and graceful. She handed him the card and said, "Uncle Hu, this is my surname and given name. Why don't you just use my given name? But please, I don't want to hear anything more that has to do with the Yang family."

From the very beginning of this conversation, Li Chengfu had been sitting off to one side and had not once interrupted. But he couldn't help wondering, "Since you don't want anything said about your relationship to the Yangs, how do you get off calling Hu Ziyun 'Uncle' if not on the basis of that very relationship?" As this thought occurred to him, he couldn't help but turn to look directly at her. Now, Xichun must have been one of those people with the proverbial ability to *hear with their eyes and talk with their eyebrows,* for as soon as she saw him staring, she smiled and addressed him directly: "To tell the truth, good sir, I feel

2. *Liu* is her family name. Her given name, *Xichun,* is composed of two characters *(Xi* and *Chun)* that can suggest something like "tethered to [*Xi*] spring/romance [*Chun*]"—and Ziyun probably interprets them this way.

that there's a contradiction at work here, for although I'd just as soon be free of the Yang connection, I still retain feelings of affection and respect for the elders of the family. By the way, are you and Uncle Hu in the same compartment?"

Chengfu laughed and said, "You flatter me. I'm in the *second*-class sleeper, but ever since we left Fengt'ai, I've been sitting here in the dining car. Actually, I'd better be going back now to see how things are going in my compartment." He stood and prepared to leave.

It was now Ziyun's place to ask him to tarry longer, though that's not at all what he wanted to do. On the other hand, if he just let him go, that would be rude and certainly no way to treat a friend. He stood, smiled, and took Chengfu by the hand. "You're in number 8, isn't it? I'll be by a little later." Chengfu nodded, said that he was in fact in number 8, and then left. Xichun also stood and accompanied him a few steps down the car. When he had gone, instead of going back to her original seat, she resumed her place at Ziyun's table.

Ziyun sat down and said with a smile, "I never expected to run into a relative on the train. Here you were, all alone in the dining car, and there I was, all alone in my compartment—a bleak situation for both of us. Now that we've found each other, wouldn't do any harm to stay here in the dining car and chat a bit longer."

"It would be an honor to sit here and benefit from Uncle Hu's wisdom."

At this point, Ziyun called the steward and ordered two teas with lemon. Sitting across from each other, they continued their conversation, but now it was stiff and unnatural, for whenever they touched on anything remotely connected with the Yangs, her expression turned cold. It always seemed that there was much she could say, but that she couldn't bring herself to talk about it. Nor did Ziyun particularly feel like investigating the affairs of the Yang family. Besides, since she wanted to avoid the subject, he didn't press it.

What Xichun did talk about was Peiping's opera houses, movies, and restaurants—in general, she was able to say something expert about all of Ziyun's favorite pastimes. Now they began chatting with something like enthusiasm, and before they knew it, they had arrived in Yang Village. Although express trains don't stop there, it is a comparatively large station, and they are required to slow down. As they approached the station, Xichun looked out the window to see what she could see—nothing save the platform lights and above them two words: YANG VILLAGE. Supporting herself on the table, she stood up with a cry of surprise. Ziyun could easily tell by her reaction that she was surprised they had already arrived at Yang Village and was worried that she hadn't yet made up her mind as to whether or not to get off in Tientsin. Pretending to be unaware of all that, Ziyun asked, "Has Miss Liu lost something?"

"No, that's not it. It's just that we're going to be in Tientsin very soon now, and I still haven't found out if there's any likelihood of anyone getting off anywhere to free up a berth."

By now, Ziyun felt he knew her well enough not to stand on ceremony. "Miss Liu, you've no reason to worry. I've already got it all worked out. If there's still no free berth when we pull out of Tientsin, I can double up with some other man on the first-class sleeper. In the first-class sleeper, nobody wants an upper berth, and that's why all the *lower*-berth tickets get sold out while the upper berths stay vacant. The result is that anyone who buys a lower berth has the whole compartment to himself. In other words, it shouldn't be too difficult for me to find an upper in another compartment. That would leave my compartment vacant, and you could move in."

"That, of course, would be ideal," said Xichun smiling,

"but I'd feel bad about crowding you out of your own compartment."

Ziyun raised both hands, palms out, in front of him and assured her that it wouldn't matter a bit. "It's nothing more than a matter of moving from a lower berth to an upper. Supposing I'd been in a hurry to get to Shanghai and hadn't been able to get a lower berth, I'd have had to take an upper anyway, right?"

Hands on her empty cup of tea, Xichun turned her eyes away and thought things over for a bit. Finally, she said, "Of course I'd love to take you up on your offer, but the train *is* pretty crowded today. Suppose you can't find an empty upper."

"Way I see it, that's highly unlikely. Look at the situation in my own compartment—upper berth's empty. If I were a female passenger or you were a male, we wouldn't even have a problem."

"If I were a man, the problem would never have arisen in the first place. I'd have had a berth as soon as I boarded at Chengyang Gate. The trouble is my gender, pure and simple."

"Well," responded Ziyun, "there's no real problem with my suggestion. On the off chance that I can't find an upper, I can sit it out tonight in the sleeping car, and you can have my compartment, and then tomorrow morning you can take my place in the dining car and I can go sleep my shift in the compartment. We can switch back and forth like that quite comfortably all the way to Shanghai."

Smiling, Xichun shook her head in negation, and as she did so her earrings swung back and forth against her cheeks, heightening her allure. "You belong to my parents' generation. Think how awful I'd feel depriving you of your berth." She paused for a moment in thought. "On the other hand, think of how lucky I was to run into a relative on board in the first place, one who helps me out with everything. All right then, I've made up my mind: I will *not* get off this train. Besides, when I get to Shanghai, there are quite a few things I'd like to have my uncle help out with there as well."

"Well, you and I do, after all, have old family ties. As long as there's the slightest thing I can do to help out, I certainly won't sit idly by. As soon as we get to Shanghai, I'll give you an address where you can always reach me." Ziyun was overjoyed to hear that she wasn't getting off the train, especially since her decision apparently had something to do with him personally.

Xichun smiled and replied, "I can't thank you enough, Uncle. We'll be in Tientsin any minute now. Hope you won't let anyone else move into your compartment. Otherwise, what you've said just now about letting me have the use of it will be a case of *drawing a picture of food to stave off hunger,* as the saying goes."

Ziyun frowned, thought for a bit, and said with a forced smile, "But it's going to seem unreasonable of me to just sit in there, hog up the whole compartment, and not let anyone else in. The best thing would be to. . . . "

"Let me make a rude suggestion. Why don't I just move all my baggage into Uncle's compartment. For the time being, I'll sit in the compartment as well. With the two of us in there no one else is going to move in."

"Couldn't be better!" Ziyun applauded her suggestion till his hands were red. "That way, even if somebody does get on in Tientsin with a berth reservation, once they spot a female relative in the compartment, they won't dare to come in. But we better strike while the iron is hot. I'll go get the sleeping-car porter to come move your stuff." As he spoke, he hastily motioned for the steward to come over with the bill and scribbled his name across it.

Xichun didn't stand on ceremony either, and before five minutes were out both the young woman and her baggage were in Ziyun's compartment.

Ziyun let her sit on the bunk while he sat on the little chair by the washstand. Xichun stretched a bit and yawned slightly. "Although it's warm in the dining car, it's not nearly as comfortable as it is here in your compartment."

"Well, you can set your mind at rest now. Even if someone does get on in Tientsin with a reservation for a berth, I'll just say that the lower berth is yours, and they'll have to go somewhere else." Xichun laughed at that.

"That's fine by me. I'll go along with anything you decide." The train was already stopped at New Station in Tientsin. Very few people got on or off, and Ziyun silently prayed that the situation would be the same at the Main Station as well. But it wasn't. Quite a few people got on the train. You could hear them constantly shuffling back and forth in the passageway outside. And a few of them actually did ask about berths, but luckily the porter said there was nothing available and got rid of them all one by one.

Once the car was quiet again, the porter knocked at the compartment door. When Ziyun let him in, he smiled and said, "None of them got past me, did they? I got rid of all of them for you. After the train's pulled out of the station, all you have to do is buy a ticket for an extra berth, and that will be that. But since we don't pull out for a long time yet, why not get off and stretch your legs a bit? Don't worry about the compartment; I'll lock it up for you."

The one thing that worried Ziyun was that Xichun might see something unseemly in the situation, change her mind again, and decide that she would get off the train in Tientsin after all. There would be nothing he could do about it. But if they were to get off the train right now and divert themselves while the train was stopped in the station, that might well put all her problems out of mind without even *her* realizing it. With this in mind, Ziyun smiled and suggested, "It's really quite stuffy here in the compartment. I think it would be a good idea to get off the train and stretch our legs a bit. You'd better put on that fur coat of yours, Miss Liu. If you go from a hot place to a cold one and aren't careful to wear enough, it's easy to catch cold, you know." As he spoke, Ziyun glanced at her coat on the lower berth, picked it up in both hands, and made ready to help her on with it.

Xichun stood and twisted herself around to the right position to allow him to put it on. "You really shouldn't keep putting yourself out on my behalf."

"On the road like this, we men are supposed to look after the fairer sex as much as we can." After he had finished helping Xichun, Ziyun put his own overcoat on. At this point, he couldn't have been more pleased with himself, for he was convinced that Xichun had fallen so far into his trap that now there was simply no *way* she'd get off the train in Tientsin.

When they stepped off the train, they discovered that a majority of the other passengers had gotten off to stroll around the platform as well. Especially noteworthy among them was the man with the dog from the compartment next to Ziyun's. He sported a leather jacket, riding breeches, and an otter cap. He held his dog's leash in his right hand and a riding crop in his left. He paced back and forth on the platform, looking proud as a peacock.

Now Ziyun was very put out with him to begin with because when the man's dog had sniffed at him earlier, far from apologizing for his dog's behavior, the man had actually laughed at his discomfort. And so it was that Ziyun now couldn't keep himself from nailing the man a dirty look. Far from being intimidated, the man leashed in his dog, looked boldly in the direction of Xichun, and gave a gasp of surprise. She lowered her head and moved to one side so as to keep out of his way. When he and his dog were some distance from them, Ziyun asked her if she knew him.

"I think my uncle himself ought to recognize this fellow

◄ "Xu, so you're on this train too!" ►

as well. He's a well-known Peiping troublemaker. Five or six years back, when his dad was still a warlord, he used to go around with a bodyguard, stirring up trouble everywhere he went. His dad has fallen from power now but still has a lot of money, and so his son still throws his weight around, though he doesn't dare openly break the law anymore. In my student days, we girls considered ourselves lucky not to run into him when we went downtown shopping. If you did run into him, he'd always find some way to take advantage of you one way or another. I once had a run-in with him myself, and that's why he recognizes me, though he probably doesn't know my name."

Ziyun smiled and said, "I'll bet Miss Liu isn't one to be cowed by a bully."

Xichun said, "When you meet up with a bully like that, you can't afford to show fear because the more you do, the more he'll take advantage of you."

As they strolled along the side of the train, before they realized how far they had gone, they were outside third class. Someone behind them called, "Xu, so you're on this train, too!" Turning around, Xichun saw a young woman with her head thrust out the window just opposite a peddler who was selling bread and beef jerky from a basket. This was Zhang Yuqing, her schoolmate from three years back. Xichun would just as soon not have been seen by her.

Leaving Ziyun for the moment, she hurried over to the window. "Zhang, why have you left home in such cold weather to go traveling? Come on down to the platform so we can have a good talk."

Yuqing pulled her purchases back through the window and said, "Can't. If I do, someone else'll grab my seat. Which class are you riding in?"

"First. Since you can't come out, I'll come in." She climbed back on the train as she spoke. When she pulled the door to third class open, her nostrils were assailed by a coachful of stagnant air. Inside the car, two rows of hard two-seat benches were crammed with passengers. From under the ends of those seats a large assortment of baskets and suitcases protruded into the aisle, making it difficult to walk.

Yuqing was seated in the corner of one of the two-seat benches and next to her a young man in student garb. An old couple sat on the two-seat bench across from them. Two facing benches, four people, eight legs. And in the space between the young couple and the old couple a large bamboo basket with a very high handle, two bulging bundles, assorted bags of fruit, and a scattering of small boxes of various kinds of snacks. As soon as she set eyes on the young couple, Xichun had a good idea of the relationship between them. She moved forward and shook hands with Yuqing. "*Now* I know why you're out traveling in such cold weather."

Smiling, Yuqing nodded and said, "I was going to send you an invitation but didn't know your current address. I'm really sorry about that."

"So you've already drunk the proverbial wine of joy?"[3]

"Of course," said Yuqing, "otherwise we wouldn't be traveling together."

Xichun looked at the young man, smiled, and said, "I haven't had the honor."

The young man immediately reached into his pocket and brought out a card, which he respectfully presented to her with both hands. The name on the card was composed of three characters: *Zhu,* his family name, and *Jin Qing,* his given name. Xichun laughed and said, "Well you're a real

---

3. "Wine of joy" *(xi jiu)* refers, of course, to wine drunk at a wedding; the wedding itself is referred to as an "affair of joy" *(xi shi).*

Jinqing all right, about as close to her as you can get, I'd say."[4]

Yuqing laughed and said, "Three years haven't changed you a bit—still full of the devil as ever. Have you been continuing your schooling the last few years?"

"Given the pressures of the economy, how could I afford to study?"

Yuqing laughed at that. "How can someone in first class be worried about 'the pressures of the economy'?"

"Well, it's hard to explain. By the way, where are you two headed?"

"Shanghai."

"Great. That'll give me an opportunity to explain it all in detail later on." As she spoke, she couldn't suppress a cough. She heard several other people in the car coughing as well. Xichun looked around and saw that the air was thick with smoke. The steam heat in the car didn't work too well to begin with, and so every window was tightly closed against the cold. To make things worse, seven out of ten passengers were smoking cigarettes, and in a nearby seat someone was smoking a pipeful of strong Kuantung[5] tobacco whose dry, biting aroma stung the eyes and throat. Yuqing realized what the trouble was and immediately pushed up the window next to her seat.

Xichun said, "Don't you think you two are going a bit too far in trying to save money? After all, you only have one honeymoon in a lifetime. At the very least you could have gone second class."

---

4. The first character in the young man's given name, *Jin*, means "close to," and the second character, *Qing*, is identical with the second character in Yuqing's given name. Hence, his name could be read as "the young man named Zhu who is close to Yuqing."

5. *Kuantung* is a term for northeast China.

Yuqing said, "Well, you don't see things the same way we do. As longtime students, Jinqing and I are thoroughly accustomed to living in straitened circumstances. This is nothing. All we have to do is put up with third class for a couple of days, and we'll be in Shanghai. It's no big deal. Besides, we're not on a honeymoon or even a 'sweet' moon for that matter. He's got a job in Shanghai, and we're going there to live—simple as that."

"But you're a Peipinger born and bred. Do you think you'll be able to get used to Shanghai? To begin with, there's the problem of housing. For ten-odd dollars, you might be able to get a garret at the turn of the stairs someplace, but it would be something not much bigger than a tabletop. And even then you'd have a cluster of little rooms over and under you with maybe seven or eight families crammed into them. People in Shanghai call it 'living in a pigeonhole.'"

Yuqing said, "You seem very familiar with living conditions in Shanghai."

"Don't judge me from the first-class passenger you see before you now. I've lived in my share of Shanghai pigeonholes myself." Just as they reached this point in the conversation, a shadow flashed by outside the window. It was none other than Hu Ziyun, and so Xichun said, "The train's going to pull out any minute. I'd better get off now. We'll come see you later on. Gotta go." She immediately broke away from them and got off the train.

Ziyun greeted her with a smile and said, "When Miss Liu first got on the train, she was very lonesome. Now that she's met me and run into some fellow students as well, I trust she's not lonely anymore."

Xichun smiled and replied, "She's a newlywed on her way to Shanghai to set up housekeeping with her husband. Running into her unexpectedly like that, I was overwhelmed with emotion." She sighed as she spoke.

"And you told her that you'd lived in your share of Shanghai pigeonholes too."

She paused a bit before replying to that one. "Isn't that the truth! That was the year I came to live with relatives. It was difficult for them because their home was already crowded without me. After a lot of deliberation, they cleaned up a little room that had previously doubled as a maid's room and storage room and made it into my humble abode. I felt I didn't have enough room to turn around. But the head of the house said that in Shanghai when one person has a pigeonhole all to herself, that can't really be counted as crowding because there are places where a whole family lives in a single pigeonhole!"

Ziyun thought that a person of her class would never go to Shanghai to live in a real Shanghai pigeonhole and thus readily accepted her explanation of the remark he had overheard her make to her friend. They made a couple of more rounds of the station, and Ziyun bought perhaps a half dozen more illustrated magazines, which he gave to Xichun. Ziyun found her quite amenable to his suggestions now, for she readily boarded the first-class sleeper and accompanied him back to his compartment without a moment's hesitation. With magazines, she'd have something to pass the time, even when they weren't talking, and wouldn't feel lonely.

The train pulled out of the station. Accompanied by one of the dining-car stewards, the conductor came around checking tickets again. When he got to Ziyun's compartment, he wanted to know why there was another person in it. "Are you two together?"

"Yes, we are," said Ziyun. "All you have to do is give her a berth ticket." He pulled out a ten-dollar bill and gave it to the conductor. His round-trip ticket had been checked once in Peiping, and now the conductor looked at it again along with Xichun's ticket, which was one-way.

"If you two are together, how come one of you has a round-trip ticket while the other has a one-way?"

When Ziyun had first started talking to the conductor, Xichun hadn't said anything, but now she did. "Of course I've got a one-way and he's got a round-trip. What's wrong with that? He's going back to Peiping, so he has a round-trip ticket. I'm not going back, so I have a one-way ticket. Does the railroad have some regulation against that?"

The conductor smiled and replied, "It doesn't matter, of course. It's just that I can't put a man and woman into the same compartment unless they really are together."

The steward from the dining car interrupted. "They are together. They really are." The conductor simply went on with the business of checking tickets, for conductors don't have the authority to investigate closely into the relationships among passengers. He simply took the money owed for Xichun's berth ticket.

After the conductor had left, Xichun blushed and said to Ziyun, "When Uncle paid for my berth ticket just now, I couldn't say anything. For if I had refused to let you pay, then the conductor would *know* that we weren't actually together and would have made me move out. Then everyone in first class would have found out about it, and I would have been absolutely humiliated."

Ziyun smiled and said, "Doesn't matter." As he spoke, he raised his head and leaned back. Then he smiled and continued, "I had the same sort of concern that you did, but I was worried about what would happen if I hadn't gotten a berth ticket for you. They would have made you move out in that case as well."

"Buying the ticket doesn't matter. But later on . . . later on, since I obviously can't stay here, what are we to say when I switch my berth to another compartment? How are we to explain that?"

Ziyun said, "Well, you really don't have to switch, Miss

Liu. When you come right down to it, I'm your elder, so what does it matter if we *do* happen to occupy the same compartment? If you want to remain above all suspicion, however, we'd better stick to my first plan—sleep in shifts."

After considering that for a while, she responded, "Well . . . I suppose that's the way we'll have to do it, then." Speaking in low tones, she pursed her lips and seemed a bit put out. Fearful that she just might change her mind, Ziyun didn't dare say anything in reply in case a misspoken word should upset the applecart. He smiled ever so slightly, took out his pipe, filled it with tobacco, and sat there smoking.

Suddenly, and totally unexpectedly, Xichun began to giggle. "Uncle's smoking habits are a bit odd, to say the least—you might even say 'double barreled.' You not only smoke a pipe, but you smoke cigarettes as well!"

Just now, Ziyun had felt that she was a bit put out and couldn't think of any good way of assuaging her feelings, but now that she had become cheerful again all by herself, there was no need for him to come up with any trick to bring her out of her funk; this happy circumstance in itself was more than enough to put him at ease. "I've always smoked a pipe," he replied with a broad smile. "I keep cigarettes on hand only so I can join guests in a friendly smoke when the occasion arises. I really admire Miss Liu's keen powers of observation in noting such small details!"

Xichun smiled and said, "Uncle admires me for my powers of observation, but if the truth were known, I'm actually the most slapdash person you can possibly imagine." At this point in their conversation, the conductor returned with a ticket for the berth, along with Ziyun's change. As soon as he had left, Xichun took the ticket and change and put them in her purse. Then she took a ten-dollar bill out of her purse and placed it on the lower berth.

Ziyun immediately realized what she was up to and got to his feet, frantically waving one hand back and forth.

"Take that money back right now. If you insist on doing that, aren't you openly criticizing me for not knowing how to act? Take it back. Think of what a rare occurrence it is for two relatives like us to run into each other on the train in the first place. It wouldn't be excessive even if I were to buy you a round-trip fare, much less a measly berth ticket."

Xichun looked at him carefully and said, "But it's not just *one* you know."

Ziyun said, "That's right. In the sleeper, you have to buy a berth ticket every night that you're on the train. But no matter how many nights it is between here and Shanghai, it's still only a very limited amount of money. My dear Miss Liu, take back your ten dollars right now." While saying this, he picked up the bill and thrust it into her hand. Although that was not his original intention, his action had an unanticipated consequence: his hand came into contact with that pale and tender hand of hers. She thought nothing of it, but for him the contact was nothing less than electrifying and set his entire body atingle. He did his best, of course, to remain calm for fear his reaction might cause her to shrink back.

She, however, taking note only of the polite part of his action, held the bill fast and said with a smile, "Well, since my uncle puts it like that, if I don't accept it, I'll be treating you as a stranger. All right then, I'll find some way of making it up to you after we get to Shanghai."

"Well, that's that then," said Ziyun with a clap of his hands. "After we get to Shanghai, Miss Liu can take me to the movies or perhaps even take me out dancing, and that will more than make up for this little favor I've done her."

Narrowing her eyes into a smile, Xichun studied him and said, "Do you mean to say my uncle goes *dancing?*"

"These days you have to know how to dance. Otherwise, there are many social events that you won't be able to attend. Does Miss Liu object to dancing?"

"If it's done to be sociable, I don't object to it. To tell the truth, Uncle, in order to socialize I've learned a bit of dancing myself." Dangling his pipe from his mouth, Ziyun clapped enthusiastically at her confession. Just then, a plinking sort of sound was heard in the passageway that reminded one of a Japanese koto.

"Time for dinner," said Ziyun. "Let's go."

"I was wondering what that was," said Xichun. "I thought it was someone's child out there playing with a toy. Guess it must be the dining-car steward tapping on a metal plate. But why doesn't he use a bell?"

Now how in the world was Ziyun to know the answer to that? Nonetheless, he replied, "The railroad gets more and more modern with every passing year, so naturally there must be some good reason for not using a bell."

"*What* reason?" Xichun insisted.

"Well . . . well, suppose a male and a female passenger are in a compartment getting romantic with each other and somebody comes along with a big old dinner bell: ding-dong, ding-dong. Wouldn't that be a pain? At any rate, that's the way I see it. What do you think?"

Sitting directly across from him, Xichun shifted around uneasily in her seat, blushed, and lowered her head. After a bit, she turned away from him entirely and began to giggle. Although she *said* nothing, that giggling was far more expressive than words.

3

▬

Bewitched

▬

▬

▬

In pursuing a woman, nine out of ten men adopt the strategy of incremental attack. Polite, respectful behavior signals the first stage. If the woman doesn't repel the attack with a definite refusal, then the second stage follows. This consists of demonstrations of great sympathy, going along with the woman's every whim, and comforting her at every turn. Consequently, a sense of intimacy and familiarity develops. If this stage of the battle plan proceeds smoothly, then the third stage swiftly follows. This begins with light-hearted double entendres that combine frivolity and understanding.

If the woman fails to immediately parry this third-stage thrust, or perhaps feels too embarrassed to refuse the man entirely, then the attacker moves easily into the fourth and final stage of the campaign, the stage the final goal of which is the woman's unconditional surrender.

The strategy of attack Hu Ziyun employed with Miss Liu was the incremental one described above. Although they had been together only three or four hours, he had already reached the third stage. His assessment of the situation went something like this: "When a husband can't get along with his wife, he'll either take a concubine or go whoring. When a wife can't get along with her husband, she'll behave in a similar fashion. If Xichun has taken this trip on the Shanghai Express because of some misunderstanding with her husband, it goes without saying that she's going to work off her rage by finding another man in order to pay him back. Given a situation like this, my attack has already half succeeded before it's even begun." His mind filled with thoughts such as these, he forged boldly ahead with light-hearted double entendres. It would appear that Xichun half understood what he had to say and half didn't. Her blushes, however, were gainsaid by the somewhat rakish appearance she presented as she sat there and smoked.

Sitting diagonally across from her, puffing on his pipe, Ziyun peeked at the young woman now and then out of the corners of his eyes. His mind was hard at work examining a group of alternatives: "As long as I've gotten this far, there's no reason I can't go a step further." While busily figuring out exactly *how* to do this, his gaze fell on her diamond ring. He had it! He smiled at her and said, "Miss Liu, that ring of yours is so sparkling. Did you buy it in Peiping?" Before Xichun could respond, he stood up and moved to her side of the table. Though he realized he couldn't make so bold as to take her by the hand, he thought that he might use the ploy of examining her ring to relish the beauty of her face close up.

Xichun seemed aware of what he was up to, for she shrank back a bit in her seat and said, "It's really not much of a ring, Uncle, but if you'll take your seat, I'll take it off and show it to you." Since she had clearly asked him to sit down, he couldn't very well just go on standing there. He had no choice but to sit back down in the seat he'd just vacated diagonally across from her. No matter how you looked at it, he had suffered a rebuff and was probably a bit embarrassed. Xichun seemed to pick up on this, for as she took the ring off her finger and passed it across the table, she gave him a reassuring smile.

In the wake of his disappointment at the rebuff he had suffered, Ziyun was crestfallen. When she passed the ring over to him, however, his spirits soared. He picked it up between two fingers, tilted back his head, and appraised it. Hefting it in the palm of his hand, he looked at it closely again and said, "Not half bad. A wonderful ring, really!" He had to content himself with studying the ring, however, not daring to make any move that might spook her. When he was finished with the ring, he didn't dare hand it to her directly for fear of suffering yet another rebuff. Instead, he put it down gingerly on the one-legged folding table that separated them.

Xichun picked the ring up and put it back on her finger. Although she had not looked him straight in the eye through all of this, while she was putting the ring back on she lowered her head and, peeking out from under her eyebrows, looked him over. When a woman looks you straight in the eye, that's nothing to write home about, but when she *peeks* at you like that and, what's more, you *know* she's peeking, that's more than you can take. Just at the point when Ziyun no longer dared to do anything, Xichun peeked at him, and that peek immediately set his mind to working again. He smiled and said, "What a refined person you are, Miss Liu, and with that ring on your finger you are even more so. Why. . . . "

Not waiting for him to finish, Xichun interrupted and said, "You're far too flattering, Uncle. I really don't deserve it." She spread her arms and stretched as she said this. "It's getting pretty late," she added. "We really ought to head for the dining car, shouldn't we?"

That *we* had a most agreeable ring to Ziyun. He immediately stood up and said, "That's right! I wasn't paying attention to anything except talking and completely forgot about eating." As they spoke, Xichun was the first to go out the compartment door, followed closely by Ziyun, who told the sleeping-car porter to lock the door after them.

As Xichun was going through the door that led from the sleeper into the next car, she suddenly stopped dead in her tracks and said, "Oh no! I left my purse in the compartment."

"What do you need with your purse?" asked Ziyun. "Thinking of taking money to the dining car to pay the bill? Well, let me tell you something, when you and your uncle are away from home together, it would be absolutely *unthinkable* for your uncle to take advantage of you by having you pay your own tab. From now on, stop treating me as a stranger, will you? Whenever you want something, just tell your old uncle what it is. I don't want you going round worrying about who's going to pay for things." Ziyun was so pleasantly caught up in what he was saying that he just stood there with his hand on the knob of the door that led to the next car without pushing it open. Standing behind him as she was, Xichun couldn't easily get around him to open the door and was reduced to standing there while he wound up his little speech.

At just that moment, a loud, brusque voice was heard calling for a porter. Ziyun turned around to look: it was none other than that short, fat man with the dog. It occurred to Ziyun that this fellow was a royal pain wherever he went. Ziyun was all set to give him a dirty look, but the man already seemed to know what Ziyun had in mind, for he stood there quite solidly, his hands thrust into the pockets of his riding breeches, and stared straight at Ziyun. Stranger still, he curled his shoulders slightly forward and laughed. Ziyun thought this most unusual: "Why is he laughing at me?" Xichun, on the other hand, actually seemed intimidated by that laugh for she blushed and forced her way around Ziyun in order to get out the door. Since, in terms of his priorities, following Xichun was number one, Ziyun didn't have time to stop and concern himself with the whys and wherefores of the man's laughter.

The next car was the dining car. Eight or nine seats out of ten were already taken. Ziyun stood there among the tables and looked around for vacant seats. "They're really doing a good business," he observed. "Look how full it is."

A steward immediately approached them and pointed to a table in the corner. "There's room over there in the corner. It's the same place the young lady was sitting before." As he said this, a knowing and somewhat impudent smile crossed his face. It was as though he knew that these two had started out as strangers and then progressed to their present state of intimacy. Feeling like a little boy who had been caught doing something he shouldn't, Ziyun was slightly embarrassed.

Xichun, on the other hand, didn't seem to mind in the least. "Uncle, when you're traveling, you have to make the best of things. Why not take this corner table?" she suggested as she sat down in the very same seat she had occupied earlier.

Ziyun thought to himself, "Running into a relative on the train is a common occurrence. Why then should I feel so timid and reluctant to sit here? What's more, the longer I stand, the more suspicious any friend who happened to see me would get." Armed with the courage of that observation, he sat down. But as coincidence would have it, his buttocks no sooner plunked down on the seat than a gale of laughter burst out behind him, causing his heart to take off at a gallop. "Who would dare taunt me to my face?" he wondered. Ill at ease, and anxious to see who in this dining car was aware of his little secret, he turned round and scanned the tables. He was instantly ashamed of himself for having been so sensitive, for it turned out that the laughter had come from two foreigners who were in the midst of a spirited conversation. It couldn't possibly have anything to do with him. When he turned back, Xichun was already going over the menu.

She smiled and said, "They usually don't have many things to offer on a train. I'll just eat whatever's on the menu with no substitutions. Why don't you decide for me, Uncle." She passed him the menu. As he took it, Ziyun discovered that the whole thing was written in a cursive scrawl—an English cursive scrawl at that! Now, Ziyun's knowledge of English was very limited to begin with. What's more, this was not the ordinary printed variety but chicken-track script at its worst. After staring at it for some time, he managed to make out two words—the one for "coffee" and the one for "soup," but exactly what *kind* of soup it was he had not the foggiest notion.

While Ziyun was mumbling to himself, Xichun took the menu back, looked at it, and said: "Let's see, what shall we eat? They have chicken soup, but why don't we have the oxtail instead? The entrée is a combination of salmon, pork chops, and roast pheasant. The dessert is rice pudding. What shall we substitute for that?"

As Ziyun listened to her, his heart melted, for he realized that she knew he couldn't read the menu and spoke of "helping" him while actually *translating* for him. What a considerate and charming young woman she really was! He beamed at her. "I'll have whatever you have and make whatever substitutions you make."

She lowered her head and peeked out at him from under her eyebrows. "Now, why would you want to do a thing like that?" she asked with a coy smile.

How was Ziyun to answer that? He just smiled. Xichun called the steward over. "We want oxtail soup instead of this, but make sure it's good and thick. We'll take the entrée just as it is, but we'd like to have the rice pudding a bit sweeter than it usually comes."

After the steward left, Ziyun smiled and said softly, "Miss Liu is a real soul mate. 'Thick and sweet'—that's the way I like things, too."

Xichun arched her eyebrows, smiled, and asked, "Why, whatever are you saying, Uncle?" Observing her expression, and listening to her tone of voice, Ziyun was totally flustered and didn't know how to respond. At this juncture, a few electric lights flashed past the windows. "We've been so interested in our talk," she said, "that we haven't been paying attention to where the train's going. I wonder what place we've come to now?"

"It's probably Yangliutsing."

"What a beautiful name for a town."[1]

"You don't know the half of it. The town is really worthy of its elegant name. Produces beautiful girls galore. In Tientsin, all a matchmaker has to say is that the girl's from Yangliutsing, and the match is already three-tenths guaranteed."

"In that case, I'll try and be born in Yangliutsing my next incarnation," said Xichun with a smile.

"Do you really think you'll still be down here in the realm of mere mortals after your next incarnation?" asked Ziyun. "A beauty like you ought to go to the moon to keep the Moon Goddess company."

"Uncle certainly has a way with words. It would be enough to make any girl happy just to sit and listen to him." Hearing her praise him that way, Ziyun was quite pleased with himself. On the crest of his elation, however,

---

1. The name suggests the interpretation "'the willows' [yangliu] are 'green' [tsing; pinyin: qing]." *Willowgreen* would make a pleasant name for a town in English as well. The town itself is known for the folk art produced there.

the steward arrived with their dinner, and Ziyun had no choice but to cancel what further he had to say.

After they had passed through Yangliutsing, the train began to pick up momentum and was soon hurtling south through the night. The flowers on the dining-car tables were a good indication of the train's high speed, for the ba-da-dump-bump ba-da-dump-bump rhythm of the cars flying along the tracks was so powerful that it set the begonias dancing in their vases.

Both Xichun and Ziyun ate their meals in silence. When Ziyun raised his eyes from his food to look at her, he saw that she was smiling at something or other. This time, Ziyun had raised his eyes, not to admire her face, but rather to savor the pleasure of watching her earrings swing and sway to the pitch and roll of the train. Since she happened to be smiling, however, he took another tack and asked, "Has Miss Liu thought of something funny?"

"I thought of something about my friend."

"Oh."

"You know, that girlfriend of mine in third class."

"What's so funny about her?"

"Well, she used to say that she'd never marry, but just look at her now. Speaking of friends, Uncle, how about that friend of yours? How come he hasn't come for dinner yet?"

"Oh, you mean that friend of mine named Li. It's probably because, like most people in educational circles, he's very considerate of others. He didn't want to disturb us. That's why he didn't come."

Xichun smiled and said, "What an odd thing to say. We're not the only ones in the dining car, after all. It's filled with people, and none of them is disturbing us. Why would *he* disturb us if he came?"

"But they don't know each other, and they're all minding their own business. If Mr. Li came, he'd sit with us and overhear everything we said, and that would be a bit inconvenient. He was probably mindful of that and thoughtful enough not to come."

Xichun laughed and said, "Talk about being overly sensitive! What could we possibly have to say to each other that Mr. Li couldn't hear?"

"My feelings exactly! But he probably *thinks* we have things we'd rather discuss in private. Actually, even if we did, why wouldn't we just wait until we got back to the compartment after dinner and discuss them there at our leisure?"

Xichun smiled and whispered with a knowing glance, "Let's not talk about such things. We really are in the dining car, you know." If she had just come right out and said whatever was on her mind, Ziyun wouldn't have been particularly excited. But he was positively turned on by her flirtatious glances as well as that feeling she projected of having more to say than she actually could in such a public place. How he longed to grab her by the waist and start dancing right here and now in the middle of the dining car! Noting that Ziyun's face had reddened as though the wine was beginning to get to him, Xichun stopped talking and concentrated on her food.

Although Ziyun continued to talk, she now seemed indifferent to him and responded to what he had to say only with an occasional "Mm." Ziyun was baffled. At times, this young matron was like a day in June, but there were also times when she was cold as a day in December. What was her attitude toward him, really? On the other hand, he had to remember that they *were* in the dining car, not the best of places to talk. All right then, he'd try again when they got back to the compartment. Having considered things thus far, he decided to call off his attack for the time being and, like her, concentrate on the business of eating. When they had finished, the steward brought the bill. Obviously well versed in the ways of society, and keenly aware of the male penchant for taking care of the female, he gave the bill to Ziyun instead of Xichun.

Giving it a cursory glance, Ziyun signed his name and said, "We're in compartment 7 of the first-class car."

"Yes sir," responded the steward with a bow. As he straightened up, he looked briefly at Xichun, as if to ask, "Is she staying in compartment 7 as well?" The steward's action was enough to fluster Ziyun a bit, though Xichun paid no attention to it at all.

"Going back to the compartment?" she asked with a smile. "Think I'll go see my friend in third class."

"Oh? I wouldn't do that if I were you," Ziyun admonished. "Third class is filthy—crowded too."

"That's precisely why I have to go there. Otherwise, my old schoolmate will think that I'm putting on airs." She walked away from the table as she replied.

Third class was north of the dining car, while first class was south of it, which meant that *her* route lay in the opposite direction to the one back to the compartment. "Can't stop her," he thought. "All right then, let her go sit with her friend for a while. What difference does it make? She'll be back before too long anyway."

And so it was that Ziyun went back to the compartment alone. A purse lay on the chair, and a woman's coat hung from a hook next to the door. Just an ordinary first-class compartment, but the addition of these two items lent it infinite charm. Ziyun pulled out his pipe and sat down opposite that high-collared, narrow-waisted coat. He sat staring at it as though lost in a trance. He was just on the point of reaching for a match to light his pipe when he became aware of a secondary consideration that immediately caused him to stop: if the compartment was filled with smoke from his pipe, he'd no longer be able to smell the perfume on that coat. He closed his eyes, flared his nostrils, and took a deep breath. Sure enough, he detected an odor reminiscent of powder and rouge. It was a scent that made him think of the person who wore the coat—thoughts that made him very restless indeed.

When he first caught sight of her, he had thought her pretty, and that was that. Then when he had begun conversing with her, he had felt that she was absolutely charming. And now—well, in his eyes, she was a woman so rare on this earth that you'd stand a better chance of finding her like in heaven. As he sat there, silently enjoying her perfume, he began going over things in his own mind again. She said she couldn't get along with her husband, that she was thinking of getting a divorce. Wonder if there just might be any secrets related to all of that concealed there in her purse? As long as I've got the chance, why not take a peek! He pulled together the two sides of the curtain on the compartment window facing into the corridor of the coach, picked up the purse on the chair, and then sat with his back propped against the door.

He pulled open the zipper. No secrets in the first compartment of the purse—only a compact, some perfume, and a hairbrush. The second compartment contained a stack of seven or eight ten-dollar bills as well as a good number of fives and ones thrown in at random. He could tell he was dealing with a wealthy young matron who had no conception of the value of money. Looking more closely, he discovered a small pocket in the second compartment that contained a piece of gold jewelry. Looked rather like a wedding ring. There was some sort of inscription on the inside, but he couldn't make out the words. It occurred to him that since she didn't wear her ring, the enmity between her and her husband must be intense.

Putting everything back, he opened the third compartment and found it filled with slips of paper bearing addresses and some bills for clothing. There was also a pink, Western-style envelope addressed to a woman in Hangchow. Ziyun was delighted. Here in this yet-to-be-mailed letter, he would surely be able to find some indication of her true feelings! He removed the letter from its envelope and found that it consisted of a single page and was unfinished.

Dear Ling:

Hope you won't be put out with me for not having written in so long. But for these past two months I've lost all spirit. I have utterly neglected myself, not to speak of friends. But divorce papers in hand, I'm well now. Yes, I've decided to divorce that man. You once told me that since the point of life is happiness, we shouldn't be concerned with riches and social position. At the time I thought you a bit too romantic and didn't want to take your advice. In the last two years, however, I've come to see that this one-sided fidelity only makes me suffer. . . .

The letter ended there. The tone of that last sentence clearly proclaimed her unwillingness to preserve a "one-sided fidelity." Before he has her firmly in hand, the thing a man likes to see least in a woman is a concern for chastity or fidelity. Because if she's not overly concerned with that, he can always devise a plan of attack. Had Xichun, for example, been overly finicky about fidelity to her husband, Ziyun would never have been able to get her to share his compartment, to say nothing of entertaining the hope that he just might be able to get her to share his bed. In that letter to her friend, she had said that "one-sided fidelity" only made her suffer. Not only was she not concerned about it, she even considered it a hardship! Since that's the way she saw things, she was probably like a small bird spreading its wings and ready to fly into someone's welcoming arms!

Ziyun stood there lost in thought as he slowly slipped the letter into its envelope. He returned the purse to its original place, sat down, and then in the course of smoking two pipefuls of tobacco thought over all that had transpired:

"No wonder she acted like that! I thought it odd at first that a young matron from a good family would make so free and easy with a stranger. I even suspected that as a lone woman in first class she might be there to trade her body for money. Judging from the evidence in her purse, however, I couldn't have been more off the mark. Trade her body for money? Could anyone who stuffs bills in her purse as haphazardly as she does care anything about money? I've got a handle on it now. Basically, she just wants to pay her husband back for his infidelities and isn't all that particular about what man she does it with, either. With a woman like that, I can play the old make-out game to my heart's content and not have to waste a penny in the bargain. A once-in-a-lifetime opportunity if ever I saw one. And just to think that it fell into my lap completely out of the blue. It doesn't get any better than this!" When he reached this point in his thoughts, he couldn't help but throw back his head and laugh out loud.

Having interrupted his cogitations, he now fished a gold watch out of his pocket and checked the time: half past eight. Since they'd finished eating at about seven thirty, that meant that she had been in third class for around an hour. Why didn't she come back? Third class was so crowded you couldn't even find standing room. How could Xichun put up with it? "Oh well," he thought, "she'll be back sooner or later. But when she does get here, I don't want her to suspect I've been going through her purse." He opened the door a crack, lay on the lower berth, and pretended to be sleeping. He waited that way another ten minutes or so, but Xichun still didn't show up. Unable to actually sleep, he rolled over and sat back up. Once again, he sat face to face with that coat of hers; once again, too, he was deliciously aware of a trace of perfume in the air.

He sat there quietly staring at the coat. He scrunched up his nose and sniffed. He couldn't have told you whether it was because he'd suddenly gone round the bend or whether he was intoxicated by the sight of that garment, but, at any rate, he suddenly stood up and shut the door tight as he could. And then he took a sleeve of the coat in one hand and began to breathe in its aroma while with the other hand he reached up and, ever so slowly, ever so lightly, stroked the collar again and again as though he were caressing his lover's hair by way of demonstrating the ardency of his devotion.

After Ziyun had been at this for a while, even he began to see it for the idiocy it was and sat back down to wait for her. But the more he waited, the more she didn't come. He began to suspect that perhaps she didn't want to share the compartment with him after all. But on second thought he realized that things couldn't be as bad as all that, for she had already moved her baggage in and he had bought her a berth ticket.

There was no point in sitting in the compartment brooding like this. He stepped out into the corridor and stood there. The compartment two doors down from his own was also occupied by a man and woman. The woman was standing in the corridor, too. She must have been around twenty. Her long, silky black hair hung disheveled down her back. She was wearing a scanty black silk robe with short sleeves. Judging from her costume, she must have been bothered by the heat, too. That robe was a bit on the small side, making her breasts jut out in front and her buttocks behind. Her slippers and flesh-colored stockings heightened the effect so that, all in all, she presented an extremely provocative sight. A male voice was now heard from within the compartment: "Why don't you come back in? You're just blocking the way standing out there in the corridor."

"Too hot," she answered. "At least I can catch a breath of air out here in the corridor, though it's not all that cool either."

"On a cold snowy day you're uncomfortable because you're too warm? Now I've heard it all."

"You don't mind the heat because, day or night, you stay in your pajamas. If I could run around in my pajamas all the time the way you do, I wouldn't care about the heat either."

That crisp, clear, feminine voice sounded very familiar. Ziyun wondered where he had heard it before. Just as he was trying to place it, the woman suddenly turned, and Ziyun had a clear view of a smooth-complected and slightly flushed oval face. He recognized it immediately. It was Li Mingxiao, the famous Peiping opera singer. What was someone like that—an unmarried virgin—doing parading around in such scanty attire and sharing her compartment with some man or other? Judging from the looks of things, there was probably no shortage of people who used trains as a location to gratify their desires. Just as he was watching her and thinking these thoughts, a hand reached out of the compartment and yanked her in. Everything might have been all right had Ziyun not been a witness to that. The playing out of this little scene, however, added most mightily to his restlessness, and he looked longingly at the coach door at the end of the corridor—still no sign of Xichun.

Now his thoughts took a different tack, and he began to wonder if perhaps he had showed a bit too much of his hand while talking to her in the dining car. Had that made her angry? Yes, that must be it! Otherwise, why would she have left like that as soon as we finished eating? Didn't even take the time to come back to the compartment and freshen up a bit before going to see her friend. The more he thought, the more uneasy he became, and the more uneasy he became, the more he started to move about, until finally he was pacing back and forth up and down the corridor. Now, the corridor was provided with a long rug, so he shouldn't have made all that much noise in the process, but somehow or other his pacing finally grew loud enough to disturb the other passengers until, one after the other, three people came out of the two compartments at the south end of the car.

The first, a tall man in military uniform, looked down the corridor and glared at him. The next two were foreigners, bearded priests in long black robes. They were looking at him, too. "Could they possibly know that I'm here waiting for a woman?" he thought. "Hold on, all I have to do is look natural, and that'll take care of them." He bent down, leaned against the brass rail that protected the windows, and stared nonchalantly into the night while humming a Peiping opera tune. The trouble with that was that when you stand in a brightly lit place and look out into a dark one, you see nothing. Even when he put his head against the glass and strained for all he was worth, all he could make out was the black shadows of trees that marked the location of villages. He heard laughter behind him. So the bearded priests had seen through his ridiculous ploy! All right then, the best thing to do would be to sing a Peiping opera aria and walk back to his compartment as though all was right with the world. And that's what he did.

Actually, the two priests were laughing over something that had to do with them personally and was entirely unrelated to Ziyun. The more uneasy he felt, however, the more he suspected that all laughter was directed at him, and the more he felt that people were laughing at him personally, the more uneasy he became. Once again, he lay down on the lower berth, gazed at that coat, and began to think of Xichun again. "What am I so upset about? If she does want to move, she's got to come here to get her things first. And when she does come, I'll be able to question her and explain things, won't I? So why get myself all worked up now?" These thoughts calmed him somewhat. He took out his pipe and filled it with tobacco. Just as he was about to light it, however, another thought occurred to him. "If she really does come back and move out, how can I do anything to stop her? And since I won't be able to stop her, I'll be reduced to sitting here wide-eyed, helplessly watching while she carts her stuff away."

At this point, he heard a porter out in the corridor say, "Where are you moving to? All right then, I'll move you over there right away. It's a lot better there than where you're staying right now."

"That's it! It's all over! She really is going to move out. I'll just have to remain calm and let her go, act as though it doesn't bother me a bit. Bide my time till I get another chance later." He put his pipe in his mouth and lay down on the berth again. He didn't even want to hear any more of what was going on out in the corridor. Nonetheless, he couldn't fail to notice a chaos of footsteps passing his own compartment and headed someplace else. He couldn't resist poking his head out into the corridor to see exactly what was going on, and when he did see, he couldn't help laughing.

4

▬

A Typical Passenger in the Second-Class Sleeper

▬

▬

▬

Since Hu Ziyun was on pins and needles for fear the young woman named Liu Xichun would move out of his compartment, everything he saw or heard suggested that this was in fact the case. Finally, when he heard talk in the corridor indicating that she really and truly *was* going to leave, he immediately thrust his head out the compartment door to see what was going on. It turned out that what was going to be moved was not a person but rather two sacks of fruit resting against the steam pipes, where they were sure to be ruined by the heat. Two porters were moving the sacks into the washroom by the coach door. It was cooler there owing to the wind that came through the cracks.

From the looks of things, his assumption that Xichun was about to move out was nothing more than a wild guess with no basis in reality. As he calmed down, Ziyun began to realize that if he continued to sit there and let his mind ramble at will, there was no telling what sort of nonsense he might dream up. His best bet would be to go to the second-class coach and have a good chat with Li Chengfu and thereby exchange all the present impressions in his mind for a fresh set. He instructed the porter to lock up his compartment but to let Xichun in if and when she came back. This was necessary because porters will not allow strangers to enter the sleeper compartments. But now, given Ziyun's instructions, there would of course be no problem for Miss Liu.

Pitching and rolling with the motions of the train, Ziyun made his way through several sections of the train to the second-class coach. Like first class, this too consisted of a corridor running along a series of compartments. Unlike first class, however, it was quite noisy: raucous voices vied in talking over each other, and wherever a compartment door was open, you were greeted by thick clouds of tobacco smoke. From some of the compartments legs were thrust at random out into the corridor, impeding your progress. Ziyun was puzzled. "Didn't Li say that second class was fairly roomy?" he wondered. "How come it's so crowded? Well, maybe it's different in his compartment." Ziyun forged ahead, checking the door numbers as he went.

When he got to Chengfu's compartment, he was in for a surprise. He had imagined that, except for Chengfu, it would be empty, that he would be able to go in, sit down, and have a good chat with his friend. As he looked in now, however, he saw that all four berths were taken and the floor space between the lower two was crammed tight with sacks, baskets, suitcases, bottles of wine, and hampers of pickled vegetables. Now, you might have thought that there would be at least some space under the one-legged table by the window. In fact, however, the area inside the triangle formed by the leg that came up from the base of the car and the little table it supported was stuffed full of every sort of thing imaginable as well. Some of the stuff even stuck out far enough to intrude into the lower berths.

As was the case in all the other compartments, the little table had originally had an enamelware spittoon beneath it. In Chengfu's compartment, however, the spittoon had been

crowded out into the middle of the floor, where it was strad-
dled by a pair of shoes that someone had taken off. Small to
begin with, the spittoon itself was filled to the brim with a
chaos of orange peels, pear pits, and crumpled balls of wax
paper that had once held preserved dried plums. All of this
in turn was covered by a sprinkling of saliva, cigarette butts,
and phlegm. Definitely not a pleasant sight to behold. The
floor—what little could be seen of it—was carpeted with
matchsticks and the shells of watermelon seeds. There was
no place you could set foot without stepping on something.

Two passengers were stretched out in the upper berths,
while Li Chengfu sat on one of the lower ones. Leaning
against the wall of the car, a cigarette dangling from his
lips, Chengfu seemed very bored. The man seated on the
berth across from him and the two passengers in the upper
berths, on the other hand, were carrying on a loud and spirited conversation in their native dialect. Had you provided
the compartment with a set of gongs and drums going full
blast, it could hardly have been any noisier. Although
Chengfu didn't say anything, you could tell by the way he
kept knitting his brows that he found all that racket
immensely annoying but had no way of escaping it.

Standing outside the compartment door, Ziyun called
out his friend's name. Chengfu immediately raised his head,
broke into a broad smile, stood up, and invited Ziyun to
come in. "You couldn't have picked a better time to drop by
for a chat. I was bored silly." Ziyun went in and squeezed
onto his friend's berth, a berth so crowded with things that
there was barely enough room to accommodate him.

Before he had a chance to say anything, Ziyun was
brought up short by a very strange odor. He frowned, flared
his nostrils in and out, and asked, "What's that smell?"

Looking at the man in the berth across from him,
Chengfu smiled and responded, "Hard to say." Ziyun
immediately realized that it must be coming from those

pickled vegetables and Tientsin-smoked chicken spread out on the opposite berth.

"Here I thought that you'd be lonesome in here all by yourself, but actually it's just the opposite—lively as can be."

"I thought the same thing when we pulled out of Peiping," Chengfu explained. "Actually, I found it comfortable rather than lonely. But there was a surprise in store for me when we got to Tientsin. An enormous number of passengers boarded the second-class sleeper, so many, in fact, that a lot of them couldn't find berths. I daresay a lot of people must have gotten on up there in first class as well. Bit crowded up there now, are you?"

It was a totally innocent question, but when Ziyun heard it, his face reddened into a full-blown blush. Seeing him like that, Chengfu realized that he must have pushed the wrong button and immediately took a different tack. "Buy any good books when we were passing through Tientsin?"

"Since I'm not the studious type to begin with, why would I be interested in buying good books? Train's not much of a place for study anyway."

Chengfu laughed and said, "You don't get it. I'm not talking about ordinary books. The 'good' books I'm talking about are bad books, if you know what I mean. Remember those vendors who got on the train back there in Tientsin along that stretch of track between New Station and Old Station? Ordinarily, they just sell run-of-the-mill magazines and books. But if you ask them on the sly whether they have any *good* books, they'll sell you sexy novels. On a long, lonely journey, don't you think 'good' books like those would be more fun than even the liveliest conversation here in this compartment?" He laughed at his own question. What he had just said, of course, was a reproach to his three compartment mates, but they weren't at all aware of it.

One of them had just been up north for the first time and

had fallen in love with Peiping opera. He was lying on the upper bunk humming arias from *Hillside Warriors, A Tale of Splashed Oil, A Journey of a Single Stage,* and *Tear-Swept Blossoms.* Hearing this, Ziyun, who was something of a Peiping opera buff himself, couldn't suppress a chuckle. Chengfu knew that Ziyun was especially amused at the off-key rendition of *Hillside Warriors* and was afraid his compartment mates might catch on as well.

"It's really inconvenient to entertain guests here in the compartment," he said. "I don't even have any tea to offer you. Why don't we go sit in the dining car for a while?" Ziyun glanced at the table: a teapot, cups, a tin of cigarettes, a box of cookies, and a box of matches, all crowded so close together that there wasn't room to stick a needle in.

"Li Chengfu has always been fastidiously neat and clean. How can a man like him tolerate this chaos?" Just as Ziyun was asking himself this question, the man in the upper berth started coughing and then raised his head as though he were going to spit. "Hold on a minute," thought Ziyun; "from way up there how's he going to be accurate enough to hit the spittoon?" But Ziyun's concern was totally unnecessary, for, calm and collected as you please, the gentleman in question reached under his pillow and retrieved a round cigarette tin. He hawked up a goober of phlegm, held it in his mouth while methodically removing the top of the cigarette tin, and then spit it in. The goober in question was very thick, and when he let go with it, it did not flow readily or completely into the waiting receptacle. Some of it stuck to his lip. He must have sensed this, for he now used the edge of the tin to shave that excess neatly from his lip. Ziyun came very close to throwing up. It obviously didn't bother the man in the upper berth in the least, for he calmly put the lid back on the tin and then returned this portable spittoon to its original place under his pillow.

At this point, Chengfu tapped Ziyun on the arm and said, "Why don't we step out for a bit?" He crowded his way outside the compartment as he spoke, and Ziyun followed. As they stood in the corridor, Ziyun asked, "Didn't you say you wanted to go sit in the dining car for a bit?"

Chengfu smiled and said, "I've changed my mind. Besides, you can't speak freely in the dining car." It occurred to Ziyun that the reason his friend offered for changing his mind was somehow lacking, but since he wasn't that keen on going to the dining car himself, he didn't pursue the matter.

"I think you're unhappy with your present circumstances," Ziyun observed.

"If I had known the second-class sleeper was going to be like this, I wouldn't have taken it."

"And you really shouldn't have either. You don't save *all* that much money by not going first class anyway. The best thing about first class is that you can sleep whenever you feel like it."

"You misunderstand me," said Chengfu. "If I didn't go second class, I'd go third, not first. I could catnap through the two nights between Peiping and Shanghai and save thirty dollars in the bargain. Why not? Money's not that easy to come by these days."

As someone who had for the last two weeks been spending money as though it were going out of style, Ziyun was in no position to refute his friend's statement, but he couldn't bring himself to second it either. Instead, he looked back through the window of the compartment door and said, "Your three compartment mates appear to be business types. You probably don't have much in common to talk about."

"They all talk at once anyway. Each of them has to fight just to get a word in edgewise. In light of that, they have no burning desire to involve me in their conversation in the first place."

"On the other hand," jested Ziyun, "people like them have a charm of their own. Don't you think? And you, my fortunate friend, have the round-the-clock pleasure of listening to them from Tientsin all the way to Shanghai!" As the two men stood there in the corridor looking into the compartment, the two passengers from the top berths came down and sat on Chengfu's berth. The third reached under the tea table and from all that chaos retrieved a box of food, opened it, and spread its contents out next to him on the berth: pigs' feet, pickled vegetables, smoked fish heads, and crab preserved in wine. Then he took a bottle of liquor from a wicker basket, poured it into a teacup, took a swig, and passed it around.

And now they began sampling the various foods on the bed with their fingers. The crab, packed in wine, was a bit on the drippy side, and, before long, wine stains began to appear on the bedding, something that didn't appear to bother them in the slightest, as they continued to chat and eat.

As Ziyun watched the three men, he became aware of a complaining voice behind him. "Damn! Next time I go traveling, if I don't have enough to go first class, I'd just as soon go third and be done with it. I'll never take second class again!" Only an overheard chance remark, yet the two men felt that whoever had said it was a comrade under the skin who had expressed their own views exactly.

Li Chengfu was the first to turn around and look. It was a middle-aged woman of forty or so who had spoken. She had not bobbed her hair in the modern fashion but rather continued to wear it combed straight back into a little bun at the back of her neck in the traditional mode. She wore a simple black silk gown with no fluting, though it did boast a row of small diamond buttons. Her face was thin, her eyebrows full. One could well imagine that those sparkling eyes were warehouses that contained a variety of formidable tricks. The earrings were tastefully small and fashioned of gold thread. Her silk stockings were flesh colored, and her shoes were slip-ons.

Although she was not what you'd call captivating, she did convey the impression of being well kempt and tidy. In Li's eyes, eyes long accustomed to the ways of the world, she was probably an over-the-hill concubine, a Soochow one at that.[1] He knew this because her Mandarin had a strong Soochow flavor to it. While Li was engaged in appraising her like this, Ziyun was giving her the once-over as well. In Ziyun's eyes, however, even though she was getting on in years, she was first and foremost a woman, and a gentleman didn't stare at women. After giving her a fleeting inspection, he politely looked away in embarrassment. She, on the other hand, was not at all inhibited and, looking Ziyun straight in the face, smiled and said, "Mr. Hu, I've not had this pleasure in a long, long time. But I'll bet you don't remember me."

Being addressed by his own name, Ziyun was thrown for a loss. He hadn't expected that this woman would know him. Nonetheless, he managed to nod his head and say with a smile, "Soon as I heard you call my name, I realized that you looked very familiar, but I can't place you." Ziyun studied the woman now and noted that her face was covered with a thick layer of vanishing cream, which gave it a very white look. On the left cheek, he noticed a scar about the size of a small thumb.

That scar brought a flood of memories back. He clapped his hands together and said, "I have it now! You're Number 6's mom. Why, I haven't seen you in years. Who would have

1. Soochow is noted for its beautiful women.

expected that you'd still be so young and fresh looking?" He turned to Chengfu. "Let me introduce you. This is Mr. Li Chengfu, and this. . . . " He stopped dead in his tracks. According to the way things used to be when she lived in Stone Alley back in Peiping, he would have called her "Number 6's mom" and referred to her behind her back as "Old Number 3 from Soochow." But that was a while back. Who was to say what line of work she was in now? And so he just plain didn't know what to call her.[2]

Women like her, however, are extremely sensitive to social situations, and, as she looked at Ziyun, she immediately realized the difficulty he must be having. And so she smiled and said, "The master of our household is surnamed Yu."

"Oh, Mrs. Yu!" said Ziyun with relief. "And how about Mr. Yu; is he still in Peiping?"

"Originally, he was with the Ministry of Communications in Peking," she explained. "But then, when all the government organizations moved south to Nanking, well, the ministry simply couldn't do without such an old and experienced public servant as Mr. Yu, and so he was transferred to Nanking as well. This time I was up in Peiping on some personal business."

"Well, in that case congratulations on your marriage, Mrs. Yu! Congratulations! You've found a good home for yourself. How many years have you been married?"

"It'll be six or seven now. In my situation, 'congratulations' are not really in order. It's just that when you're a woman, you can't go bumping around from pillar to post all your life. Sooner or later a woman's got to get properly married to someone so she's got a place where she belongs, a place to call home."

2. Hu Ziyun had, no doubt, known her back in Peiping as the "mother" (procuress) of a prostitute known as Number 6; since in her younger days, before becoming a "mother," she, too, had been one of the girls, so to speak, Hu might also have referred to her as "Number 3 from Soochow."

"Are you going to Nanking, Mrs. Yu?"

"No, actually I'm going to Shanghai. The master of the house has gone there and sent a telegram asking me to join him; otherwise, I'd never travel in weather as cold as this."

"Since your husband's in the Ministry of Communications, why are you going second class?"

"Things aren't what they used to be, Mr. Hu. The railways aren't under the jurisdiction of the Ministry of Communications anymore. No more free rides, I'm afraid. But still it depends on individual cases. For instance, I have met a few wives whose husbands aren't even in the Ministry of Railroads but who have nonetheless managed to travel free. Speaking of that, Mr. Hu, what's a rich man like yourself doing in second class?"

"Well, actually I *am* in first class. But as for rich—that's an adjective I can't lay claim to anymore. My present situation is not at all what it used to be either. On the other hand, I've gotten so accustomed to going first class that I can't break myself of the habit all at once. I've come back here to visit with my friend, Mr. Li. He's in the compartment right next to yours."

Mrs. Yu frowned and said, "When it comes to second class, the best thing is *not* to. If you do, you're likely to end up in a compartment like mine. There's a Russian woman in there who's straight out of a dance hall somewhere. Smokes like a chimney and drinks like a fish. Green eyes, blond hair, thick makeup—enough to scare anybody to death. And then, as if that weren't enough, we've got one of those female student types, too. Looks down on everybody. She's in the upper on my side. She's set the feet of her ladder smack dab in the middle of the floor and won't let anybody move it. Up down, up down—whenever she feels like it, and she couldn't care less that her up-downs might inconvenience someone else. To round things out, we've got a woman with bound feet on the way to Nanking with a couple of brats in tow who do nothing but piss, fight, cry, and shit in their drawers. I tell you, that compartment's given me one hell of a headache. But what can I do? I'm reduced to padding up and down here in the corridor, and then when I get tired of that, I go sit in the dining car. Listen! Those brats have started bawling again. Last time I rode the train, I had two Soochow women for compartment mates, the kind of people I could talk to. But which, pray tell, of the three monsters I have for roommates this time would you have me chat with?"

Hearing her go on like this, Chengfu couldn't keep himself from laughing. "Judging from what you say, Mrs. Yu, even the three roommates I'm stuck with actually seem a bit preferable!"

"Now in third class," continued Mrs. Yu, "it's true that people are packed in like sardines, but at least the coach isn't divided into compartments, and you've got more open space, and even the air's a little better. In second class, people are jammed together, sealed up in little boxes."

"That's not entirely true either," commented Ziyun. "I had a look at third class a while back. They're so crowded a person doesn't even have room to stretch. And they certainly don't have a corridor like this where you can stand and talk."

Mrs. Yu laughed at that and said, "Haven't gone third class yet. Don't know when I'll have *that* pleasure."

"Well, maybe you won't, but if you ever do, you'll find lots of women like the one in your compartment with the bound feet. But at least you won't find the kind of female student who looks down on everyone. Now don't get me wrong. To be sure, I don't have to worry about where my next meal's coming from, but that's not the only reason that I blame people for not being willing to part with a little extra money. I criticize them because it's really true that when you're out in public, you're going to find that people are going to be better behaved wherever it costs a little more to get in. Take movie theaters, for example. Go to one where tickets are a dollar, and once you're inside you won't hear so much as a cough; go to one where the tickets are only a dime, and as soon as you set foot inside you'll hear so much racket that you'd think someone had turned a basket of ducks loose."

"But I hold the government responsible for that," opined Li Chengfu. "It has nothing to do with poor people themselves. If education were universalized and everyone had an opportunity to be educated, then you'd find that the poor would behave as well as anyone else and be just as concerned with sanitation, too. It doesn't do to look at any problem just from one's own subjective point of view. You never see the whole truth that way."

"Wait a minute," said Mrs. Yu laughing. "As Mr. Hu well knows, I'm virtually illiterate myself, lucky if I recognize a total of two or three words. I certainly don't have anything you could call 'education,' but I *am* very fussy about good sanitation, and I *certainly* consider myself well behaved."

"She's not exaggerating a bit," said Ziyun. "You know, I suppose all *three* of us can be counted as typical passengers."

Mrs. Yu didn't quite understand what he meant. Chengfu smiled and said, "Mr. Hu surely can't be talking about *Chinese* passengers when he says 'typical.' I daresay those men in my compartment drinking liquor and eating crab are really the 'typical' ones. As for women. . . . "

He was interrupted by the voice of a woman speaking in a heavy local accent as she called for a porter. A porter came running and saw a female head with two buns, one at each side, thrust out from a compartment door. The woman smiled at him and said, "Why don't you get a broom and come in here and clean up?"

The waiter looked into the compartment, stamped his feet, and said, "Oh no! Don't tell me he did it again!"

"It's that woman with the bound feet I told you about," Mrs. Yu said to Ziyun in a low voice. "We told her to make sure to take the kids to the toilet whenever they have to go or at the very least to call the porter and have *him* take them. She agreed, too. But her two-year-old suddenly squatted down right there in the compartment and let fly. Happened so fast his mother couldn't have stopped him even if she wanted to."

Li Chengfu said, "It goes without saying that the kid must be allowed to let fly anywhere he pleases at home."

"If we go on in line with what Chengfu was talking about," Hu Ziyun added, "this woman is your *typical* female passenger, and her child is a *typical* Chinese child." The two men had a good laugh over that.

From behind them someone else said, "The Chinese are a hopeless lot." When they turned around to look, it was a young man dressed in Western clothes. His hair was plastered down and shiny, and a long gold chain dangled from his watch pocket. Two things negated the general impression of sophistication and modernity that he was obviously trying to project with his slicked-down hair and Western suit: he was a pockface[3] of the first order, and his lips were curled so far out and away from his upper and lower teeth that one saw more of the inside of them than the out. "I think it imperative," he continued, "that we have an inspection team on every train. The Chinese have no sense of pub-

---

3. A "pockface," or *mazi,* was a person who had had chicken pox in childhood—few infants were inoculated against the disease at this time—and bore the lifelong scars of the disease, the most striking of which was often a face as pockmarked as the moon. Owing to the prevalence of inoculation in contemporary times, *mazi* are not often encountered anymore.

lic responsibility. If I were a member of the train crew and I saw anyone disrupting public order, I'd make them toe the line right away." He stood up straight and tall and took hold of the lapels of his Western jacket in a gesture that announced that *he* at any rate stood firmly in the ranks of the righteous.

Seeing that he looked like a student, Chengfu thought that he couldn't very well just ignore him, and so he responded, "With all the more pressing things that the railways have to do, how could they find time to look after these trifles? Take that stretch of track between the Old Station and the New Station in Tientsin. There's nothing but unsightly mud holes on both sides of the track. And as if that weren't enough, you've got all those coffins that people have deposited there, a clear and present danger to sanitation as well as being a terrible eyesore. And it wouldn't take all that much money to cart away the coffins and fill in the mud holes either. But from the time of the Peking government[4] down to this very day, no one has given the problem any attention. Especially during the regime of the Peking government, you'd wonder why *something* wasn't done, for then you had highly placed government officials riding back and forth across that stretch of track all the time, but did even *one* of them say anything about the problem? The Chinese people's way of seeing things has always gone something like this: make big problems into small problems and small problems into not-at-all problems; better to stay still than to act; and better to have one thing too *little* to do than one thing too many. And so, as long as people can get by without doing anything about something, they will. It seems that nobody is really interested in progress."

The young man with the pockmarked face kept nodding his head in vigorous agreement. Just as Chengfu finished

4. For a chronology of these events, see chap. 1, n. 1.

speaking, a pasty-faced young man in a Western suit hurried toward them and addressed the pockface fellow with a "Hello!" after which he continued speaking in English. He and pockface shook hands and then, speaking English for all they were worth, went into a compartment together. Li Chengfu stared after them for a while and then said in a low voice, "These are your typical *modern* passengers. To be sure, we'd be in a hell of a mess if all Chinese were like that woman with the bound feet, but are these modern Chinese who have forgotten how to speak their own language any better?"

Mrs. Yu was totally uninterested in the turn that this conversation had taken and would just as soon not continue with it. Therefore, she looked at Hu Ziyun and said, "I'm certainly in no position to invite you into my compartment, so why don't we go to the dining car and have a good chat?" Ziyun hesitated to respond, for he was afraid that if they went to the dining car and Liu Xichun saw them together, she might very well get the wrong idea.

5

■

Some Confusion with Regard to Status

■

■

■

In the second-class sleeper, if you run into a friend and take him back to your compartment for a chat, you're bound to disturb your fellow passengers. Your best alternative, then, is to ask your friend to the dining car. But now, when Mrs. Yu issued an invitation to do just that, Ziyun remained silent and didn't respond to it one way or another. For some reason that even he couldn't put his finger on, Li Chengfu was made uncomfortable by Ziyun's silence.

As a woman from a well-to-do family who was rather skilled in the social graces, Mrs. Yu, however, immediately picked up on the fact that her proposal occasioned some sort of difficulty for Ziyun. Consequently, she immediately changed the topic of conversation: "Hey, we'll be pulling into Tsangchow pretty soon. Tsangchow's famous for its fruit. I don't remember whether it's apples or pears they produce, but I do remember that they are very, very large."

"No," said Ziyun. "It's Potou that's famous for its pears, while Tehchow's known all over for its watermelon. As a matter of fact, from Tsangchow on south, every station has fruit of some kind. If you want to talk about fruit, the honey peach grown around Yucheng is something else."

"I just thought of something else," Mrs. Yu continued.

"On the banks of the Yellow River you can buy a kind of white sugar that's famous along this route."

"No," laughed Ziyun, "you've got it mixed up again, Mrs. Yu. You're thinking of that stretch of the Yellow River that lies on the Peiping-Hankow line. The Shanghai Express doesn't stop along the Yellow River."

Mrs. Yu tilted her head back, thought about that for a moment or two, and then replied with a laugh, "You're right. I do have it mixed up. People who travel a lot often make that kind of mistake. They'll take a stop on one railroad line and misremember it to another." By this time, her motion to remove to the dining car had been uneventfully tabled. And after exchanging a few more words, each went his own way.

Ziyun just couldn't get his mind off Miss Liu. Could she have gone back to the compartment? He kept turning possibilities over in his mind as he walked, and before he knew it he had already traversed the dining car. "Not here," he thought. "Must still be in third class visiting with her schoolmate. Better go look for her there. But I have to have some reason for going there. Can I come straight out and say that I went there to look for her?" He turned and walked back toward third class. As he was sorting things out, he hesitated and then stood still. One of the stewards saw him and misunderstood his reason for stopping, thinking that he'd come to get something to eat and was deciding where to sit. "All the chairs are comfortable," he said. "There's no one around this time of day, so you can have your pick."

The steward's words brought Ziyun abruptly out of his reverie. "Must look like a damned fool wandering into the dining car at this time of day!" he thought. "No, no, that's not it," he said to the steward. "I thought there was somebody here waiting for me, but since there isn't, I'll just leave." Flustered, he turned around and quickly walked away. He had originally intended to go to third class, but in his confusion he had turned around again and was actually walking in the direction of first class. Ziyun didn't realize his mistake until he had walked through the door and into the first-class coach. "Oh well," he thought, "long as I'm here, might as well go back to the compartment." He slid the door open and headed inside. When it had opened only a small crack, an aroma compounded of cosmetics and perfume wafted into his nostrils.

Sure enough, wasn't that a woman with her hair fluffed out over the pillow on the lower berth? He didn't say anything, but a smile of utter joy appeared on his face, followed by a gasp of surprise. Liu Xichun's face appeared in profile, her eyes were shut tight, and she seemed to be having a very sweet sleep. But the corners of her lips twitched ever so slightly as Ziyun came in, as though she were smiling. The smile lasted for ever so short a time before she was fast asleep again. "A smile like that isn't a dream smile," thought Ziyun to himself. "When you smile in a dream, there's no inhibition. In a dream smile, your mouth just suddenly widens into a big grin. Besides, when she smiled just now, her long eyelashes twitched a bit. It would be total nonsense to describe that as a dream smile."

He stood in the middle of the compartment, head lowered, and studied Xichun's face. He raised his shoulders and smiled. Liu Xichun lay with her head against the pillow, still pretending to be asleep. An inspiration suddenly came to Ziyun, and he began talking to himself. "Even though it's pretty warm in this compartment, it's not a good idea to sleep without any covers." Thereupon, he took the woolen blanket folded at Xichun's feet and pulled it gently up over her.

Now, on the train they enclose their blankets in a sheet so that the woolen hairs don't prickle people. In his haste to be of service to Xichun, however, Ziyun forgot to make sure that the outer wrapping was in place, and when he pulled it even with her shoulders, as luck would have it, an exposed corner of the blanket came to rest against her nose so that a woolen hair tickled the inside of her exposed nostril. She stood it for as long as she could, then when she couldn't take it any longer, she burst out laughing, flipped onto her back, and sat up while straightening her hair with one hand and rubbing her eyes with the other.

Laughing, she looked at Ziyun and said, "The one thing in this world I can't *stand* is being tickled. Now how on earth did you know a thing like that, Uncle?"

Observing her casual state of dishabille, Ziyun was keenly aware of a certain lack of modesty on her part. What's more, she obviously knew that he had been toying with her in the business of the blanket and apparently thought that it was *all right* for him to trifle with her in such an intimate fashion. Deciding to strike while the iron was hot, he sat down close to her on the bed. "Actually, I didn't tickle you on purpose. It's just that your clothing *is* a bit on the sheer side. As long as you're sitting, it's nothing to worry about, but if you lie down, it's easy to catch cold. That's why I put the blanket over you. I *was* a bit careless, though, and let a bit of wool tickle your nose." As he spoke, he reached down and held onto the edge of the berth for support. Then he turned his body so that he faced more toward Xichun.

She had kicked off her high heels before lying down, and now she extended her silk-stockinged feet under the berth to feel around for her slippers. Not finding them, she stretched her legs out straight. Out of the corner of his eye, Ziyun caught sight of the slippers under the berth. He bent down, fished them out, and presented them to Xichun. Shrinking back from him ever so slightly, she smiled and said, "Why Uncle, I really don't deserve such attentiveness."

"It's nothing," replied Ziyun. "The slippers were right at hand. It's not as though I expended a lot of energy to get them."

"Although it didn't cost you any expense of energy, slippers are *lowly* things that one wears on the feet."

"So what if they are slippers? They're still something you wear on your body just like anything else." As he spoke, he leaned over and picked one of them up and was about to put it on her foot.

With a serious expression on her face, she pushed him away with both hands and said, "Uncle! I simply will not allow you to be so attentive. If you go on waiting on me hand and foot like this, I won't dare stay in this compartment any longer."

Since Xichun's expression was fully as stern as her words, Ziyun blushed and put the slipper down. Her expression relaxed a bit as she slid her feet into the slippers. She went to the washstand, took the washbasin down from its hook, and turned on the water.

An old hand at social relationships, Ziyun realized that if he said nothing after suffering her rebuff, that would clearly indicate that his intentions had not been honorable in the first place. "Miss Liu," he said in a very calm and natural voice, "if you want to wash your face, why not let me call the porter and have him bring you some hot water? You're not going to get any hot water out of those pipes."

"No, I'll do just fine this way. Washing with cold water is just as sanitary anyway." As she spoke, she twisted around and smiled at him. Since she had her back to him as she stood at the washstand, Ziyun had assumed that she was angry. Much to his surprise, his remarks, which he had framed with an eye to smoothing things over, had actually worked; what's more, they had even earned him a charming smile in the bargain.

"Well then, you're in luck, Miss Liu," he said with a

happy grin, "for at least there *is* water in the pipe. I remember once on another trip I woke up around noon with the same idea you have now. 'I'll just wash up with cold water and let it go at that,' I told myself. To my surprise, however, when I turned on the tap, I got nothing but the most terrifying pow!-pow!-pow! you've ever heard. Then the tap started foaming at the mouth—scared me half to death, I'll tell you! Actually, if you're going to give passengers washbasins and running water, then you ought to have a plentiful supply of both hot and cold water on tap whenever they need it. And if the railroad officials find *that* too troublesome, then they ought simply to do away with the whole business. You're lucky that just now you didn't get that pow!-pow!-pow! the way I did, or you'd be good and scared for sure."

"Oh, I'm not as easily frightened as all that," said Xichun. "If I were that timid, I'd never have dared make this trip from Peiping to Shanghai all by myself in the first place." As she spoke, she washed her hands and then took her purse from the tea table and put it on the washstand. She took out her powder and rouge and made herself up again. As Ziyun watched her, he couldn't help wondering, "Who is it that she's making up for?" It was the kind of question that was better left unasked, and so that's how he left it. Sitting slantwise on the sofa, he smiled, smoked a cigar, and gazed at her back.

Tap-tap-tap—just as he was on the point of saying something, there was a light knock at the door. Thinking it was the waiter bringing a thermos of hot water, Ziyun responded offhandedly, "Come on in." Much to his surprise, and embarrassment as well, it turned out to be Mrs. Yu. He was in a tough spot, for what was he to say if Mrs. Yu asked if Xichun was his wife? If he said she was his wife, Xichun would surely refuse to go along with it. On the other hand, if he said she *wasn't* his wife—well, a strange woman in his compartment, a woman with whom he had obviously spent the night, wasn't all that easy to explain either.

Now, Mrs. Yu wasn't born yesterday. When she saw him hesitate, she took a step backward, nodded in greeting, and asked, "Is it convenient for me to come in?"

Before he could answer, Xichun, treating the woman as a friend of Ziyun's, smiled and said, "Please do come in." Mrs. Yu nodded toward Xichun in acknowledgment and entered the compartment. What was Ziyun to do? Couldn't very well push her back on out. He got up and yielded his spot on the small sofa to her. Xichun immediately hung the washbasin back on its hook, offered Mrs. Yu a cigarette, and poured her a cup of tea. She was acting exactly as she would act if she really was Ziyun's wife! Ziyun was delighted, for now there was no need for Mrs. Yu to ask who this was, and, besides that, he got a little bonus out of the situation to boot.

Just as expected, Mrs. Yu was not in the least suspicious about their relationship but simply smiled and said, "No need to be so polite on my behalf. It's just that I am an old friend of Mr. Hu here and haven't seen him in a very long time. Bumped into him just now, but you really can't have much of a chat standing in a corridor on a train, so I came to pay him a visit." Since the little sofa was only large enough to accommodate one person, Xichun had no choice but to sit down next to Ziyun on the berth, an action, of course, that emphasized the wifely impression she conveyed to the other woman. Blowing out a mouthful of smoke, Mrs. Yu looked all around the compartment and commented with a smile, "You two certainly do travel light."

"I'm not going to be in Shanghai very long," explained Ziyun, "so there's no point in taking a lot of stuff I won't need. Besides, you can get anything you want in Shanghai. Just as long as you've got the money, inside three or four hours, you can find yourself a bride, get married, buy furniture, rent an apartment, and set up house! So if I need anything, I can always pick it up when I get to Shanghai; there's no point in taking a lot of things with me."

"Yes," said Mrs. Yu, "but taking a woman along on a trip is always somewhat of a bother." Ziyun had no idea as to how to react to that one. He just smiled and peeked at Xichun out of the corner of his eye. She didn't seem to take it at all amiss.

Her response, however, wasn't completely in accord with the smiling expression she wore as she delivered it: "I'm afraid I can't go along with that, Mrs. Yu," she said. "Modern women are perfectly capable of traveling alone just as men do."

"Now isn't that the truth!" exclaimed Ziyun as he brought his palm down on his thigh in an enthusiastic slap of agreement. "Why Mrs. Yu, you yourself are a good case. You're traveling all by yourself, right?"

Mrs. Yu laughed and replied, "This doesn't count as *real* traveling. I hop on at Ch'ienmen in Peiping, and before I know it I'm at North Station in Shanghai. But on most trips there are things that aren't all that easy for a woman to take care of by herself. It's much more convenient if she has the man of the house with her. Wouldn't you say so, Mr. Hu?"

Ziyun raised his right hand, scratched the side of his head for a minute, and then asked, "Mrs. Yu, how is it that *Mr.* Yu didn't come along with you?"

"Although it *is* better for the man of the house to accompany a wife, it's also important that he make a living. North to south, south to north—if I required Mr. Yu to accompany me each and every time, who would take his place at work? You, Mr. Hu, are a capitalist living on your own money. You don't have a boss over you, and you can do as you jolly well please. But you've got to remember there aren't very many people who enjoy a situation like yours."

Xichun sat in silence on the berth as though she were

doing her best to think of some way of correcting Mrs. Yu's misunderstanding with regard to her relationship to Ziyun, but she didn't seem to be having any luck. Ziyun had a good idea as to what Xichun was doing, and so he tried to move the conversation in another direction. "Mrs. Yu, where are you going to stay when you get to Shanghai?"

"Our husband always stays with a friend of his. I've already sent that friend a telegram so that he'll come meet me at the station. Staying with a friend is always preferable to staying at a hotel. Where are you staying, Mr. Hu? I'd like to know so I can come visit." Although she said "Mr. Hu," she looked at Xichun as she spoke, as if to say that she'd like to visit her as well. Xichun stood up, got a cigarette, and started to smoke.

"Well, I used to stay at the San Tung, but Shanghai gets more and more modernized with every passing day. There's a new one opened up on Szechuen Road called the New Asia that's fairly modernized, but I've heard another one just opened for business on Nanking Road. They call it the Park. I've heard tell it's more than twenty stories tall with the most up-to-date appointments imaginable. This time I'm going to give the Park a try."

"I think I'll enjoy trying it out, myself," said Xichun. It was a remark that caused Ziyun's heart to skip a beat.

Mrs. Yu smiled and said, "I hear tell it's quite a classy place. If you two stay there, then I'll ask the old fellow who's man of our house to take a room there as well. We'll all be together! Won't that be a lark?"

Xichun stretched out her legs and, smiling at everyone, let her slippers dangle back and forth on her toes. Ziyun was smiling, too. How those dangling slippers excited him! He controlled himself and said to Mrs. Yu, "Since you seem to have Mr. Yu so well in hand, why didn't you get him to spend a little more and get you a first-class ticket? See how much more quiet and comfortable it is up here."

Mrs. Yu said, "Actually, I'm the one who wanted to save money. Has nothing to do with him."

Xichun said, "If you find second class too irritating, Mrs. Yu, just come up here for a chat whenever you feel like it."

"Sure I wouldn't be disturbing you?" asked Mrs. Yu.

"What could be more disturbing than the day-and-night hung-dung hung-dung of the train going over the tracks, and what could be more *pleasurable* on a train than the conversation of another woman? Please come whenever you feel like it." From both the tone and the content of what she had to say, it seemed to Ziyun that Xichun was passing herself off as his wife. That came as a complete surprise. At the beginning of this conversation he had to go to the bathroom but hadn't dared leave the compartment for fear that Xichun might reveal their relationship to Mrs. Yu for what it really was. Now, however, he was confident that she didn't intend to do that and felt safe in leaving the compartment to go to the toilet, and so he did.

As he left the compartment, Mrs. Yu squinted her eyes together and smiled at Xichun; then she shifted her gaze in the direction of the briefcase in the rack just above the compartment door. The leather was purple, and the metal parts were made of shiny white brass. It was neat and clean, as though it were advertising to people that it contained something most precious. When Mrs. Yu looked at the briefcase, Xichun's eyes went to it as well. She covered her mouth with one hand and smiled. The silence of the two women as they sat in the compartment awaiting Ziyun's return was interrupted only by occasional low-keyed laughter.

When Ziyun returned, Mrs. Yu stood up and said, "It's getting pretty late; I really ought to be going now. You two ought to be calling it a day as well." As she spoke, she pulled the compartment door to one side and started out into the corridor. Xichun shook her hand.

"See you tomorrow, then," said Xichun. As she shook

Mrs. Yu's hand, Xichun's own hand trembled a bit as though she were very nervous about something. Squeezed in behind Xichun, Ziyun couldn't step forward to say anything to Mrs. Yu, but as she left he heard the last thing she said very clearly.

"See you tomorrow, Mrs. Hu."

Xichun turned around, lowered her head, and sat down on the little sofa as though very embarrassed by that "Mrs. Hu." Ziyun made a conciliatory gesture and said, "I'm really terribly sorry about all that, Miss Liu. Because I really wasn't sure what you had in mind, I didn't know how to go about correcting Mrs. Yu's misapprehension as to our relationship." Still looking down, Xichun cupped the fingers of her left hand in her right hand and gently massaged them. She seemed to be pouting ever so slightly as well. Ziyun lowered his voice and meekly said, "I hope you'll find it in your heart not to blame me."

"I didn't say I *blamed* you. It's just that I regret having moved into your compartment in the first place. It would seem inappropriate for me to move out now, but somehow even more inappropriate if I didn't."

"There's no need to upset yourself," said Ziyun. "I'll just explain the whole thing to Mrs. Yu tomorrow, and that will be the end of it."

Xichun pursed her lips, shook her head gently in negation, and said, "That would be the most *in*appropriate thing you could do!"

"We're in a sticky situation no matter how you look at it. But we *could* always fall back on that rough plan I had to begin with: I'll go sit in the dining car, and you sleep here," Ziyun suggested.

"Oh no!" said Xichun as she gesticulated her negation of the plan with both hands. "What kind of stupid thing would that be? If it came to that, I'd simply move out. But that's not such a good idea either; if it were, I'd have long since moved out."

"Move out? Don't even say such a thing. Just now you were gone for so long that I was sick to death with worry that you actually had moved out."

"I must confess I don't quite understand your reasoning, Uncle. Suppose I really *had* moved out. What could that possibly have to do with you personally? How could something like that possibly be serious enough to make you 'sick to death with worry'?" She faced away from Ziyun as she spoke, as though she were deliberately avoiding looking at him. Then she fished a cigarette out from the tin on the table and let it dangle from her lips as though on the point of lighting it. She did not, however, actually strike a match, and after a bit she put the cigarette back down on the table.

"You've got me wrong," said Ziyun. "I didn't mean it *that* way. Of course, it would have nothing to do with me personally. It's just because, because. . . . " As he continued to speak, he didn't reach for his pipe as he usually did but rather for the tin of cigarettes. Just as he did so, without thinking, Xichun gave him the cigarette she was holding between her fingers. Ziyun took advantage of the opportunity to look closely at the expression on her face. She appeared not the least put out.

On the contrary, she smiled and said, "I've already smoked too many cigarettes today. I was afraid if I smoked this one I might get dizzy, and that's why I didn't light it. Why don't you smoke it for me?"

When he first took the cigarette, Ziyun thought nothing of it. But when he picked it up and looked at it, he saw that it bore fairly heavy traces of lipstick—lipstick from her lips. He immediately broke into a broad smile, bowed, and said, "Thank you, thank you so much!"

"Uncle, I don't understand this either. Why in the world

should you thank me? After all, these are *your* cigarettes."

Ziyun answered, "Because, because. . . . "

"You don't have to because-because me. I think I understand anyway. Besides, that last time you because-becaused me, you didn't finish what you had to say anyway."

Sitting on the bottom berth, elbow on the tea table, chin supported in his palms, cigarette dangling from his lips, Ziyun sat and gazed at Xichun. He smiled and said, "Because, because when two friends are together and their conversation is congenial, they become ever more intimate; and if their conversation is *not* congenial, then they'll go their separate ways. There was nothing holding them together in the first place. And yet that's not *entirely* true either. I seem to remember two lines from *The Story of the Stone* expressing the exact opposite point of view: 'If we *weren't* fated to meet in this life, then why did we run into each other in the first place; and since we *were* fated to meet in this life, then how could this relationship come to naught?'"[1]

Xichun gave a faint smile, shook her head, and said, "Better not talk literature to me, Uncle. I know from nothing about it."

"Actually, I'm not all that much older than you are," said Ziyun. "Why should you have to call me 'Uncle' all the time?"

"Well, it would seem a bit too distant if I were to call you *Mister* Hu, and I don't think I ought to."

"Why say *Mister* at all, then? Just call me Hu Ziyun, and be done with it."

---

1. *Shihtou ji* (The story of the stone) presents one of the great love stories of world literature. This eighteenth-century novel by Cao Xueqin (also romanized as Ts'ao Hsüeh-ch'in) is also popularly known as *Honglou meng* (Dream of the red chamber; or, A dream of red mansions) and is available in several English translations.

"I'd dare do that even less."

"Why *wouldn't* you dare do that? After all, we're not *blood* relatives to begin with, and we don't have to worry about who's one up on the other in the generational pecking order. The only reason you call me Uncle in the first place is because I'm distantly related to people in the family you married into. But, as a matter of fact, our relationship is really friend-to-friend. So what's using a friend's name got to do with daring or not daring?"

Xichun didn't say anything. She stroked her face thoughtfully, and as she did so, her diamond ring caught Ziyun's eye again. "That ring of yours is beautiful; may I see it?" He reached out as he asked, making it a bit too obvious that his real intention was to hold her hand.

She shrank back and said, "Mr. Hu. Please go up to the top berth and get a good night's sleep. It's pretty late, you know." From the way she drew back her hand, Ziyun thought he might be in for a scolding. Discovering that was by no means her intention, he gave a loud and satisfied laugh.

6

Middle of the Night in Third Class

As the present writer has previously said, the war of aggression that man wages against woman is carried out in a three-stage campaign. In the space of these few short hours, Ziyun's attack against Miss Xichun had already reached stage 3. His time was as good as the train's—an express train at that! Such an achievement, of course, is not to be sneezed at. On the other hand, however, if you put any single man and any single woman together in a room not much larger than a bushel basket where they are as snug as bugs in a rug and then try to fix the responsibility for the inevitable development of such a situation on one side or the other—well, that's not the easiest thing in the world to do.

Hurtling ever faster through the cold and star-filled night, the train passed over the Tsangchow plain. The cars bobbed and swayed with an accelerating rhythm until their pitch and yaw settled into a steady swaying motion that rocked the passengers into dreamland. Like the train itself, the degree of comfort provided by that swaying motion could also be divided into three classes.

In the first-class sleeper, some of the compartments had only one passenger, others two. In all of them, the heat rose to 38° or 39° Celsius,[1] well above a person's normal body heat. The springs supporting the berths were so soft and gentle that you would have thought you were riding on clouds.

In the second-class sleeper, the temperature was the same as in first class, but the berths themselves—and there were four instead of two—were smaller and more cramped. The springs under them were a bit on the stiff side as well. While you could say the people in second class were sleeping, you *couldn't* compare it to riding on clouds. Moreover, there were four passengers in each compartment, and, for the most part, they didn't know each other. But the most striking difference from first class was the unsavory odor of the compartment. The discomfort one experienced was occasionally further magnified by a snoring compartment mate.

Down in third class, of course, there were no compartments. In the daytime you sit on a wooden seat that accommodates two passengers; and at night—you sit on a wooden seat that accommodates two passengers. Xichun's fellow student, Zhang Yuqing, and her husband, Zhu Jinqing, also sat on one of those seats for two. Leaning back, they closed their eyes and slept.

Among animals, each species has its own way of sleeping. The horse, for example, sleeps standing up, birds in a squatting position, and the bat hanging upside down. For human beings, however, the normal pattern is lying down. But if the human beings in question happen to be riding third class on the train, the pattern is broken, and they have to sleep sitting up. Normally, any sudden change in a habit of long standing makes people very uncomfortable. With the third-class passengers, however, heaven looks out for their

1. 38° or 39° Celsius comes out to an incredibly high 100°–102° Fahrenheit.

welfare, for when the train is pitching and swaying for all it's worth, their nerves become so utterly exhausted that they quite naturally close their eyes and go to sleep. And so it is that when third-class passengers are tired out, their hard wooden seats transform themselves into the spring-supported berths of first class, and they, too, voyage gently into dreamland.

Shoulder to shoulder, Zhu Jinqing and his wife slept sitting up. Jinqing's head rested back against the headrest at the top of the seat. Yuqing was somewhat shorter, and her head didn't reach up that far; therefore, she pillowed it against her husband's shoulder and slept that way. She occupied the seat next to the window, and the steam pipes ran right past her feet. As the night deepened, those pipes seemed as tired as the passengers and put out only a minimal amount of heat. Yet, no matter how slight, heat after all *is* heat, and the person closer to the pipes is at least somewhat warmer. Thus, although Zhang Yuqing and her husband were both third-class passengers, she was third class, grade A, while he could only be counted as third class, grade B.

After one o'clock in the morning, even Jinqing couldn't hold out any longer, and he actually fell asleep. But sleeping with your head thrown back against the headrest inevitably takes its toll, and after being in that position for a long time he was brought partially awake by an ache in his neck. At some point, his hand had apparently slipped down behind his wife's back because that's where it was now, pressed hard against the seat by her body weight; his hand was in such a tingling state of numbing sleep that he could no longer move it. Under the pressure of his wife's head, his right shoulder had gone to sleep as well.

The feelings of people riding a train are somewhat different from ordinary folk. When we ordinary folks are sound asleep in the peace and comfort of our homes, the slightest sound will wake us. But put us on a train, and things are different. The normal sound of a train hurtling down the tracks is something like roaring wind and pelting rain punctuated by loud claps of thunder—incredibly noisy. In the midst of that din, however, passengers actually do manage to sleep. But let the train stop in a station, and all that racket will for the moment be silenced, and the pitching and rolling will cease as well. At that point, shocked by the sudden change, we are actually awakened by the silence!

Sometime after two in the morning, the Shanghai Express stopped at some station or other, and Jinqing woke up. He was looking out the window when Yuqing woke up as well. As she opened her eyes, she realized that she had been sleeping with her head on her husband's shoulder. Her body was still cuddled against him. She immediately raised her head and surveyed the other passengers draped every which way and that on the seats around them. Some of those who weren't sleeping stared openly at Yuqing and her husband. And, strange to say, their stares actually felt embarrassing.

Covering her mouth with her hand, she yawned a bit, smiled at her husband, and said in a low voice, "Must have been in a daze. Guess I fell asleep without knowing it."

Only now was her husband able to retrieve his right hand, which had been pinned behind her back. With his left hand, he slapped it lightly over and over again. "You went to sleep without knowing it? That's what everybody does. The secret to riding third class is not to think about sleeping but rather to concentrate on staying awake as long as you can. Then when you can't take it any longer, your eyes will drop shut, and you'll sleep. Works that way because as long as you're not concentrating on sleeping, you'll feel much better because you won't be aware of the discomfort you're suffering because you don't have a bed."

"Well, that's one way of looking at it, but no matter

what, the kind of forced sleep you get that way isn't really good sleep."

Continuing to slap the back of the hand that had gone to sleep behind his wife's back, Jinqing said, "When you're traveling, of course, your sleep, food, and drink are never going to be what they are at home."

Yuqing laughed and asked, "Did I put your hand to sleep leaning on it with my back?"

Jinqing smiled. "Doesn't matter a bit. I like it when you're comfortable leaning against me."

Yuqing noticed that the two passengers across from them began to shift around in their seats. She didn't think it appropriate that they hear what her husband had just said. She tapped on his leg to signal as much and then changed the subject. "Where are we now?" she asked as she pressed her face against the window and looked out into the blackness.

"Well, if you go by time," Jinqing answered, "we ought to be someplace past Potou and about to arrive in Tehchow."

"Tehchow's famous for its roast chicken. Why don't we get off and get some?"

"Their pears aren't bad either," her husband added, "and in summer they produce lots of watermelon as well. But you're not going to buy any of it in the middle of the night like this. It's not that the merchants don't want to get up and do business. It's just that if everyone on the train is asleep, where are they going to find customers?"

"Where are they going to find customers?" She repeated her husband's question and then answered it with a smile, "In *third* class, that's where. People in third class don't sleep all that much in the first place. Besides, it would give us a chance to get off the train and stretch our legs a bit. After all, we're not like the people in first or second class, who are sound asleep at this time of the night."

Zhu Jinqing thought about that for a while and then gently patted his wife's hand and said with a smile, "I really ought to apologize for being so tight with money. Doesn't cost *that* much more to go second class."

"You've got me all wrong," said Yuqing. "I wasn't saying that I was jealous of people who go first or second class. I was just pointing out that no matter what business you're in, you make your money when ordinary people like you and me buy things. To be sure, people of the bourgeoisie spend their money too, but, after all, they are a minority, and you can't make money doing business with a minority. Haven't you noticed that the people who sell food in the various stations always hang around the third-class coaches? That's where they do their business."

Jinqing said, "That goes without saying. If the railroad had to depend on selling first- and second-class tickets, they wouldn't stay in business very long. Quite often a first-class coach won't have more than ten people in it, but when a third-class coach is full up, it'll hold two hundred! Add up the value of all the tickets, and it's in third class that the railroads make their money. Only trouble is, in third class you've got no place to sleep."

Yuqing laughed at that. "If they did have places to sleep, there'd be just as few people as there are in first class, and the railroad would soon go broke that way too." As the young couple got into the comfortable swing of this conversation, their voices grew loud enough to attract the attention of some of the other passengers. They quickly realized what was going on and stopped talking. Now that their voices no longer broke the silence, the train seemed almost abandoned as it waited in the small station for a train coming from the opposite direction.

There was a fairly large stretch of open countryside between the station and its town. If you looked out the window, you first saw the dark shadows of tall trees and then the figures of station attendants, lanterns in hand, trudging back and forth on the platform. Although separated from them by a glass window, you could hear their steps on the platform as clearly as you could hear the heavy breathing and intermittent snores of the third-class passengers.

Jinqing laughed. "Know what? I've got a great title for a poem: 'Feelings Engendered in the Depth of Night upon Hearing People Snoring in the Third-Class Coach While Stopped at a Small Railroad Station.'"

Yuqing burst out laughing. "How in the world could one ever have such a long title for a poem?"

"But it has to be that *long* to express the charm of it all. And it has to be *hearing people snoring*—and they have to be snoring *in the depth of night*—to make the *reader* feel sleepy too. If the train weren't *stopped*—or if it were stopped at a *large* station—that snoring sound wouldn't call forth that same feeling of intimacy either. And so it has to be a *small* station where you can hear everything with complete clarity, for only then will it *engender* the feelings I have in mind."

After listening to what he said, Yuqing carefully turned it all over in her mind and decided there was something to it after all. She opened her eyes wide and conducted an inspection of the coach. Although most of the passengers were leaning against their seats and were either halfway or fully asleep, their bodies were stretched or constricted into such a variety of positions that not a single one of them looked comfortable. Of those who had managed to stay awake, some were heavy lidded and constantly yawning, while others were sitting all awry with their heads drooping this way and that and saying nothing. A few passengers doggedly supported themselves in upright postures and had cigarettes dangling from their mouths, but you couldn't find a trace of life in any of their expressionless faces.

Jinqing said, "At a time like this, you can see that a second-class ticket's being more expensive by half than a third-class one is not all that unreasonable. If we do well in Shanghai, then when we go back to Peiping for a visit, we'll go second class for sure."

Yuqing smiled and said, "You seem to have become something of a second-class fanatic. That's all you talk about."

Jinqing raised his hands high above his head, yawned, took a good stretch, and said: "As the saying goes, *When deep feelings are stirred, they come forth in the word.*" Before Yuqing had a chance to respond, an earthshaking roar was heard in the distance. After listening attentively, she asked what it was. Jinqing replied, "It's the train we've pulled in here to let go by. If you listen carefully to a sound like that, it's really fascinating. The louder it gets, the closer it is, but if you listen to it from another place. . . ." As he continued with his explanation, Yuqing put her head back on his shoulder and got ready to go back to sleep. Jinqing sighed gently and said in a low voice, "Well, as the saying goes, *When a couple's poor and humble, anything they do takes a tumble.*"

At this point, the other train thundered past the station and then, just as fast as it had come, sped away again. The sound startled Yuqing. She raised her head, looked at her husband with heavy lids, and smiled. Then she put her head back on his shoulder and went back to sleep. His wife's head on his shoulder felt *very* good. He began to feel that the saying *When a couple's poor and humble, anything they do takes a tumble* was not nearly so true as another one that held that *When a couple's poor and humble, their feelings are too rich to crumble.*

Once the other train was past, the Shanghai Express continued its southward journey. Jinqing had so much to think about that he couldn't sleep and just sat there reflecting on his various experiences during this trip. He thought of Miss

Xu up there in first class. One had to grant her that she was free and easy in her social interactions, that she dressed in expensive clothes, and that she traveled first class, but when you came right down to it, she was not nearly as pretty as his own lovely wife. The most peculiar thing about Miss Xu was that she said she had changed her name to Yang. How did that happen? She hadn't said anything about marrying anyone name Yang. Jinqing couldn't figure it out.

"But if a person's goal in life is material comfort," he thought to himself, "you might as well stop talking about moral integrity. After all, how much was that worth a pound? I have some good friends who work in the Transportation Office myself. If I were willing to do harm to the public good for my own private purposes, those friends would have given me two free tickets on second class. But that's not the way a person ought to act. What gives me the right to ride a train operated by the national government without paying?"

As his thoughts took this tack, his spirits headed off in the direction of righteous indignation, and he stamped his foot lightly on the floor, but it was enough to awaken his wife. She raised her head and said, "I'm sorry. Went to sleep on your shoulder again, didn't I?"

Jinqing smiled and said, "Before we were married, having you sleep with your head on my shoulder is the kind of thing I could only *dream* about."

"But now you find it annoying?" she asked.

"That's not it at all. I stamped my foot just now because I was wondering why the two of us don't deserve to go second class. Then I wouldn't have to put you through all this."

Yuqing immediately took his hand in hers and said, "I don't want to hear such nonsense. To be sure, we might be in a tight spot right now, but we ought to step back and think about all those folks less fortunate than ourselves. What are *they* supposed to do? Besides, traveling third class on a train isn't even a 'tight spot' to begin with."

Jinqing took her hand in his and said, "I wouldn't have said anything unless you'd asked me. Anyway, I think there are lots of people in both first and second class who don't have it as good as we do."

"More than that," answered Yuqing, "I'll bet there are lots of them who aren't as happy as we are either. But, whatever the case, I think you ought to take a good look around the coach. Everybody's asleep except us! We're sure to annoy them with all our talking. Now go back to sleep!"

Jinqing looked about, decided she was right, and went back to sleep. When he woke again, there were electric lights outside the window: they had stopped at another station. What pleased him most, however, was that the two passengers directly across from them on the same side of the aisle had gotten their luggage together and were preparing to get off the train. People said that this was Tehchow. Jinqing hurriedly pushed his wife away from him in order to wake her. "We're at Tehchow. Let's get off and have us some Tehchow chicken," he said with a smile.

Yuqing, who had been leaning against her husband's side, sleepily opened her eyes and murmured, "I want to sleep. I don't care if they've got Tehchow ambrosia; I still want to sleep." As she spoke, she arranged her hair, then, holding her husband's hand between hers, cuddled up against him as before. As he looked at her, he could not remember ever having seen her look so charming and lovable.

It was all he could do to bring himself to push her away. However, if they didn't occupy the two-person seat directly across from them as soon as those passengers packed up and left, someone else was bound to come and take it. It was an opportunity they couldn't afford to pass up. Gently, he took hold of her shoulders and moved her off to one side so that he could stand up. After all, although his poor young wife had said that going third class was no big thing, physically she really wasn't up to it. And if at this moment someone were to offer her a berth in second class, he was pretty sure she wouldn't hesitate for a moment. Wasn't she already lying there on the seat sound asleep? Jinqing took off his overcoat and staked his claim to the seats across from them by spreading it out over them.

He reached down, took his wife's feet off the floor, and cradled them up onto the seat so that she was lying on it in a semifetal position. Then he folded her coat into a pillow and gently placed it under her head. When he had everything arranged to his satisfaction, he sat down across from her. As he happened to turn his head, he made eye contact with an old man sitting in the seat across the aisle from him. The old fellow wore a long gown with a *magua*[2] over it and sported a long beard that he constantly stroked as a slight smile played about his lips. Jinqing thought the old fellow was probably amused at the fussy way he was looking after Yuqing. "Traveling away from home is always bothersome," said Jinqing to the old man. His intention in saying this was to announce that this woman was his wife and that he wasn't engaged in any improper behavior.

The old man continued stroking his beard and then said with a smile, "Had you two figured out from the beginning. You've both been very close and intimate from the time you first set foot on the train. Had a certain poise about you as well. Guessed right off that you two were a loving couple who hadn't been married all that long. Thought you were

2. A *magua* (lit. "horse [*ma*] jacket [*gua*]") is also called a "Mandarin jacket" since it was originally worn by important people. The Manchus brought it into China, and, as its name indicates, it was originally worn as a riding jacket. By the time of this novel, however, its presence simply signaled that the wearer was formally attired. The old fellow is all dressed up.

probably on your honeymoon." Since there was no reason for Jinqing to try to put anything over on the old fellow, he nodded his head in affirmation.

"Honeymoon trip? You've hit the nail on the head! To those old experienced eyes of yours, we must look somewhat foolish."

"Not a bit of it." The old fellow shook his head. "Although I may be old, my *heart* isn't. As a matter of fact, I'm making this trip down south to get married. When I come back, I'll have a bride with me too, and we'll be on *our* honeymoon!"

"You must be pulling my leg," replied Jinqing with a smile.

The old fellow put on a very serious expression and said, "I am by no means joking. Don't judge me by this beard. As a matter of fact, I'm still only sixty-two. I'll bet I've got another good twenty years left in me. Trouble is, my own kids have all run off to set up their own households and left me alone as alone can be. Business hasn't been all that great these past few years either, so what the hell, I up and decided to add another string to my lute."[3]

"So that's the lay of the land. As you describe it, it's really quite natural, too. Is the bride from Shanghai?"

The old fellow laughed until the original wrinkles around his eyes doubled in number. He stroked his beard and replied, "No, she's from Soochow. A real 'Soochow maiden' born and bred!"

Jinqing smiled broadly at that. "A Soochow maiden? Marvelous, marvelous. And exactly how old a teenager is this young maiden?"

The question caused the old fellow to tilt back his head and roar with laughter. Fortunately, the train was already

---

3. "To add another string to one's lute" was a standard expression meaning to remarry after the death of one's wife.

under way so that his outburst was hardly noticed against the already considerable din. "How in the world could I get a teenager? It's like this: she was engaged at one point, but the marriage fell through, and now she's an old maid of thirty-eight." As Jinqing carried on this conversation, he never took his eyes off his lovely wife. Although she was wearing a pair of heavy cloth shoes, her legs were covered only with a pair of silk stockings. Thinking that she might not be warm enough, Jinqing got up, took his coat from under him, spread it over his wife's legs, and then sat back down on the bare seat.

Continuing to stroke his beard, the more the old fellow watched this, the younger grew the thoughts that welled up in his breast. Jinqing sensed that his traveling companion was priming up for an extended conversation. Once the old fellow got under way, there would probably be no stopping him, and eventually they'd end up disturbing the other passengers. Jinqing pointedly yawned and then curled up on his seat and prepared to go to sleep. Trouble was the seats in third class weren't very wide, and it became quite obvious that no matter how he tried to shrink himself, there was no way that that seat would accommodate someone as tall as he was in a sleeping position. Jinqing had no choice but to sit up, lean against the window, and stretch his legs out across the seat. Though he closed his eyes and tried to sleep, his present posture was not at all comfortable, not nearly so pleasant as cuddling with his wife had been, her head on his shoulder. Since he was only supported from one side, whenever the coach pitched and yawed, his upper body swayed partway off the seat.

He opened his eyes and looked at his wife curled up on the other seat. Sound asleep. As a matter of fact, all the other passengers were sleeping as well. Even the sixty-two-year-old headed to Soochow to be married had one voluminous sleeve of his *magua* stuffed under his head for a pillow and was now sound asleep. "Don't even know if I'll still be in this world when I'm sixty-two," he thought. "But there he is headed happily south to get married! Even plans on living at least twenty years more! Taking third class south now, but I wonder if he'll still be doing third class when he comes back north with that Soochow bride of his? Probably not. Bet she wouldn't be able to go through thick and thin with a man the way this bride of mine can."

When his thoughts reached this point, he began to feel sorry that he had put his lovely wife through the inconvenience of such a difficult trip. He made up his mind that when they got to Shanghai, he would work as hard as humanly possible, and then, later on, when he had made some money and they went back up north again, he'd take her back in second class, or maybe—dare he even think of it?—maybe even first class! "I can see it now," he thought. "She'll be dressed like the beauty she is, and I'll put her in a first-class compartment. Might even be a couple of children frolicking around the compartment as well. What a day that will be!" It was as though once he had the fantasy, the reality followed hard on its heels. Sitting on a first-class berth supported by soft springs, he crossed his legs and was incredibly comfortable. The springs eased him up, and then they eased him down. He rode as comfortably on top of them as if mounted on a cloud. But just at that moment a monster grabbed his legs and unceremoniously yanked him down from his downy mount. The intensity of that shock was beyond all description. He opened his eyes and looked around. Where had his cloud gone? Quite obviously he had been dreaming, for he was still seated on a hard wooden seat in third class.

Standing before him was a soldier in full uniform. Bandoliers loaded with ammunition crossed the man's chest, and he held a rifle in his hand as he sat down gruffly next to Jin-qing. This soldier had probably swept Jinqing's feet down from the seat while he was still sleeping. Also fully armed, a number of his comrades were seated here and there in the coach as well. Jinqing quickly realized that these armed troops had boarded the train in order to protect the passengers so that they might safely put back their heads and sleep while the train continued to race through the long night. Fortunately, this comrade proved quite civilized. Though he did rest one of his feet on Yuqing's seat, he and his comrades did not occupy any seat originally held by a woman.

Jinqing raised his arm and looked at his watch: 3:30 in the morning. All the other passengers, of course, had long since gone to sleep. Even those little lights below the baggage racks were now lost in a dark slumber. Jinqing looked out the window. Everything was as dark as though it had been painted black. The ba-da-da ba-da-da of the train's mad gallop down the tracks was enough to strike fear in anyone. Fortunately, the soldiers scattered among the passengers did give one some feeling of security, for they all sat up straight and unafraid.

"But when you come to think of it, the passengers here in third class are mostly poor," he thought. "Doesn't matter if you protect them or not. If you want to protect people, it ought to be those in first and second class. They have lots of stuff with them that's worth stealing, and if you kidnap them, then they themselves would be worth a pretty penny too." Actually, had he only known, he was needlessly concerned on their behalf.

Outside the compartments in first and second class was a corridor just wide enough to allow the passage of one person. At both ends, the corridor made a dog's leg before connecting to the doors between the cars. In both corners formed by the turns, there was a jump seat that could be pulled down. In first and second class, those jump seats at either end of the cars were occupied by a soldier in a warm leather coat and with a Mauser automatic at his side. It would be very difficult for anyone to get into those cars.

The two entrances to first class were especially well guarded. One might have thought that it was some sort of *yamen*[4] stoutly defended by two loyal government guards. And though it was deep night, the guards' eyes were wide open, and their hands rested on their Mausers as they sat on their jump seats. The doors to the first-class compartments were tightly closed, and, though there were windows in the doors, they were so closely curtained by green felt that not so much as a breath of air could have gotten through.

There was one compartment between Hu Ziyun's and the guard at this end of the car. At a time when everyone was sleeping, the sound of laughter reached the ears of the guard at Ziyun's end of the car. This was nothing unusual, of course, because many passengers had brought their family members along, and it was only natural that if they couldn't sleep, some of them would while away the time in conversation.

About half an hour after that, a compartment door made a creaking sound as it was slid open from the inside. Out stepped a young matron wearing a pink silk nightgown decorated with embroidered blue flowers. Below, all you could see were flesh-colored silk stockings on feet that were thrust into slippers of white embroidered satin. Her hair billowed down over her shoulders, partially covering her cheeks. As she entered the corridor, her four limbs seemed drained of strength, as though she were ill. Supporting herself against the outside of the car, she lurched her way unsteadily down the corridor. Judging from the looks of things, she was probably headed to the bathroom.

4. In traditional China, *yamen* were government offices.

And then the upper half of a man's body appeared protruding through the doorway of the same compartment. He was over forty and sported a small moustache. Beneath a terry-cloth kimono with a large, loosely tied belt at the waist, he too was in his pajamas. Supporting himself against the door, he looked toward the woman in the corridor and called after her, "Hurry back. You aren't wearing enough. Watch out you don't catch cold."

She turned and gave him three words in response: "It doesn't matter."

The male was obviously very concerned with her welfare for he waited for her by the door to the compartment until she returned from the toilet. Then he rushed forward, took her by the hand, and said with a smile, "It doesn't matter, huh? Then why is your hand so cold?"

The young matron smiled at him and said, "I'm grateful for all your concern. When we get to Shanghai, I'll pay you back." Holding hands, the man and woman went back into the compartment.

Seeing all this, the guard at the end of the car was thoroughly confused. Since this man and woman were in the same compartment, they had to be man and wife. The wife comes out to go to the bathroom; the husband watches over her like a hawk the whole time—nothing unusual about that either. But why had she said she'd pay him back when they got to Shanghai? If she wanted to pay him back, she could pay him back this very night, or tomorrow morning. Why did she have to wait until they got to Shanghai to pay him back? The guard was so puzzled that he actually felt a bit depressed.

How could this guard have known that the couple was in reality none other than Hu Ziyun and Liu Xichun, two people who hadn't even known each other twelve hours earlier when their relationship to each other had been just as distant as the guard's relationship to them now? While the guard continued to wonder about them, their compartment was once more sealed up tight, though a bit of light did manage to escape from the curtained glass door. Before long, however, even that was gone. Obviously, they had turned the lights out. The fates of the two people in that compartment were like the fate of the Shanghai Express itself as it hurtled blindly through the night.

7

Everyone Ill at Ease

In the full depth of night, there was nothing worth recording either inside or outside the Shanghai Express. Even in describing the compartment occupied by Hu Ziyun and Miss Liu we can come up with only a single sentence: *Nary was heard so much as a word.* By sunrise, they were already on the Yellow River Bridge. Ziyun looked out the window and saw the mighty waters of the Yellow River surging eastward. The dikes on both banks of the river were tall as mountains. Many boats were moored by the muddy bank on the south side. They had flat, wide decks from which tall masts stretched skyward and swayed back and forth, magnifying the rocking motion of the boats under them. It was really quite a sight. Ziyun turned back to the berth, took Xichun by the shoulders, and tried to shake her awake. "Wake up; we're almost in Tsinan. Besides, you really ought to get up to see the Yellow River."

She raised two bare arms above her head and stretched. Sleepy eyed, she looked at Ziyun, smiled, closed her eyes again, and said, "I want to get a little more sleep."

"The sun isn't quite up yet, and both banks of the Yellow River are still hidden in the morning mist. It's really quite beautiful."

Xichun kept her eyes closed, flipped over on the berth, and said, "You talked and talked all evening before I went to sleep yesterday, and you're *still* at it."

Ziyun drew the blanket up over her shoulders. He took the washbasin off the rack and prepared to wash up. He filled the basin half full and tested it with his hand. He drew his hand back in alarm for the water was ice cold. He immediately rang for the porter and asked for some hot water. The porter who was on duty last night had gone off to get some sleep. The new one came in, noticed Xichun on the lower berth, and couldn't keep himself from staring at her. Noticing the look in his eyes, Ziyun was rather upset. Putting on his sternest expression, he said: "Just pour the water in the basin and go! We have no further need of you here."

Xichun turned over on the berth and asked, "Ziyun, are we in Tsinan yet?"

Ziyun answered, "Almost. Why don't you get up now."

The porter thought this little exchange sounded exactly like the talk you'd hear between a man and his wife. He decided that he had been mistaken about the woman on the lower berth. Nor did he dare look at her again. Having been rebuffed by Ziyun, all he could do was leave.

Whatever the porter had or hadn't done, it certainly didn't bother Xichun. She got up, washed, combed her hair, and then opened her purse and took out her various weapons—bombers, tanks, smoke bombs, and so on. There was nothing magic about her purse that enabled it to hold all these weapons of war; we are merely talking about her compact, combs, rouge, lipstick, and the like. Those men in the world who have been utterly destroyed by women will readily agree that their cosmetics are in fact death-dealing instruments of war. After exhibiting her consummate skill in the handling of these various weapons, Xichun returned them all to her purse. By this point, the train had already pulled into Tsinan station and been stopped for quite some time.

There was the usual chaos of passengers getting on and off the train. After ten minutes or so, the crowd on the platform thinned out, and Ziyun suggested, "Since the weather's so fair and there's no wind, why don't we take a turn around the platform?"

"But it's nice and warm in here and quite cold out there. If we go out, we might catch cold, isn't that right?" As she said "isn't that right?" she gave him a smile that showed her snowy white teeth off to advantage. Ziyun was, of course, aware of the truth of all she had said, but he was feeling dizzy, perhaps because he had already smoked too many cigars this morning, and wanted to get outside to clear his head.

"Well, we'll be all right as long as we bundle up a bit. Quite a few other passengers have gotten off already. Look outside." When she looked, sure enough, some foreigners were strolling along the platform, and the young man with the dog in the compartment next to theirs was out there, too. He was wearing a heavy jacket and a large hat that appeared to be made of something like the fur of a porcupine. He controlled his large dog by hanging onto the heavy leather leash with both hands.

"If you're afraid of dogs," said Ziyun, "we don't have to get off."

It was a very ordinary sort of thing for him to say, but, strange to tell, it seemed to disturb Xichun. Her face flushed a deep red, but then, almost immediately, she recovered her composure and said, "Actually, I would like to get off and then walk down the platform to third class and visit that friend of mine." Thereupon, they bundled up, put on heavy overcoats, and got off the train. As they walked out of the first-class sleeping car, their warm faces were suddenly assailed by ice-cold air, and yet, everything considered, they found it rather refreshing. Ziyun supported her under the arm and helped her down to the platform.

Thanks to special permits issued to them by the Bureau of Railroads, there were a few vendors plying their trade right there on the platform. Shoulders huddled against the cold, they took slow and measured steps along the side of the train. Baskets with various foods for sale dangled from the crooks of their arms, while their hands were held out in front of them, each buried deep in the opposite sleeve and thus well sheltered from the wind.

Further off, just outside the wooden paling that separated the station from the street, there were many other vendors, each behind a little stand from which they carried on their business. Most were clustered in the vicinity of the third-class coach, and many of the third-class passengers walked over to the fence and bought snacks from them. Ziyun smiled and observed, "Nowadays, young people are forever talking about abolishing classes, but that's a lot easier said than done. Even vendors divide themselves into classes. Those with clout leisurely conduct their business inside the station, while those without it have to content themselves waiting for customers there outside the paling."

Xichun said, "Actually, it's a difficult situation for the railroad to deal with. If you let all the peddlers in, you'd have utter chaos on the platform, and that would be most inconvenient for the passengers. On the other hand, if you didn't let a single one in, that would be inconvenient for the passengers as well because some of them don't want to have to get off the train to buy things." Xichun was quite full of herself as she spoke and came across as someone thoroughly familiar with the ways of the world. Without her realizing it, her voice grew ever louder as she went on with her explanation, and she became so wrapped up in what she had to say that she ceased to pay attention to anyone around her. At this point, the young man with the dog walked up next to her.

The young man stared at her for a moment and smiled ever so slightly. One could tell from the way he smiled that there was more than a little contempt in the gesture. Last night, Ziyun had felt that this young fellow was contemptible because of the way he always kept his eyes glued on young women. At that time, however, Ziyun had felt in no position to intervene. But now, because he felt his relationship with Xichun had deepened, anyone who treated her with a disdainful attitude was insulting him personally. Therefore, he stopped dead in his tracks and nailed the young man with a dirty look.

Water off a duck's back. The young fellow retained his poise and didn't seem to mind a bit. At this juncture, his dog came over quietly, stretched out its neck, and began sniffing around Xichun's feet. The young man yanked in the leash for all he was worth and warned the dog, "Watch out where you sniff! Careful *you* don't get taken in, too!" His remark made Xichun flush red clear to the base of her ears, and she hurried away.

"Did he frighten you?" asked Hu Ziyun. "If he ever lets that dog of his sniff at you again, he'll have me to answer to!"

After Xichun watched as the young man got back on the train, she turned back to Hu Ziyun and said, "He's nothing but a hoodlum; why sink to his level? Besides, acting the way *he* does, somebody's bound to clean his clock sooner or later anyway." As she spoke, she kept turning and looking back as though afraid he might follow her and try to overhear what she said. She disguised her discomfort by changing the subject entirely: "Look at that foreign woman. See all the bread, bananas, and pears she's bought!" Xichun pointed over toward the second-class car. "From the looks of things, she doesn't plan on using the dining car. Foreigners try to save money just like anyone else."

Ziyun laughed and said, "That's a White Russian. She's in the same compartment as Mrs. Yu. I wouldn't be at all surprised if somebody bought the ticket for her."

"Your mentioning Mrs. Yu reminds me. Since she came to visit us yesterday, we ought to return her visit today."

"Might not be up yet," suggested Ziyun.

"Doesn't matter. As one woman to another, I can go into the compartment even if she isn't. But you really ought to get back on the train. It's too cold out here for you."

Without thinking, Ziyun put his hand through her arm for he really didn't want her to go. At just that moment, however, Li Chengfu got down from the train and walked toward them. Seeing his old friend, Ziyun loosened his hold for a moment, and Xichun took advantage of the opportunity to pull away and walk down toward Mrs. Yu's compartment. Ziyun had to content himself with striding forward to welcome Li Chengfu. "Good morning," said Chengfu. "Got off to stroll about, I see."

Ziyun hesitantly stroked his chin as though thinking of what to do next. Then he smiled at Chengfu and said, "Well, with a woman in the compartment, in lots of ways I'm not as free as I was before. That's why I got up a little on the early side. You've come out for a walk, too, huh?"

"By now, I must have been *through* Tsinan at least twenty times without ever having gotten out of the station. But I always make it a point to get out and stretch my legs so that at least I can console myself with having walked along the Tsinan platform if nothing else."

"From here on south," said Ziyun, "every station is warmer than the one before. You can take a stroll every time the train stops if you want to."

Seeing that Xichun was no longer with them, Chengfu

smiled and said, "Traveling is much easier to take when you have someone to chat with. But in that compartment I'm in they like to chat way *too* much. Can't get a word in edgewise."

"Why don't you talk with that Mrs. Yu in the compartment next to yours? She loves to talk and is pretty knowledgeable about most things as well," Ziyun suggested.

Hearing Ziyun say this, Chengfu looked around and, having assured himself that there was no one near, said to him in hushed tones, "Mrs. Yu says that she is a married lady, but I'm not so sure. I think her background is somewhat questionable, and the less one has to do with her, the better."

Ziyun laughed and said, "You worry too much. She comes out of one of the back *hutongs*[1] in Peiping, I'll grant you that. But you'll find a lot of women who come out of those Peiping *hutongs* who make very good wives. Just because a person's had a bad start doesn't mean she's condemned to amount to nothing her whole life." Chengfu mulled that over for a bit and smiled—but he didn't say anything.

At this point, a man wearing a gray cotton robe shoved his way through the crowd and, holding a battered old felt hat in his hand, approached Ziyun. "Manager Hu," he said, bowing toward Ziyun. Hu Ziyun looked at the man carefully. His face was gaunt and as emaciated as it would have been if he had just recovered from some serious illness. His eyes were sunken, and his cheekbones protruded sharply. His beard was a scraggly affair that amounted to only a few measly strands. Since, like his hair, it was still black, you could tell that it was *not* something he had grown because he felt he was at an appropriate age to do so, but was rather

---

1. *Hutong* is the word used for "lane" or "back street" in northern China and is especially associated with Peiping (modern Beijing). Here, Ziyun is saying that Mrs. Yu—back in the days when she was known as "Number 3 from Soochow"—once worked as a prostitute in a back alley in Peiping.

the result of not having shaved. On first sight, Ziyun didn't recognize him, but when he heard his voice, he realized that it was Shi Ziming, a man who had once worked as his own administrative secretary.

Ziyun nodded in his direction and said, "Must be two years since I last saw you. I almost didn't recognize you."

The man frowned, sighed, and said, "I won't try to hide anything from you, Manager Hu. These past two years I've had one piece of bad luck after another. It's only been two years, but I'm afraid I've aged at least twenty. No wonder you didn't recognize me at first."

"Where are you headed?" asked Ziyun.

"I came to hunt up a friend of mine here in Tsinan. Turned out he was away, and I waited over two months for him to come back. But now, with the year coming to an end and winter coming on, I can't afford to wait any longer. I'm headed back to Nanking."

Noting that Shi Ziming's gray cotton robe was heavily stained with cooking oil and ink, Ziyun didn't really want to continue the conversation. "All right, then. We'll run into each other on the train again after a while."

"Yes sir," said Ziming before bowing and walking away.

Chengfu said, "Lots of young people are unemployed these days. I think this man belongs to their ranks."

"I never imagined that he'd sink so low. Back when he was working for me, he used to sport Western suits and looked sharp as a tack. Used to be that when he met people, he was always poised and self-confident. I hadn't thought that poverty could so change a man's attitude. Now when he meets people, he seems to positively grovel."

Chengfu smiled and said, "There's a lot of truth to the old saw that *Cash is courage and clothing is clout.* Since he has neither courage nor clout, it's no wonder he can't make much of a showing for himself." Talking in this fashion, the two men had already made two rounds of the platform.

Ziyun felt that he'd been out in the cold long enough. He smiled at Chengfu and suggested, "Let's knock off the walking and go to the dining car for a cup of coffee."

Since he hadn't invited him to go to the first-class sleeper but had suggested the dining car instead, Chengfu felt that Ziyun must be trying to hide something from him. He cupped one hand inside the other in front of him and made a slight bow in Ziyun's direction: "No! I'll have to beg off of that one. I can't even drink strong tea, and I'm even less used to drinking coffee early in the morning on an empty stomach. The train's about to pull out. Think I'd better head back to my compartment. Have to keep an eye on things in there." Having said that much, he turned and walked toward the train.

Feeling somewhat abandoned, Ziyun stood there immobilized. It seemed to him that no matter what he did lately he always ended up feeling somewhat at loose ends. Even in interacting with friends he felt the same way. After a few brief remarks, Chengfu had just up and left him standing there alone. Ziyun felt that he must have said something that offended him. The train was starting to move now.

"When I have a little time," he thought, "I'll have to go to the second-class sleeper and say something or other to smooth things over." With thoughts such as these in his mind, Ziyun made his way to the second-class sleeper along the outside of the train. He looked inside, but with the weather as cold as it was the windows were all sealed tight, and looking into a relatively dark place from a bright one he couldn't see a thing. Then his thoughts took a different tack. "Chengfu just got on the train. If I go running to his compartment immediately, isn't that going to be a bit too obvious?" And so, after he climbed aboard the second-class coach, he turned around and headed for first class instead.

The way the train was put together, the dining car separated first and second class, and so, to get back to his compartment, Ziyun had to go through it. Unexpectedly, as he pushed the door to the dining car open, the first thing he saw was Xichun sitting at the first table. She was facing toward him and sipping lemon tea. Mrs. Yu, with her back to him, was seated across from Xichun and, of course, didn't see him enter the car. She was in the midst of saying something to Xichun: "No matter what, the best thing is to do it before we get to Soochow. But we can't make it too soon either because. . . ."

Xichun cut her off mid-sentence. "Oh look, Mr. Hu is here! How did you happen to come in from this end of the car?" She shifted her eyes immediately away from Ziyun and looked meaningfully toward Mrs. Yu, who, seeming rather disconcerted, quickly reached up, straightened her hair, and wiped her lips with a napkin.

Mrs. Yu stood up and said, "You've come at just the right time, Mr. Hu. Sit down and have a snack with us." She both blushed and smiled as she spoke. Looking at the two women, Ziyun was puzzled to find that they both looked somewhat dismayed. But then his thoughts took a different tack: "Feeling confused and at loose ends myself, I have no real basis for trying to judge how others feel just by the way they look. My best bet is simply to calm down so that I don't end up making a fool of myself."

Thinking in this way, he managed to compose himself before smiling at Mrs. Yu and explaining, "I was taking a turn around the platform just now when the cold began to get to me, and I scurried back into the warmth of the train as soon as possible." He took his coat off as he spoke, and Xichun, not at all trying to keep above suspicion by hiding their relationship, immediately took Ziyun's coat in her own hands and placed it on the seat. What's more, she then scrunched over to one side to make room for him to sit

◄ "The best thing is to do it before we get to Soochow." ►

down. Ziyun had originally felt the situation somewhat awkward owing to the presence of Mrs. Yu, but, seeing that both women seemed very matter-of-fact about the whole thing, he felt it wouldn't do for him to be too timid. And so without any qualms he sat down next to Xichun, which placed him directly across from Mrs. Yu. He couldn't help feeling there was something rather unnatural about her appearance, for her face reddened and turned pale by turns.

"Mrs. Yu isn't feeling all that well," explained Xichun. "I had to drag her out of her compartment. There are simply too many people crowded into that little space, and the air is absolutely stifling—enough to make *anybody* dizzy. I thought that bringing her to the dining car would refresh her a bit."

At this point, the said Mrs. Yu actually did assume the look of someone who was ailing: placing her left elbow on the table and supporting her head with her left hand, she raised her right hand and tapped several times on her forehead the way one does when suffering from a headache. "The steam pipes on these trains are far, far too hot," she said with a frown.

"Then let's have the steward bring her a nice cold, carbonated drink," suggested Ziyun. Xichun gave him a little kick under the table; she also stole a glance at him, while a slight smile played around the corners of her lips. Her obvious intention was to make him feel good. Ziyun realized what she was doing, and he smiled back at her. Ziyun ordered a cup of hot tea for himself.

As Ziyun sat there and kept them company with his tea, he couldn't help feeling that the conversation had a very detached quality to it. There would be long stretches of silence before even meaningless social commonplaces were exchanged. Ziyun considered this rather odd, but then his thoughts took another tack: "There must be things that

Xichun finds it hard to talk about with nothing more than the status of 'girlfriend.' Here she is, sharing a first-class compartment with a man. How can she readily explain that to her friend? No wonder their conversation is a bit strange and strained. Perhaps the best thing I can do is to make myself scarce so that they can talk more freely."

Ziyun picked up the check and signed it. Then he took his overcoat, said good-bye to Mrs. Yu, and returned to his compartment. Once inside, he yawned several times and stretched. His eyelids were becoming very heavy. Tossing his coat on the bottom berth, Ziyun flopped down on it. The train had been under way for some time now, and the hypnotic rocking of its cars afforded tired passengers a sweet sleep.

Ziyun's feet hung over the side of the berth. In his sleepy state, he was vaguely aware of someone taking off his shoes and then lifting his feet onto the berth. He guessed, of course, that this was Xichun, but he was so very sleepy that by the time she had finished arranging his feet, he had totally lost consciousness.

When he awoke again, Xichun was seated by his head, reading. When she saw him open his eyes, she said, "Wow, you really had yourself a sleep! You've been out of it for a long time. Do you know we're almost in Taian now?"[2]

"Got up a bit too early today. What's more. . . . Hey, how come you didn't lie down for a while, too?"

Xichun got up and pulled their compartment door tightly shut before answering, "I didn't want to climb over you to get to the top bunk, and the lower one would be

2. Taian (pinyin: Tai'an) is in Shantung (pinyin: Shandong) Province south of Tsinan. This is where one stops to visit Tai Shan, most important of China's "five sacred mountains." It is also the hometown of Jiang Qing, Mao Zedong's last wife and leader of the notorious "Gang of Four" that misruled China during the Great Proletarian Cultural Revolution (1966–1976).

uncomfortably small for the two of us, so I sat here and read."

Putting a hand on her shoulder, Ziyun pulled himself up to a sitting position and said, "It's all my fault for going to sleep on the lower bunk. Here I left you all by yourself with nothing to do but sit."

Xichun covered her mouth demurely with one hand and smiled. Then she rang for the porter and asked for a hot towel. After Ziyun had cleaned his face with it, she poured him a cup of hot tea. Sipping the tea, Ziyun gazed at Xichun's face and smiled. "You've had a whole day to look at me now," said Xichun. "Recognize me yet?"

"In the beginning, these eyes of mine were always greedy for your great physical beauty. I'm beyond that stage now; now I'm appreciating your character, the *kind* of person you are. You know, you have all the qualities it takes to be an ideal modern woman *or* a traditional one. In sum, you are the kind of woman who's cut out to be a good wife and mother. I can't figure out for the life of me why in the world your in-laws should have anything against you."

Xichun knitted her brows. Noticing that Ziyun's cup was empty, she took it and smiled. "Would you care for more tea?"

"I would like another cup, but I don't want to bother you."

Xichun took his cup and filled it. "Why would that be the slightest bother? Now that I know there's a man in this society of ours like you, a man who really understands a woman, how could I *ever* find him bothersome? When it comes to that, I'd gladly be your slave, for that matter."

Ziyun took the cup and said, "Such lavish praise. I don't deserve it."

"Lavish? You've never been as frustrated and disappointed in life as I have, so you don't really understand. But suppose for the moment that you were as frustrated as I have been, and further suppose that just when you were feeling the worst, someone came along and comforted you. You'd be more thankful to that person than you would be even to someone who had just plucked you from the jaws of death and saved your life. That's why I am so ecstatically happy this morning, so happy that I even seem a bit drunk. On the other hand, I feel sad as well. By fits and starts, it's as though everything is going my way and then suddenly *not* going my way. I'm happy and miserable by turns. You can probably tell the way I feel just by looking at me." Her eyes reddened a bit as she spoke.

Holding the warm cup of tea in both hands, Ziyun gazed at her and said, "But why should you be down in the dumps?"

Although there were no tears in her eyes, she looked as though her suffering was genuine. She took a handkerchief from her purse, rubbed her eyes a bit, and said in a low voice, "You mean you can't guess? Here I am—a supposedly proper woman—conducting myself with what could well be construed as impropriety. How can I face myself?"

Ziyun put down his teacup, placed one hand over hers, and patted her on the back with the other. "You're much too honest and hard on yourself. In a modern society such as ours, you can't allow yourself to be tied up in knots by old-fashioned Confucian morality. After all, how many decades of life are we allotted in this old world anyway? In the few that we *do* have, we should make every day as happy as we possibly can. What's the point in making yourself miserable? Besides, it's different for women than it is for men. Girls aren't taught the importance of being happy. And then, when they do realize how important it is, it's too late! After all, if a woman wants to be happy and to enjoy life, she's got to do it in that decade between twenty and thirty."

Xichun laughed and said, "According to you, I'm just at the right age to enjoy myself right now."

"Well, isn't that the way it is?"

"Actually, I quite agree with you," said Xichun. "But this morning, for some reason or other, I have this strange feeling. . . . I just keep feeling ill at ease."

"Yes, and just as I was beginning to feel totally at ease, you said all those negative things and made *me* feel ill at ease, too."

"Everyone on the train seems to be feeling ill at ease. What do you think the reason is?"

Just as Ziyun was about to launch into his explanation, a knock was heard at the compartment door. Thinking it was the porter, Ziyun slid it open with easy assurance. Much to his surprise, however, the person who stood outside was not the porter but Shi Ziming, the former employee that he had earlier run into on the platform. The latter, conscious of his place, did not enter the compartment but rather remained in the corridor. Shi Ziming took off his hat and bowed toward Ziyun; then, catching sight of Xichun, he gave another bow.

He even said something to her by way of greeting, but it was in tones so low that it was difficult to make out, but it seemed to be "Missus." Ziyun didn't seem the least offended by Shi's lack of decorum in addressing his wife directly. However, he did begin thinking to himself: "On the platform when I told him we could talk later on when we got back on the train, it was only talk. Didn't really want him to come. What do I do now? Invite him in? I really don't feel like it. How about taking him to the dining car and having a talk with him there? But, shabby as he is, how can I pull that off? The steward would take one look at him and know that he's from third class. According to railroad regulations, third-class passengers aren't supposed to go to the dining car in the first place."

Just as he was hesitating, Xichun, not objecting in the least to the man's obvious poverty, nodded toward him and invited him in. Shi Ziming bowed again in her direction with a smile and said, "There's no need for me to come in. I'll be just fine standing here in the corridor." Ziyun was worried that Xichun would lead him into the compartment anyway. If nothing else, he didn't want the man's sweaty odor to foul the little room. He hurriedly packed his pipe with tobacco, held it between his teeth, and then, picking up a box of matches, walked to the doorway and stood just outside the compartment in such a way as to block access to it. He lit his pipe and blew out a cloud of smoke.

"So you're headed for Nanking, eh? There are scads of people going there to look for work. Arrive by the thousands every day. What makes you think there are enough organizations in Nanking to place so many unemployed?"

Shi Ziming gave a forced smile and said, "You're right, of course. It's going to be very tough to find a job there. I realize that. You might say I'm like somebody buying an Air Force lottery ticket—taking a long shot." Pipe clenched firmly between his teeth, Ziyun granted him a slight smile. "In the past few years," Ziming continued, "Manager Hu's business has really taken off."

"Commerce and industry are in a state of economic depression right now throughout the entire world. I'm afraid the words *taken off* are not applicable," Ziyun responded.

"Ah," said Ziming with a note of genuine regret, "I should never have left Manager Hu for what I thought were greener pastures. If only I'd stayed under your direction, I'd be sitting pretty right now. But it's too late to be sorry about that now, I suppose."

"What's the point in bringing up the past?" asked Ziyun.

"In Tsinan, I got so bogged down," explained Ziming, "that it was all I could do to pull myself free. Fortunately, a friend came up with a train ticket. I've learned my lesson, though. Never venture into a strange place where you don't have that many friends on the off chance of making it big." These words pleased Ziyun immensely, and he nodded his head several times in hearty agreement. "I've got the train ticket all right, but the trouble is when I get off the train, I don't have any money for a hotel."

That set Ziyun off. "Since you're going there looking for work, what's the point in trying to put on airs by living in a hotel? Stay in a friend's house."

"You're right, of course, and perhaps I can do that later. But I can't very well go hole up in a friend's place the minute I set foot in town. I've got to have some money on me when I get there so I can afford a hotel for a day or two. It's really hard for me to ask this, but I wonder if you could spare some cash? I can't promise to repay you right away, but later on, as soon as I have a job, I'll. . . ."

Ziyun didn't wait for him to finish. He thrust out his chin and, still holding his pipe in his teeth, said, "Well, I'm sure you can appreciate that as a traveler I don't carry much cash with me."

Ziming bowed every so slightly, smiled, and replied, "Of course. But I wouldn't dare make so bold as to borrow any sizable sum from Manager Hu. If you could see your way clear to letting me have as little as ten dollars, I'd be eternally grateful."

Ziyun frowned, gave a scornful laugh, and said, "It's not that I want to keep on criticizing you, but I really should point out that that's the trouble with you—you don't know the value of money. Do you really consider ten dollars a small amount?"

"No, it's not. It's not. You're right, of course," replied Ziming compliantly.

"I don't have any money to give you," said Ziyun. "You'd better make other plans." Ziming had not expected that

Ziyun would respond with such a cold and clear-cut refusal. He stood there in the corridor confused and not knowing which way to turn. Ziming's gaunt face was past all blushing, but it did break out in a cold sweat. Hu Ziyun, on the other hand, seemed to grow more composed by the minute. Pipe still clenched between his teeth, he stood perfectly still and, apparently feeling thoroughly at ease, slowly blew out a stream of smoke.

8

Those Who Ask for Help Are Also Willing to Give It

A woman's heart is difficult to fathom. Sometimes she is cruel, sometimes kind. That same vicious mother-in-law so fond of disciplining her daughter-in-law is the same woman who can often be heard piously invoking the name of Amida Buddha; and that same prostitute who will lead an honest youth down the primrose path to destruction until he has utterly squandered the family fortune is the very same woman who will on another occasion stuff bills into the hands of some pauper on the street whom she has never met before.

Xichun sat inside the compartment and saw how Hu Ziyun was doing his best to block Shi Ziming's entrance. She also overheard his indifferent response to Shi's request for a loan. "This jerk named Hu is a miser," she thought to herself. "When an old friend with a kind and pleasant face asks to borrow some money, you simply don't refuse him, no matter what the circumstances. If I were Shi Ziming, I'd give Hu a good piece of my mind. All Hu has to do is skip two meals in the dining car, and he'd have enough money right there to rescue an old friend and a fellow passenger to boot." She reached up to the head of the berth and got her purse. Then she called to Shi Ziming and said, "I can help out a little." She took out a ten-dollar bill, reached around Hu Ziyun, and handed it to him. Beaming, Ziming bobbed up and down in a series of chaotic bows as he respectfully received the bill in both hands.

"I really don't deserve this," he said several times with deferential politeness.

Ziyun said nothing, but as he watched Xichun give Ziming the money he flushed a deep red. Ziming himself felt that the whole situation had taken an embarrassing turn and didn't want to linger around too long. Somewhat puzzled, he thanked Xichun again and walked away.

"I don't feel right about letting you spend your money like that," said Ziyun. "I'll pay the ten dollars back to you later."

"Doesn't matter. It's only a few dollars. Aren't you embarrassed about using a word as heavy as *repay* with regard to such a paltry sum?"

"Don't get me wrong. It's not that I don't want to help the man. It's just that he lost his job in the first place because of his opium habit. And I can tell he's still smoking the stuff even now. A man like that's hopeless. That's why I didn't take his request seriously." Xichun didn't react to this explanation one way or the other, just smiled. Since it was a very unpleasant situation for Ziyun, he managed to avoid looking her in the eye by leaning against the window and staring off into the distance.

Having unexpectedly obtained ten dollars, Ziming was surprised and ashamed at the same time. Hu had been so cold and his wife so generous. When you go seeking a favor from someone, you really never know what direction to take. Mentally going over everything that had happened since he decided to approach Hu for a loan, Ziming made his way back to third class.

Quite a few local passengers had gotten off at Tsinan, and, consequently, third class was not nearly so crowded as it had been. Ziming took a seat one row up from Zhu Jinqing. As soon as he sat down, Ziming began to think again about how he had come to borrow that money. He had started to think about borrowing money from his former boss as soon as he discovered the latter was on the train. He had thought about it for a long while before working up the courage to actually go to first class and ask for the money. He remembered how indecisive he had felt before going to see Ziyun and how embarrassed he had been when he finally did see him. The one thing you can't afford to be in this world is poor. And if you are poor, the one thing you can't do is to ask people to help you out.

He slowly drew a crumpled wad of red paper out of his pocket. Actually, it was a pack of cigarettes that had been tucked down into that pocket for so long that it now looked like a shapeless wad of red paper. From it he fished out something white and thin as a piece of string. He tried to finger it back into shape. Then he took out two broken matchsticks, lit it with one of them, sat back, and enjoyed a leisurely smoke. While he was smoking, a smile kept playing around the corners of his lips. At just this juncture, carrying a pot of hot water, a porter came down the aisle and walked past him. Ziming took the cigarette out of his mouth and called, "Porter!" The porter turned, took one look at him, and, without responding, turned away again and kept on walking. Knowing that sooner or later he would walk back this way, Ziming sat there looking down the aisle. Sure enough, before too long, the porter came back.

Ziming called, "Porter! Bring me a pot of tea." Only then did the porter stop and look him over.

"You want tea, too?" he asked. "You'll have to wait a bit." Having said that much, he took the large pot of hot water and walked off once again. Ziming smiled and thought,

"Seeing the ragged clothes I'm wearing, he added that *too* when he asked me if I wanted tea."

Seeing this little drama unfold, Zhu Jinqing waxed more than a little indignant and said, "Damn!" Then addressing himself to Ziming, "If you'd like some tea, sir, why not use ours?" He gathered up the pot and a cup from the seat next to him and passed them to Ziming.

After thanking him profusely, Ziming said, "When a poor man goes traveling, he has to be prepared to bear insults at every turn."

Jinqing smiled and responded, "In the world today, people respect the clothes and not the man. It's really pitiful."

Ziming poured himself a cup of tea and slowly sipped it. Then he said, "It's no wonder, too. Twenty minutes ago I wasn't even qualified to drink tea, but now I am. That's because I borrowed ten dollars from someone up in first class. The value of a single pot of tea is not likely to exceed ten dollars, I trust."

Jinqing said, "These porters all seem to have the same way of looking at things. If you're neatly dressed, you could probably drink down your tea, not pay anything, and they wouldn't have the guts to ask you for a penny. But if your clothes are shabby, they won't pay any attention to you even if you do have money."

"What's more," added Ziming, "if you're shabbily dressed and happen to have any money, they'll probably think you stole it." Jinqing and Yuqing both laughed at that.

Just then, the porter in question came back their way, and Jinqing called him over. "What regulations do you people observe in selling tea here in third class?"

Having noticed Jinqing and Ziming talking together, the porter had a good idea of what lay behind the question. Nonetheless, he smiled and answered, "What's there to regulate with a simple thing like tea? If you keep the pot a short time, we charge a dime or two. If you keep it a long time, then you give us a dollar or maybe two, according to how well you liked our service."

"That's it? You don't have any requirement that a passenger be well dressed before you'll serve him tea?"

Ziming looked at Jinqing with a smile and said, "Young sir, there's no need for you to be indignant on my behalf. It's simple, really. These porters sell as much as they can as fast as they can. They're out to make a profit. If you're shabbily dressed, it is possible that you might drink it down and then not pay, and they'd lose their investment."

Listening to the two of them discussing him like this, the porter began to feel embarrassed and explained, "It's not that I wasn't willing to make tea for this passenger; it was just that I'd run out of hot water. That's why I ignored him. But since he's still waiting for his tea, I'll go make him a pot." Having said that much, good as his word, the porter made some tea and brought it to Ziming.

All the passengers within earshot thought all of this a most interesting diversion. Even the sexagenarian who was going south to get married stroked his beard and commented, "Proves the truth of the old proverb: *One thing is perfectly sure, you're better off dead than poor.* When we're born into this old world, we don't demand that we get the best situation possible, but, on the other hand, we don't come into it looking to suffer either. If we meet with suffering everywhere we turn, then every day we live is just one more day of pain—might just as well be dead."

Ziming laughed and said, "Don't see it that way myself. Peiping people have a saying that I like a lot better: *Don't care what they say, a bad life beats a good death any old day.* As long as you're alive, you can always struggle. And if you struggle, who's to say that someday you won't struggle your way into the good life? On the other hand, let's suppose you *do* have a miserable life, and then let's take it a step further and suppose you let yourself *die* that way. Well, if you want to talk 'miserable,' *that's* what I'd call 'miserable.' As far as I can see, you might just as well never have lived in the first place."

Jinqing looked at Yuqing, smiled, and said, "Looks as though we've found an ally." A bad life or a good death? With a question like that to sink their teeth into, some other passengers within earshot began expressing their opinions as well. You say this, and I say that, and before long there's a stimulating conversation under way.

By this time, the train was nearing Taian. If you looked eastward, off in the distance you could already see Tai Shan. Though still high in the afternoon sky, the sun was partially obscured behind it. That side of the famous mountain facing the train lay hidden in its own dark shadows.

At last the train pulled into Taian. A quaint town with a wide pedestrian promenade and an old watchtower, it was framed from behind by the great mountain itself. Pointing out the train window, Jinqing exclaimed, "Yuqing! When we come back up north, I'm going to take you on a tour of Tai Shan."

Yuqing smiled and said, "When we come back up north, you're going to do way, way too many things. If we did every last one of them, it would cost us somewhere between three and five thousand dollars."

Jinqing sighed and said, "See how utterly useless we are! We can't even dream of saving a small fortune of three to five thousand." As husband and wife discussed this, they noticed that, head thrown back, the old fellow kept stroking his beard and smiling. He was obviously thinking that *he* had a sum like that. Looking at him, Jinqing's thoughts took a different turn. "Maybe," he thought to himself, "a small fortune wouldn't be all *that* enjoyable. After all, the old fellow is still riding third class just like we are." His discourse changed direction as well: "You know what? The hardest place to figure out what class a person belongs to is right here in third-class coach. Somebody who's a real moneybags might ride third class for the savings. And somebody who has to struggle to come up with enough to buy even a third-class ticket *has* to ride with us because there is no fourth class."

"Do you think everybody in first and second class is rich?" asked Yuqing. Then she answered her own question: "I doubt it. Some people buy a first- or second-class ticket because they want to put up a good front. And I'll bet you'll find some people in first and second class who couldn't afford to buy even a *third*-class ticket if they had to pay for it themselves. But because of some special circumstance or other—the job they hold, for instance—they get to ride in first or second class without spending a dime of their own money."

As they were talking, Shi Ziming, who had gotten off the train when it pulled into Taian, now boarded the train again with a large number of paper packages of various sizes. He dumped everything onto his seat: a roast chicken, seven or eight boiled eggs, a stack of *shaobing*,[1] twenty-some pears, two cartons of cigarettes, and a box of matches. Jinqing couldn't hold back a broad smile. Ziming picked up two pears and offered them to the young couple.

Ziming smiled as he said, "Know why I bought so much stuff? I'll be honest with you. I'm like the proverbial poor kid who's suddenly come into a fortune—doesn't know which end is up, and doesn't know what to buy first. I haven't had a five-dollar bill on me for the past six months. And with a ten spot burning a hole in my pocket, I felt absolutely rich. I split it with a fellow passenger and got off to see what I could buy. As soon as I looked at anything, the peddler would come running after me, and I bought it. Then I got worried that the train was going to leave without me, and I hurried back on without buying a lot of other

1. *Shaobing* are wheat flour griddle cakes topped with sesame seeds.

things that I really did want. Don't think I spent an arm and a leg for all this stuff either. Very little, really. Add it all up, and it's still well under a dollar."

As he talked, he began tearing the chicken apart. He put a leg in his mouth with his left hand and began chewing as he poured himself a piping hot cup of strong tea with the right. "You know," he continued with a smile, "if you don't get too hung up on how sanitary it is, eating and drinking like this isn't half bad." He picked up his teacup and finished it off in one gulp. Jinqing looked at him and smiled, vicariously enjoying the experience. Ziming said, "I'm a good example of the old saw: *For a thirsty man water's a treat, and a hungry man knows how to eat.* You know eating that chicken leg and downing that tea just now was more satisfying than having the best wine in the world. As I say this, it occurs to me that I ought to thank that Mrs. Hu. If it hadn't been for her, I don't know how long I'd have to wait before putting anything in my stomach." Having said this much, he told the story of how he borrowed money from Mrs. Hu.

Not long after that, Liu Xichun came down to the third-class coach to visit Yuqing. At just that moment, Ziming happened to turn his head in her direction. Catching sight of her, he immediately stood up and said with a smile, "Oh, Mrs. Hu's here. Too bad the third-class coach is so dirty." He slid over to one side with the intention of making a place for Xichun. She, however, never took her eyes off her friend.

Yuqing stood and said with a smile, "Have a seat. I kept wanting to go up and visit you in first class, but every time the thought came to me, I'd lower my eyes, take one look at this simple getup I'm in, and decide I really didn't have what it takes for first class. So I kept thinking about it, putting it off, thinking about it some more, and just never got around to it."

Jinqing stood up, nodded at Xichun, and walked off to

take another empty seat. Taking advantage of Jinqing's thoughtful action, before Xichun had a chance to say anything, Yuqing quickly stepped toward her friend and took her by the hand. "The seat situation here in third has loosened up quite a bit now, so why don't you sit down here right next to me? Ever since we left school, everything has been smooth sailing for you, and it looks as though you've met with success at every turn. But me. Well, I'm as down on my luck as I ever was. Come on and have a seat. You know we've never really had a chance to sit down and have a good heart-to-heart since we left school. Be a shame if we let this opportunity slip by."

Xichun sat down, but as she did so she glanced over at Ziming and said in a low voice, "I thought there were just the two of you."

"That's right, just the two of us. That man is just somebody we struck up a conversation with a little while back."

While Xichun chatted with her friend, her eyes darted back and forth as fast as the shuttle on a loom as she surveyed every last nook and cranny of third class.

Although it was early in the day and quite chilly, the steam pipes in third class weren't putting out much heat. Xichun was wearing a lined cheongsam, to be sure, but coming from first class, which was like an oven, here in third class her back felt cold. Here in third class all the passengers were bundled in thick clothing, and they all held their arms out in front of them with each hand tucked well into the opposite sleeve for warmth. A woman who had not gotten enough sleep that night was stretched out across two seats with her arm crooked under her head for a pillow. One could readily imagine how uncomfortable she must have been. Some male passengers sat up semistraight and pillowed their heads back against the seats, while light snores emanated from their nostrils and threads of spittle dangled down from the corners of their lips.

The passengers in the worst shape, however, were those fresh from the countryside. The men among them wore cotton robes that reached to their knees and were tied at the waist with sashes. Everywhere you looked on their bodies, their clothes were wrinkled and lumpy as though little mountains had been randomly scattered beneath. On their heads, they sported either felt hats or watermelon caps,[2] all of which were encrusted with thick layers of dirt.

The heads and feet of the country women were even more remarkable and gave one a different kind of feeling. Their hair was done up so that it hung down the back like a crow's tail, and their bound feet looked like the long pointed kind of triangle that students sometimes use in geometry classes. Their pant cuffs were tied tightly round their ankles, making their legs and feet look for all the world like the wooden sticks used to pound clothes when doing the laundry.

All the country folk spoke in down-home accents that no one else could understand. Many held long-stemmed pipes with little metal bowls between their teeth, while drool dripped from the corners of their mouths. Bowls gurgled intermittently as pale wisps of smoke floated through the air. When the women spoke, they exposed large yellowed incisors spotted with decay. The very sight of their open mouths was enough to nauseate one. Xichun glanced at them very quickly and immediately turned her head away so as to expectorate. As soon as she lowered her head, however, she discovered that the spittoon had been dragged from its original position to the edge of someone's seat. One can well imagine what the inside of that spittoon looked like. Even the *outside* was coated with a thick layer of just plain snot and sputum; empty cigarette packs, pear pits, and crumpled

2. Skullcaps, so called because they resembled the rind of half a watermelon.

pieces of paper were scattered both inside and around its unsightly perimeter. The floor was covered with chicken bones and the empty shells of watermelon seeds. The word *intolerable* wouldn't even come close to describing it.

Xichun immediately took a handkerchief from a pocket in her dress, covered her lips, and spat into it. Pinching the handkerchief together, she frowned and was about to say something or other to Yuqing when suddenly the door into the car blew open. Apparently, the last person in or out hadn't shut it all the way. The wintry wind cut a swath through third class, and everyone's body tightened up defensively, proclaiming a voiceless, "Cold!" Luckily, someone close to the door got up and closed it.

Xichun looked earnestly at her friend and asked, "Since you two are on your honeymoon after all, why go third class just to save money? This is really too much. Sanitary conditions are a lot more important than the money you might save. What happens if you catch something and come down sick? What are you going to do then?"

Yuqing smiled at that. "But most people go third class. If something terrible happened to everyone who rode third class, there'd be a huge number of tragedies on each and every train. As I see it, it's really not all that bad." As she was speaking, the door to third class blew open again. This time, it was Ziming who rushed forward to close it.

As Ziming turned around, Xichun found herself looking him straight in the eye. Since she had to say something, she nodded and smiled: "So you're riding in third class as well."

Ziming bowed and said, "I can't thank Mrs. Hu enough for the money. I'm in no position to repay your kindness now, but in the future. . . . "

Xichun brushed his remarks aside with a wave of her hand. "Please don't talk like that; you're embarrassing me." She immediately lowered her head and continued her conversation with Yuqing. "Do you have an address in Shanghai yet? I'd really like to establish a small circle of good friends there."

Yuqing smiled at that. "Part of your small circle of good friends? There's nothing we'd like better to be sure, but how can people like us associate with a wealthy young matron like yourself?"

Xichun's face seemed to flush slightly at her friend's reply. Nonetheless, she forced a smile and said, "Sounds as though you don't *want* to. Well, in that case, I'd better take advantage of the opportunity I have now to ask you for something I'd really like to have."

"Well, I know you're not going to ask me for money, so just name it."

"Don't know whether you happen to have one on you or not, but if you do, I'd like to have a photograph of you two together."

"It just so happens that I do. Ordinarily, we'd have put such things in our trunk when we packed, but this was an exception because we had some new ones taken just before we left Peiping and didn't get them back from the photographers until just before we left. Had to put them in our traveling bag at the last moment." As she spoke, she pointed to the baggage rack above them.

Xichun looked at the traveling bag her friend was pointing to and said, "Great! May I have one, then?"

Zhu Jinqing overheard her words and immediately came over and stood on the bench opposite the two young women and made ready to take down the bag. Xichun waved her hand to stop him and said, "There's really no hurry. We have a whole day and a night before we get to Shanghai. Later, when Yuqing comes up to my compartment for a chat, she can bring it with her." She gave Yuqing a good-bye handshake and stood as if to leave. Just at that moment, however, the porter came through the door, followed by the ticket taker. Yuqing said, "Can't leave now. If you do, they're going to think that you got on without a ticket and are trying to avoid being checked."

Xichun sat down with a smile and observed the ticket taker. He held a punch in his right hand and, passenger by passenger, thrust out his left and said, if he bothered to say anything, "Ticket." When he got to the country people, he noticed that wedged in among them was a girl of thirteen or fourteen. Her face was pale and bony. A discolored braid hung down her back like a hedgehog's tail. One look was enough to tell that she was suffering from some sort of disease. As the ticket taker approached them, she concealed herself behind one of the women, and that, of course, attracted the ticket taker's attention all the more. He was especially attentive in checking the country people's tickets. Turned out that the seven of them had only six tickets— from Tsinan to Hsuchow.

When he inquired about this, a man whose face was covered with stubble stood up and asked with a forced smile, "Does a child have to have a ticket, too, sir?"

"What are you trying to pull?" the ticket taker asked back. "Why *wouldn't* a child need a ticket? If they're over four, it's half fare, and if they're over seven, a full fare. This kid's easily over ten. Why wouldn't she need a full fare?"

Holding his long bamboo pipe in both hands, stubble face bowed at the ticket taker and said, "Good sir, be kind to us. We're poor folk and can't afford to spend that much."

"If you can't afford it, you shouldn't bring her on the train in the first place. The nation runs the railroad, you know. What would happen if we gave everybody a free ride? Where do you think this train came from? Did heaven somehow or other rain it down out of the sky just for you to ride? And the engineer, where did *he* come from? Did heaven kind of send him along to run the train for you? Say, what do you do for a living, anyway?"

Stubble face thought that the ticket taker was trying to find out if he had any money; just *maybe* the ticket taker was trying to decide whether he'd be mister nice guy. And so he answered, "I'm just a two-for-a-nickel small-time business-man."

"What kind of businessman?"

"Run a little noodle store."

"What do your noodles go for?"

"Thirty to forty cents a *jin*."[3]

"How about if a kid goes to buy your noodles?"

"Same price."

"Aha!" exclaimed the ticket taker with a gotcha smile. "If kids have to pay for noodles like anyone else, what makes you think you can bring one on the train to ride for free?"

The man hadn't expected the conversation to turn to noodles in the first place, and then, once it had gone that far afield, he hadn't anticipated that it would turn back to the girl and her lack of a ticket. Not knowing what to say next, he raised his hand and scratched his stubble. At this juncture, everyone in third class, including the military police who accompanied the ticket taker, burst out laughing.

The woman behind whom the child was hiding, feeling that she was the butt of the joke, became very angry. Supporting herself with one hand on the child, she stood up and, looking very glum, addressed the ticket taker: "Whada ya want? If we had the money, we'd *buy* her a ticket. My brother-in-law's a soldier, and when he's away from home, he *never* buys a ticket. If he was with us, there's *no way* you'd make this kid buy a ticket."

The ticket taker fixed her with a glare. "Just listen to you! You really know how to be a pain in the butt, don't you? Well, you people are gonna buy this kid a ticket, and

---

3. In 1935, a *jin* was one and a third pounds.

that's that! Otherwise, when we pull into the next station, off she goes!" As he spoke, he looked back at the third-class porter as though issuing him an order. He left the country people and came over toward Zhu Jinqing.

Xichun said, "I'm in first class. I came here to visit my friend. I don't have my ticket on me, but if you're worried, you can go to first class and check it there."

The porter beamed at her and answered for the ticket taker, "Yes, yes, I know you. You're in compartment 6." The ticket taker glanced at her without comment. Before long, he had checked everyone in third class and went back to the group of country people. "All right, I've checked everyone else. Now I want to straighten things out with you people. What have you got to say for yourselves?"

Two middle-aged men in their group stood up. Both cupped one hand in the other before their chests and pumped them up and down in a chaos of submissive bows to the ticket taker. "Sir, we really and truly don't have any money," said one of them. Besides, what difference does it make if this big old train carries one extra little passenger?"

Fixing the man with a glare, the ticket taker pointed his punch at him and said, "This is official business we're conducting here, not some family affair. Haven't you got that straight yet? The way you see it, one passenger can take another along for free. I take you, you take me. There's no *end* to it. Who's left to buy a ticket? Don't waste my time with such nonsense. *Buy . . . a . . . ticket!*" He fairly shouted each of these last three words. The woman who had spoken before was now over in the corner of the seat doing her best to evade the whole thing. Head lowered, her expression was now indifferent as she sat with her arm around the girl's shoulders. The girl herself was so frightened that she sat in a squatting position all curled up into a little ball.

Hearing the ticket taker's words, the woman pouted and said in low tones, "We haven't broken any law. Why do you have to act so high and mighty? You can't *kill* us just because we won't buy a ticket."

The ticket taker quickly realized where her words were going and said, "Can't kill you? You're right there. But I *can* throw you off the train. No matter what, when we pull into the next station, I'm going to put your daughter off the train. If that doesn't suit you, then one of you can get off in her place. The bottom line is six and only six passengers are going to ride on six tickets."

Tears streaming down her face, the girl burst into loud sobs. The ticket taker stood up straight and angrily stalked off. Xichun's words had been interrupted by this incident. Now she stood up and prepared to leave, but Yuqing reached up and stopped her. She had no choice but to sit down again. All eyes in third class were now focused on that group of country people. After observing them for some time, Ziming said to the stubble faced man, "Elder Brother, it's not going to work. This is public business. No matter how tough you are with him, you're just not going to be able to pull it off. At the very least you should buy a half fare. You've got everybody in third class worrying about you! If he actually does throw your daughter off the train at the next stop, he's within the law."

The girl had already stopped crying and was now wiping her face with her sleeve, but hearing Ziming bring up the subject again, she started sobbing again. Her father said, "Even if he does throw my kid off the train, I can't reach into my pocket and pull out money I don't have."

At this point Zhu Jinqing came over and joined them. "Come on now, this is getting ridiculous. Do you mean to tell me that you're prepared to throw away a daughter rather than buy a ticket?"

The man answered, "What do you *want* me to do? The only other thing we can do is to get off the train with her."

Ziming said, "Actually, if you put it the right way, he'll

let you get by with a half fare. A half fare from Tsinan to Hsuchow can't run more than three or four dollars. Surely you can come up with that." As he spoke, he took another glance at the woman. She grabbed a bamboo pipe out of someone's hand and, without putting in any new tobacco or even lighting what was there, sucked intermittently on the mouthpiece as she sat there, leaning back against the seat in apparent indifference to the whole affair. Ziming put his hand in his pocket and felt around. Now he gave the daughter a critical once over. She was pressed in as close to her mother as she could possibly get. As he looked and pondered, he caught sight of the Chufou Station off in the distance. If, in fact, the girl was to be thrown off the train, that's where they'd do it.

Ziming couldn't take it any longer and said to the father, "Elder Brother, we're almost there. What are you going to do?" The man raised his hand and scratched his stubble, but said nothing. Ziming turned back to Zhu Jinqing and said in a low voice, "Judging from how calm they look, they really don't realize how serious the situation is. I think I'll help them out to the tune of a half fare. Good idea?"

Jinqing couldn't have been more surprised by what Ziming just said. He immediately stood up and shook Ziming's hand. "Are you really thinking of doing that?"

"Doesn't amount to anything. The money *really* belongs to Mrs. Hu, anyway. I'll just pretend to myself that she gave me a few dollars less than she actually did, and it won't even bother me. I'm poor myself, and I know how much it means when someone helps you out when you're out on the road. I'm going to get them a half fare." Overhearing all this, Xichun didn't express an opinion one way or the other. When Zhu Jinqing heard these words, on the other hand, he tightened his grip on Ziming's hand and pumped it up and down with great enthusiasm.

9

Honeyed Words

The girl's father, who wasn't seated too far from them, over-heard every word of this and immediately looked in their direction. A slight smile played across his face, and there was just a hint of movement on his lips, as though he were about to open his mouth and ask Ziming for that half fare. At precisely this juncture, however, the ticket taker, leading the porter behind him, came once more to where the country people were sitting. The ticket taker fixed them with a stare and said, "Well, we're coming to the station. Are you going to buy a ticket or not? If you don't, one of you has got to get off."

The girl's father said, "If I had any money, I'd have bought a ticket long ago. If I had any money, why would I get into this hassle with you in the first place? If you want us to get off, we'll *get* off!"

Seeing that they had agreed to get off the train, there was really nothing more for the ticket taker to do. Nonetheless, he said, "If you're bound and determined to get off, that's your business. Can't blame us for that. But seeing how neatly you're dressed, I find it hard to believe that you don't have any money." As he spoke, he reached over and tugged at the man's jacket. He hadn't intended anything by this except to emphasize the quality of the jacket. The father, however, seemed to find this quite threatening and jerked back from the ticket taker's hand. Clang-clang-clang! Somewhere between ten and twenty silver dollars came spilling out from the space between the outside and the inner lining of his jacket. And now, not only he, but all the people in his group as well, bent over and scrambled to retrieve the coins rolling about on the floor.

The ticket taker extended one leg at a confident, "I-thought-so" angle and smiled at him. "Cotton jacket's a good place to carry silver dollars for safekeeping, but you have to keep checking to make sure the lining and the outside of the jacket are firmly stitched all the way around and haven't developed a hole somewhere."

With an investigative hand on her husband's jacket, the man's wife stomped her foot and said, "There's no hole in the stitching. It's just that I didn't tie the end real good and proper. The whole thing's come undone!"

The ticket taker thrust his hand out toward them and said, "Well, what have you got to say for yourselves now? *Buy a ticket!*" The other passengers in the coach exploded into a general convulsion of mirth. It will be readily imagined how pleased the ticket taker was with himself. He smiled around at everyone in the coach and said, "Ladies and gentlemen, *you* be the judge. Are we people in charge too *strict,* or are the passengers too *tricky?*"

The man said nothing to the ticket taker but turned to his wife and began to swear. "Bitch! You can't get a damned thing right. Ask you to sew up a few silver dollars in the jacket lining, and you can't even do the stitching right. Well, it'll be a wonder and a half if I don't give you a good beating when we get to Hsuchow!"

The ticket taker said, "Hey, I don't want to stand here and listen to your babble. Let's stick to the subject. *Buy a ticket!*" The man looked around the car. None of his fellow passengers had the serious and sympathetic expressions that they had worn just a minute before. On the contrary, they all seemed happy as larks, except for the one who had volunteered to help him. That fellow looked very unhappy indeed. The ticket taker had the man just where he wanted him, and there was no escape. The man put on a smile and asked if he could buy a *half* fare. The ticket taker refused at first, but then so many of the other passengers exhorted him to let the man off with a half fare that that's just what he did. By the time this little comedy ended, the train had long since pulled into the station at Chufou.[1]

Curiously, all that had just transpired made Xichun very sympathetic to Shi Ziming. Originally, she had been chatting with Yuqing and her husband and had totally ignored him. But now she asked him, "Where are you going to live when you get to Nanking, Mr. Shi?"

Ziming immediately stood up and replied, "I'm really not sure yet. But as soon as I *do* find a place to put up, I'll be sure to write Mr. Hu and let him know." Xichun smiled but said nothing in reply.

Then she turned to Yuqing and said, "I really ought to be on my way. I'd like to invite the two of you to join me in the dining car for supper."

Yuqing waved the invitation aside, saying, "No, that won't work. According to railroad regulations, third-class passengers aren't allowed into the dining car. The way I hear it, if the ticket taker finds one of us up there, he'll charge us to upgrade our tickets."

"Oh?" said Xichun. "Do they really have that sort of restriction? In that case, why don't you come up to the compartment later? We can sit down and have a good chat. That'd be all right, wouldn't it?"

1. As the birthplace of Confucius (551–479 B.C.), Chufou (pinyin: Qufu) is one of the most famous towns in all China.

Yuqing frowned and replied, "I'm really sorry, but we third-class passengers don't dare leave the third-class coach. If we do, someone's likely to take our seats before we get back."

"Well, if you're not sick of my company," said Xichun, "I'll come back and see you again later." She took Yuqing's hand warmly in her own and then took her leave.

If you go from third class to first, you have to go through the second-class coach to get there. As Xichun passed the open door to Li Chengfu's compartment she paused. He was sitting inside smoking. He noticed her outside the door and knew that he ought to say something or other, but how was he to address her? In his confusion, he hurriedly stood up and nodded toward her in greeting.

"Why don't you come up to our compartment for a visit?" Xichun asked.

"With all its rocking and swaying, the train has me so completely pooped that it seems as though I've really done nothing but sleep the whole trip," replied Chengfu. Xichun had intended only to say a few polite words to him and then be about her business; hence, she turned away with a smile and continued on her way toward first class. At precisely this moment, Mrs. Yu stepped out of her second-class compartment and gave Xichun a meaningful glance. Xichun smiled and made her way on up to the door between coaches.

As she was about to go out the door to the next coach, she turned and saw that Mrs. Yu had followed her. Thereupon, Xichun said to her in a low voice, "Chinkiang would be best. As I see it, *neither* Wusih nor Changchow would be as appropriate as Chinkiang. Otherwise, it'll have to be Soochow."

Mrs. Yu looked furtively in both directions before responding in hushed tones, "Just saying Chinkiang or Soochow doesn't cut it. We ought to fix on a definite place once and for all."

"All right then, wait till we get to Pookow, and I'll tell you then."

"Judging by the direction you're coming from, you must've been visiting third class again, right? I'm surprised to find that a first-class passenger like yourself is so fond of going to the third-class coach."

"Well, everyone's got her own way of seeing things," said Xichun with a smile as she took her leave of Mrs. Yu. When she got back to first class, she was in for a surprise: no matter how she pulled, the compartment door wouldn't open. Locked tight. She was on the point of saying something, but nothing came out but a gasp. A conductor standing off to one side explained, "Mr. Hu actually *is* in the compartment. Probably locked the door so he could take a nap."

"Changing my clothes," explained Ziyun in a loud voice from inside. "Wait a bit, and I'll open the door." Xichun didn't ask him to hurry but rather just stood patiently leaning against the door. She heard a bump, followed by a light and long scratching sound of a small case being placed in the upper of the two baggage racks. Obviously, he had taken it down and was putting it back. She knew, however, that the case in question was too small to hold clothing.

Before long, wearing a broad smile, Hu Ziyun opened the door. Xichun determined at a single glance that he had not in fact changed his clothes. Purposely avoiding saying anything about that, she asked: "Ever been sight-seeing in Chufou? Have you visited the Temple of Confucius?" She walked in as she spoke and flopped down on Ziyun's berth.

Still beaming, Ziyun sat down next to where she was lying and then flopped back on the berth and whispered gently, "Aren't you just a teensy bit tired?"

She extended one hand, gave him a light pinch on the buttocks, looked at him out of the corner of her eyes, and said with a pout, "Why should I be tired? I'm still bright eyed and bushy tailed." Her eyes closed slightly even as she spoke. She yawned, and then she yawned again.

"Bright eyed and bushy tailed, huh? Then what's with all this yawning?"

"When you're riding on a train and get bounced around from one end of the day to the other, who doesn't get tired?" she asked.

"If you're tired as all that, how come you pinched me?" asked Ziyun.

"Well, let me put it this way," said Xichun. *"Teensy bit tired?* is an ordinary question to begin with, but the way you asked it, it was something else—something fully deserving a pinch."

"You must have been thinking along those lines yourself, and that's why you *heard* my question the way that you did," answered Ziyun mischievously.

Xichun gave him a good shove with both hands and said, "Sit up, and behave yourself! I'd like to take a good rest."

"But it's almost lunchtime. You can have the compartment all to yourself and take a good rest after lunch. Won't that work out?"

His question gave Xichun an idea. "The compartment all to myself? And where, pray tell, will you be all this time?"

"I'll go visit Chengfu for a while. But even if I didn't do that, I certainly wouldn't be so unreasonable as to pester you while you're resting. I'd just take a book, climb into the upper bunk, and read."

"I think you're right, there. It really would be better if you kept me company while I rested. And if you do go visit Li Chengfu, make it short. If you drag it out, I'm sure to get lonely in here all by myself."

"Aha!" said Ziyun in triumph. "So you also realize that a person can get lonely in here all by their lonesome. In that case, then, why is it that whenever you go out, you stay so long and just leave me to my own devices? Don't you think *I* get lonely, too?"

"Gosh, you don't know when someone's doing you a favor, do you? I stay away so long precisely because I want it to be nice and quiet in here so that you can get yourself a good rest."

"Now I see what you're up to," said Ziyun. "You're hinting that you want me to stay away from the compartment so it'll be 'nice and quiet' and you can get yourself a good rest."

"Me?" asked Xichun with a coy smile. "Well, to tell the truth, I would like it if you'd let me have a little peace and quiet, too." As she spoke, she glanced furtively at Ziyun. He was smiling.

"Nothing could be easier. If you had only come straight out and told me that's what you wanted, why *of course* I'd let you have all the peace and quiet you wanted. But why in the world did you have to beat around all those bushes before you came to the point?"

Xichun didn't say anything in reply. She just closed her eyes and stretched out for a good rest. Just then, a dining-car steward came into first class and the sharp clang-clang of metal against metal as he walked past announced that lunch was being served. Ziyun gave Xichun a gentle nudge and said, "Let's go. It's lunchtime."

She smiled but kept her eyes closed. "I'd like to rest just a little longer."

"But you can come back and go to sleep right after we eat."

"Oh, all right," she said. "But you go on ahead. I'll be there in ten minutes or so."

Ziyun thought to himself, "Women often have secret little women's stuff that they have to take care off. Maybe Xichun needs ten minutes by herself for some such reason.

If I insist on dragging her along, she may get put out with me." He smiled and said, "All right then, I'll go on ahead, but don't make me wait forever. I'm absolutely starved." By the time he finished saying this, he was already headed down the corridor.

As she lay there motionless, Xichun feigned total indifference as to whether he went or stayed. Her eyes, however, were wide open and firmly fixed on that traveling case on the baggage rack just under the ceiling. She waited a full two or three minutes before locking the door. Then she took the little ladder used for climbing into the upper berth, propped it against the bunk, and climbed up. Reaching over the upper bunk, she yanked on a small sack crammed in next to the little case until she had freed it up enough to rummage around inside with her hand. She pulled out two oranges.

Hearing the sound of leather shoes in the corridor, she came back down the ladder, opened her own traveling bag, took out a dress, and changed. When she was done, she glanced at her own watch and noticed that ten minutes had gone by. Not wishing to break her promise to Ziyun, she hustled off to the dining car.

After they had finished lunch and returned to the compartment, Ziyun noticed that there were two oranges on the little tea table by the window. "What a forgetful fellow I am!" said Ziyun. "A whole bag of fruit, and I forgot to offer you any. Since oranges are native to the south anyway, wouldn't it look weird to bring them back down from the north again? Have some!" He picked up an orange, peeled it, and was already breaking it into sections as he spoke. He offered one to Xichun.

She smiled and said, "Let me warn you, when it comes to things like eating fruit, I'm not one to stand on ceremony. Before lunch, I climbed up and swiped two of your oranges.

But I'm pretty much a rank amateur as a thief because after I took them down I forgot to eat them and left them right here on the tea table as evidence to convict myself."

"All that explanation for two measly oranges! Why should we two be so finicky about what's yours and what's mine in the first place? As a matter of fact, if you don't object, I'd even like to go a step further. I'd like to see the two of us always facing the world together, shoulder to shoulder."

"How could a girl ask for anything more? Shoulder to shoulder with a banker—how could I possibly *not* come out winners on that one?"

A cigar dangling from his mouth, Ziyun leaned against the wall of the compartment. "So you take me for a rich banker, huh? Someone out for a good time, perhaps? Well, that's not what I am, and that's not at all what our relationship is about. If you want to know the truth, it was a feeling of *sympathy* that first got me interested in you."

Xichun now assumed a serious expression, nodded at him, and said, "Sympathy? That's just the way it happened, too—a feeling of sympathy. You know, you can always put your trust in me, for I'm not one of those people you've hired to work for you. Let me frankly share my thoughts about this with you. In this boundless universe, I was unable to find *anyone* who really understood me. And then you came along and expressed your sympathy at every turn. How could I *not* fall for you? And now you can't possibly imagine how happy I feel hearing you say that you *always* want to stand shoulder to shoulder with me. The only trouble is. . . . " She suddenly stopped and lowered her eyes.

"Since we're beginning to really understand each other, why go only so far and then hold back? Go right ahead and say anything that's in your heart."

"The only trouble is that I—as a woman—have so casually taken up with you that I'm afraid you must think less of me for it."

Ziyun seemed astounded by her remark, for he suddenly straightened up, leaned forward, and said, "What kind of thing is *that* to say? It's because we *both* fell in love that we have the relationship we do now. If you want to talk about who's responsible, then if there's any fault, it's all on my side. I'm the one who began to be infatuated with you."

Xichun lowered her head and said in low tones, "In one regard men and women are the same—neither can fall in love within the space of five minutes. If you go back over our relationship in your own mind, you'll see that from the time you first ran into me in the dining car, I had no way of getting away from you because you stuck to me like glue."

"That," said Ziyun, "was only because you're so beautiful. But I've already said the responsibility is entirely on my side. You're not to blame in the least. And yet it *is* very rare that the woman is the one who discovers that a couple has fallen in love."

Xichun laughed and said, "The way you put it is that although you should bear the responsibility, you can still be forgiven because I'm the one who discovered it. In that case, if *you're* not responsible and *I'm* not responsible, then exactly who *is* responsible?"

"It's quite obvious," said Ziyun, "the God of Love!"

Xichun glanced at him and observed, "You really know how to talk, don't you?"

"I'm perfectly serious. I've always felt that when a man and a woman come together, fate's at work somewhere. It's not something that comes about because of human will. Take us, for example. If we didn't both board this train yesterday, if it weren't for the fact that you couldn't find a berth, and if I didn't happen to have an empty one, there's no way that we would have gotten together. But now—and who would have thought it?—because of the three conditions I just spoke of, here we are, together! And we have no one to thank for it but the God of Love."

"But this is only the first act of our play," objected Xichun. "If the momentum we have built up continues, who's to say whether the ending will be a comedy or a tragedy?"

"How could it possibly be a tragedy? I don't quite understand your way of thinking. Do you think I'm the faithless sort of fellow who would abandon you after the novelty wore off?"

"No," answered Xichun. "But who can tell how things will turn out in the future?"

Ziyun took the cigar out of his mouth and put it down on the tea table. With a loud clap, he slapped both hands down vigorously on his upper thighs, sat up ramrod straight, and said, "If I have the slightest intention of ever abandoning you, let heaven above punish me with the most miserable and painful of deaths!"

Xichun quickly crossed over to him and put her hand across his mouth. "Hearing you take an oath like that makes me feel downright awful. It's as though I were forcing you to take an oath." Pulling her hand away, she sat down as close to him as she could get and said in the gentlest of tones, "*I'm* the one who might create the tragedy, not you. You know what the situation is in that family I married into. In order to win my personal freedom, I decided I wasn't going to put up with it any longer. I couldn't put up with it any longer. At that point, of course, I had to think of some way of breaking free, but even now it's hard to say if I'll really be able to pull it off. My relationship with you has strengthened my resolve. Even if I die trying, I'm going to find a way out. But if it turns out that I can't make it through this crisis, then I'm afraid I'm the one who's going to end up acting out a tragedy."

Ziyun took advantage of the opportunity presented to squeeze one of her hands tightly in his own. "You mustn't think like that. Where there's a will, there's a way. Just stick to your guns and forge ahead. Smart as you are, there's no crisis that you can't handle."

"But despite all your kindness and support, there are bound to be difficulties later on."

Ziyun picked up the cigar that he had just put down on the tea table, took a couple of puffs, and furrowed his brow as he thought over what she had just said. Then he nodded and said, "There's something to what you say because the people in my own immediate family, as well as my close friends, are all one generation older than you."

Xichun immediately waved her hand in negation and said, "No, that's not it. The generational difference doesn't bother *me* in the least. I'm not worried about how *I'll* relate to people of your generation; I'm worried about how *they're* going to relate to me." As she spoke, she picked up the teapot from the tea table and poured two cups. She passed one cup to Ziyun and then picked up the other. Ziyun thought this tea especially fragrant.

"When you say you're worried about how my people are going to relate to you, you must be thinking about my wife back home. Let me assure you, that problem is easily solved. She's got money, and besides that she has children as well, so I can just send her on back to her own family."

"No! No!" objected Xichun vehemently. "Nowadays, you see a lot of that—women taking husbands away from their wives. I can't think of anything more immoral! Is it worth it to elbow another woman out of the way, send her to hell, just to satisfy my own desires? I don't *want* to be your wife. Besides, to tell the truth—as long as I don't go hog wild— I have more than enough money to last me a lifetime. What's more, I am entirely capable of taking care of my own affairs. I don't need some man to show me how to do it. What *I* want goes more like this: after I'm completely free, I'd like you to be my intimate friend. And you can take that intimacy to any degree you want. In name, however, there will be no relationship between us. What I'm worried about, the *only* thing I can see that might stand in our way, is that your wife might hear about me and become jealous anyway. That's beyond my control, of course, but it does worry me."

Though a smiling Ziyun outwardly kept his calm, inwardly he was so happy he could have turned somersaults. "You're too good to me. How can I ever pay you back?" Xichun had already finished her tea and put down the cup. She took Ziyun's cup, filled it from the pot, and respectfully passed it over to him using two hands. He received it respectfully with both hands as well. "You're so generous I hardly know what to do."

"It has nothing to do with 'generosity,'" she explained. "It's just that you've provided me so much consolation that I'd like to return a bit of it to you. I've been through the wringer with this thing called love. It's made me realize that in a relationship between the sexes consolation has to be a two-way street. Whenever the relationship is one-sided, it is bound to fail."

Ziyun gulped down the tea in a single swallow and nodded his head with great enthusiasm. "You couldn't be more right, just *couldn't* be! You know, listening to you just now brings to mind an old friend of mine. He used to say, 'When they think of romantic love, most people like to think in terms of teenage girls. That's a great mistake. All teenage girls understand is how to play and how to pout, but they're a long way from understanding love and even further from knowing how to really console a man.' That friend was right. Just look at the way you have consoled me! How could I possibly bear to ever part with you? And as to that wife I have at home, you can set your mind to rest on that score. I'll be sure to find a way of keeping her out of the way so that you'll feel more comfortable about the whole thing."

Xichun smiled and asked, "But why do that? The way I see it, once we become intimate friends, that ought to be enough. Why take it any further? What *you* want is my body. All right, I'm prepared to give it to you. That should settle everything. Why think about going any further with the relationship?"

Ziyun smiled and said, "Perhaps you don't understand the psychology of the male. Men want to *own* their women. If our relationship were just friend to friend, then you could abandon me anytime you felt like it. If I were still head over heels in love with you at the time and you just up and decided to dump me, what would I do? I won't try to bamboozle you by saying something dramatic and extravagant like I'd kill myself or become a monk. But even so, the psychological blow I'd suffer would be awfully difficult to bear."

Xichun smiled. "There's something to what you say," she granted, "but, nonetheless, it's always a good idea to take a long view of things, for it's hard to tell how they'll develop later on. But at this stage of the game, I'd prefer not to be as definite as you'd like me to be."

"There's something to what you say as well. When a man and a woman first fall in love, they're so close nothing can come between them. But, unavoidably, as time goes on, the feelings of one or the other may well change. Given the way I feel about you, however, I don't see how that could possibly happen. Your learning, your looks, your character—every category earns at least eighty points. Where on earth could I ever find anyone better?"

As they were chatting, Xichun leaned back against the lower bunk and closed her eyes. Gradually, her body grew still, and she seemed to be sleeping. Cigar dangling from his mouth, Ziyun glanced at her again and began to think about what had just transpired. "In everything she said just now, why did the advantage always fall so one-sidedly to me? She has the sort of intelligent face that suggests a woman thoroughly versed in the ways of the world. Why then is she so prepared to let me have all the advantages in our relationship? Why? Yes! Yes, that must be it! Although she doesn't seem to care about money, money is—in and of itself—a powerful attraction. She thinks I'm a banker, and from her point of view getting hooked up with a banker is bound to bring some sort of economic advantage sooner or later. Up until now, of course, she hasn't used a single penny of my money, but as time goes by I bet that's going to change. On the other hand, she claims to have her own money, and that must certainly be the case, otherwise—as a woman especially—she'd never have been willing to part with the extra cash it takes to ride first class. It's woman's nature, after all, to economize at every turn, but she doesn't. It must be true, then, that she has her own money, and her taking up with me—a strange male—can't be explained in those terms. Other than the fact that she's young and has physical needs that must be satisfied, I wonder what part is played in all of this by her desire to pay her husband back? I wonder. Well, no matter how you cut it, I come out winners on this one." Having arrived at this point in his reasoning, he couldn't help giving a contented chuckle.

He turned and looked at Xichun. Her face was slightly flushed and her eyes closed tight. "She really is all tuckered out," he thought. "I'd better let her get a good rest." Suddenly moved by a genuine feeling of tenderness, he stood, picked up her dangling feet, and lifted them up onto the berth. Although the compartment was quite warm, he worried that, despite the heat, she might catch cold in those sheer silk stockings. Ever so gently, he covered her legs with a blanket. Another glance confirmed him in the feeling that she was genuinely worn out.

He quietly drew the door open, stepped out into the corridor, and just as quietly pulled it closed behind him. No sooner had he done so than Xichun's eyes flashed open and she sat bolt upright. As she raised one hand to arrange her hair, her enigmatic gaze fell briefly on the rack above. In the space of each and every one of the succeeding five minutes, she kept glancing back at the rack. "Doing what I plan to do," she thought, "is this a case of a man taking advantage of a woman or a woman taking advantage of a man?" She was about to arrange the ladder so she could climb up and get some oranges when she heard someone knocking— pum-pum-pum—on the compartment door. "Couldn't possibly be Ziyun," she thought to herself, for he'd have no need to knock. "Must be Mrs. Yu." With a smile of greeting, she calmly opened the door. But when she came face to face with the person outside, she started noticeably, surprised. It was the young man with the dog from the next compartment down.

Before Xichun had a chance to say anything, he smiled and said, "How are you, Miss Chen?" Having no desire to let him come inside, Xichun pushed her way into the corridor and blocked his access to the door.

"I'm not named Chen now," she said with a blush.

"How's that? Not named Chen now, you say? Well, I've learned something I didn't know before: some people have a *now*-name and a *then*-name as well."

"I got married, and I'd appreciate it if you didn't let on that you recognize me. If you had brought your wife along, I'd do as much for you—wouldn't let on that I knew you."

"Oh, I see," said the young man. "When people get married, they just dump all their former friends. I never knew that before either. Thank you."

Ignoring this last remark, Xichun drew the door to behind her, stepped to the other side of the corridor, leaned on the railing, and gazed out through the window. The train had already passed through Chufou and was beginning to roll through the plains where, here and there among the wheat seedlings, one could make out splotches of snow. Off in the distance, the weak rays of the winter sun shone on scattered villages surrounded by leafless trees. The branches shifted back and forth in the wintry wind, and behind them one could make out buildings of various sizes and even a haystack or two. It was a scene of rare and poetic charm. Whenever the Shanghai Express roared past a nearby village, peasants clad in coarse padded clothing would stop and gaze.

"Separated only by a pane of glass, we gaze at the peasants, and the peasants gaze back at us," remarked the young man, who had also been leaning against the rail observing the passing scene. "Even though, physically, we're quite close to each other, we live in two entirely different worlds. I'll bet they envy the well-dressed people they see on the train. But, as I see it, there's nothing worth envying because their hearts are far purer than those of the train passengers who pass them by."

It was a remark that she couldn't very well not answer, but it was also a remark that she couldn't very well answer either. She fixed him with a stare.

10

A Bit High

A popular saying goes, *It's the sore lump that gets the bump.* The idea is that any bruise or swelling you have is bound to be the very spot you bump accidentally. That's not really true, of course, but people think it is. For instance, how about all those places on the body that *aren't* bruised? Don't *they* knock up against things every day as well? Sure they do. But the thing is, when places that aren't bruised or swollen get bumped, they don't hurt all that much, and people don't mind.

Xichun was not free from such "a sore lump" herself—a psychological one. And, as luck would have it, she had to go and bump her sore lump against the young man with the dog. Every time he said anything, every time he looked at her, she felt that he had something up his sleeve and became very jittery. All she had to do was catch sight of him, and she would blush or lower her head. Ziyun became put out with man and dog alike. When he noticed that Xichun looked as though she'd like to get away from the man every time she saw him, Ziyun began to feel even more uncomfortable. He decided that she *must* know him, though their relationship was probably only a superficial one.

At this juncture, Xichun was out in the corridor watching the scenery roll past outside. The young man with the dog also seemed to be watching it. Though he was some distance down the corridor from her, she felt that his real intention in standing there was to make things difficult for her. Just as she was trying to think of some way of ridding herself of this devil, along came Ziyun. Pipe in his mouth, his steps were slow and deliberate. He stopped right next to her and gave the young man a hostile stare out of the corner of his eyes, a stare that announced, "This woman is taken; don't get any ideas!"

When Xichun saw Ziyun coming, she seemed thrown for a loss. The blush the young man's presence had initiated now spread clear back to her ears. Hastily pointing out the window, she said, "See how cold it is out there." Not bothering to wonder whether you could actually see the cold, Ziyun looked in the direction she had pointed. The young man, however, saw through her ploy. Tapping his foot rhythmically on the floor of the corridor, he rounded his lips and launched into an aria from *Romance of the Jade Palace*. This time, Xichun managed to come up with a plausible question: "What's that station up there?"

"Must be Yenchow," answered Ziyun.

"Big station?""

"Yes, it is. We could get off and walk around a bit. Spending the whole day on the train like this, I feel cramped, too."

"For that matter, wouldn't do any harm to go back into the compartment and lie down for a bit," she suggested with a smile. "Standing here with the train bumping up and down under us, I'm beginning to feel a bit out of it." She walked back inside the compartment as she spoke.

The young man's demeanor underwent a change. He scratched his head and didn't seem able to decide what to do next. Paying no attention to him, Ziyun followed Xichun back into the compartment and drew the door shut.

Stretching out on the lower bunk, she propped her feet against the wall.

Ziyun began to explain why he had left the compartment. "A while back, I thought you'd gone to sleep and didn't want to disturb you, so I went into the corridor, pulled the door closed behind me, and left."

Xichun laughed. "The noise you made closing the door is what woke me. And then, in here all by myself, I got pretty bored; that's why I went out into the corridor. How come you came back again?"

"Went to see Mr. Li, and found him asleep. Thought I'd come back here, get a little pipe tobacco, and then go sit in the dining car."

"Why not just stay in here?"

"Well, I might be a bit thick, but I'm still smart enough to hear between the words of what a person has to say— even one as smart as you. You wanted me to get out of here so you could have the compartment to yourself for a while, right?"

The blush her face exhibited in the corridor had subsided, but now, when she heard Ziyun say this, it returned with a such a vengeance that she no longer dared look him straight in the eye. Not having the foggiest notion of the import of the question he had just asked, Ziyun pressed her for an answer: "Well, did I guess right?"

She lowered her head and peeked at him out of the corner of her eye. Noting that he was still smiling and in a jolly mood, she said, "What are you getting at with a question like that? You don't mean to tell me you think I was trying to get rid of you so I could be up to my own little tricks while I was alone in here, do you?"

Ziyun laughed heartily. "Now why on earth would I think a thing like that! I just thought you didn't me want me to disturb you so you could have a good rest. I thought that's what you had in mind, too, and that's why I left." At this point, Ziyun lowered his voice and pointed in the direction of the compartment where the young man with the dog was staying. "Although that fellow with the dog has his eye on you, I've long since realized that you're doing your best to *avoid* him, so how could I possibly suspect anything in that regard?"

By steering their conversation in a direction Xichun hadn't anticipated, Ziyun had provided her with a new tack to take. "He's always following me," she said. "I don't know what to do. From here on out, why don't you just stay here in the compartment with me? Or if either of us has to go out for anything, let's go out together. That way you'll have no reason to worry—or dare I say it?—even be suspicious."

"I've never gone in for jealousy. I'm just not the type," said Ziyun with a laugh.

"Which way do you think it's better," asked Xichun, "that I think you *are* jealous or that I think you're *not* jealous?"

"In a relationship between a man and a woman," expounded Ziyun, "there has to be love before jealousy comes into play. The more one's love is concentrated on the love object, the more jealousy one will have. And the more. . . . "

"There you go with another lecture," said Xichun. "I meant well in suggesting that you might be jealous. I'd think you'd be only too glad to admit it."

Ziyun nodded his head repeatedly. "Yes, yes, yes—I admit it."

"Well, as long as you admit it, we can do something about it. From now on, just stay here in the compartment. There's no need to go out."

"Does that mean I can't even go to the *toilet?*"

"That's an exception, of course. But it would be best if you didn't even do that."

"What a marvelous contract you're drawing up,"

observed Ziyun with a smile. "How about extending it to a hundred years?"

Xichun closed her eyes. "Let's not talk anymore. I really would like to rest." Interlacing her fingers, she rested her hands against her abdomen and lay there motionless. Apparently, she had dropped off to sleep.

The train pulled into Yenchow. Through the window, one could see a couple of foreigners walking up and down on the platform. Ziyun put on his overcoat, quietly opened the door, and went out into the corridor. He knew that Xichun wasn't really asleep but made it a point not to disturb her anyway. When he got off the train, the first person he ran into was the young man with the dog. Another man in Western garb was speaking to him. "You always get off the train at every station," commented the other man. "Regular as clockwork!"

"Since I can't very well let him relieve himself on the train, I've got to get off and give him a walk at every stop." He gave a little tug on the leash as he spoke, and the dog responded by jumping up on him with its front paws. It stuck its pointed nose in his face and gave him an enthusiastic sniffing. Noticing this, some people standing nearby on the platform chuckled. When he saw Ziyun headed in his direction, the young man laughed and said, "My liking for this four-legged creature is nothing. Everyone has something he likes, maybe even goes a bit ape over. No harm done. Gives his friends something to kid him about. He's certainly not going to suffer any great loss in the process." Ziyun thought that this last remark might well be a barbed comment directed at his own person, but since he also thought that it was motivated by jealousy, pure and simple, he chose to ignore it.

By this time, he was at the window outside his own compartment and looked inside to see what Xichun might be up to. As luck would have it, she was sitting up looking outside, and they ended up face to face. She waved. Ziyun moved his mouth close to the glass and asked, "How's it going? Didn't get to sleep, huh?" She pouted and looked at him rather harshly as though she were very angry. Ziyun had no option but to get on the train and go back to his compartment.

"Not very good at keeping your word, are you? Promised not to go out without me, and the very next minute—pfft, off you go!" She pouted once again and looked away from him. Ziyun took hold of his lapels and was about to take off his overcoat when Xichun stopped him. Her frown turned to a smile as she said, "Don't! You've just come in from outside and might catch cold." She pulled him down next to her.

"I'm really pleased to see that you are so reliable," said Ziyun with a smile. "All I can say is I won't do it again."

"Well, that's more like it," she said as she poured him a hot cup of tea. After he had finished drinking it, she helped him off with his overcoat.

"You're such a great comfort to me," said he, "that as long as you're at my side I don't feel like going anywhere." True to his word, he stayed in the compartment and chatted with her all the way to Hsuchow.

It was she who was first to suggest that they leave the compartment. "The train stops in Hsuchow for a good long time. Why don't we get out, stretch our legs, and get some exercise?" She helped him on with his overcoat as she spoke. Since she had effectively taken the initiative away from him, he had no choice but to follow her off the train. This station was especially crowded with travelers. All you had to do to bear out the truth of this was to observe the steady stream of people moving across the overhead bridge that crossed the tracks: some carried large, unwieldy net packages, while others balanced heavy trunks on their backs. Down below them, great crowds shuttled—sha-sha-sha—back and forth across the concrete platform. Although this was an open-air station, the cold air did not bite the face as one might have expected. Outside the station proper, here and there, you could see weeping willows.

Fortunately, the station at Hsuchow was a large one, and Ziyun and Xichun were able to find places on the platform where the crowd was thin enough for them to stroll about quite freely. Ziyun took a few deep breaths and said with a smile, "It really was much too hot on the train. Head feels all swollen and dizzy. When you get out like this and a fresh, cool breeze blows across your face, you feel a lot better."

"Actually, it's also due to where we are," Xichun expanded. "Once you've crossed the Yellow River, it gets a lot warmer. Look, the trees outside the station even have green leaves on them. I don't know what the reason is, but I feel really great myself. I wasn't aware of how good I felt until you said that. I agree, it must be the air."

Ziyun shook his head in disagreement. "That's not the only reason. If I were traveling by myself, I'd feel down in the dumps no matter *how* refreshing the air might be."

Xichun drew even closer to him as they walked along. Her full head of billowy, fragrant black hair had been close to him to begin with, and now as they walked along she nestled in even closer so that their two bodies became virtually one. When she heard him say this, she turned her head, looked up into his face, and said with a smile, "Hmph! There you go again, really laying it on thick!"

"No! I was just telling it the way it is. Don't you feel the same way yourself?"

Xichun knocked her head lightly against his chest and said, "Actually, I do, though I don't understand the reason myself. This heart of mine is not easily moved, but you've moved it to such an extent that I don't know what to do anymore." They continued in this intimate vein as they walked along. Before they realized it, they had come to the end of the platform and stopped dead in their tracks. Xichun laughed and said, "If the platform hadn't come to an end, I'll bet we could have gone on like this all the way to Pookow."[1] She took him by the hand and led him back in the direction from which they had come. Off in the distance, they saw that Mrs. Yu had also gotten off the train and was strolling about on the platform. Just as they prepared to hail her, she caught sight of them and headed over to greet them.

Mrs. Yu laughed and said, "Well, here's a husband and wife who know how to enjoy themselves!"

"We just got off so we could stretch our legs and get our circulations going again."

"You know, I felt a bit uneasy about getting off because with four people in the compartment there's no way of locking it and I brought along quite a few pieces of luggage. If some of it disappeared, where would I go to look for it?"

"Oh, that reminds me," exclaimed Xichun. "The two of us just got willy-nilly off the train and forgot to tell the porter to lock our compartment. Not too good an idea. I'd better go back and check on things."

"I'd like to invite you both for lunch," said Mrs. Yu. "See you later in the dining car, okay?"

Xichun agreed, took her leave of Ziyun, and got back on the train. This left Mrs. Yu with Ziyun on the platform. He, too, of course, acceded to her invitation. Mrs. Yu asked Ziyun, "Is she your first wife?" Ziyun merely smiled. "She looks a lot younger than Mr. Hu. What a lucky man you are to have such a young and beautiful wife."

1. Pookow (pinyin: Pukou) is on the northern bank of the Yangtze River, while Nanking is on the southern one. Until 1968, when the Yangtze River Bridge was completed, the only way to get from Pookow to Nanking was by ferry. The bridge has a roadway on top and a railway below. In the 1930s, the Yangtze River would have been the southernmost limit of the stroll that Xichun so fancifully imagines.

"Aren't you and your husband separated by quite a few years as well?"

"That's right. He's over twenty years my senior. I don't mind that a bit. Between husband and wife, love's the most important thing. You can overlook anything else. To put it somewhat vulgarly, the older a husband is, the more he'll spoil his wife."

"Then it's a safe bet that Mr. Yu spoils you rotten, am I right? I ask because otherwise it probably wouldn't have occurred to you to make that comment about how an older husband treats a younger wife."

Mrs. Yu smiled and replied, "Since you've got it all figured out, there's no need to ask."

"But if you look at it the other way round," continued Ziyun, "why would a younger woman marry an older man in the first place if she didn't expect some spoiling?"

"Now, that's telling it the way it is. By the way, Mr. Hu, that wife of yours looks like she came from some sort of student background."

"How can you tell?"

"Well, she carries herself like an educated person, and there's a certain elegance to her speech as well. It's quite different from that of someone like myself, who can't read a word."

A self-satisfied smile spread across Ziyun's face as he said, "Not only is her knowledge of Chinese culture deep, but she speaks foreign languages as well. She's the kind of person who can acquit herself well in any social situation."

"You're really a lucky man, but I'm starting to feel a bit chilly out here. Let's get back on the train and continue this in the dining car."

Wouldn't do to be so ungrateful as to refuse an invitation from Mr. Yu's wife, thought Ziyun to himself as he got on the train and followed her to the dining car, where lunch was already being served. They found a table and sat down across from each other. The steward came over and inquired, "Just the two of you?"

"Three," answered Ziyun. "But I really find the Western food you serve in here hard to take. Yesterday, I saw some passengers eating Chinese food. Just give us three orders of Chinese food."

"You have to order Chinese food in advance," said the waiter. "It's too late now."

"Well then, we'll order Chinese food right now," said Ziyun. "We'll go back to our compartments, and wait until all the Western meals have been served and eaten, and then come back for our Chinese food. That would be all right, wouldn't it?"

The steward hesitated for a moment, then, placing one hand on the table, lowered his head and smiled at Ziyun: "The Chinese food here in the dining car isn't all that great."

"They sell Chinese food for a dollar a portion and Western food for a dollar and a half," explained Mrs. Yu, "so naturally they don't want you to eat Chinese food. We might as well order from the Western menu." Hearing her say that, the steward took a menu from another table and handed it to Ziyun.

One look was enough! Scrawled every which way and that he saw nothing but—English! Now, Ziyun did know a word or two of English, but his knowledge was very—even exceedingly—limited. After staring at the menu for some time, by straining for all he was worth, he was able to make out the word *soup* at the top and *coffee* down at the bottom, but, as to what came in between, he had not the vaguest notion.

Too embarrassed to ask the steward for a translation, he mumbled, "Hardly see anything I like. We'll wait for a bit anyway. We've got a third person coming." The steward walked away, and Ziyun put down the menu.

Observing his annoyance, Mrs. Yu commented, "What are the Chinese people coming to, anyway? When they talk to each other, they use a foreign tongue, and when they write menus for their own countrymen, they scribble them out in a foreign language."

Ziyun laughed and replied, "What are the Chinese people coming to? Practicing up to be *wang-guo-nu*,[2] that's what! Later on, when we fall to foreign invaders, we won't be allowed to speak the Chinese language or to write Chinese characters. But it won't matter a bit! We'll have been in practice for it a long time. And that also explains why *Chinese* people on a *Chinese* train traveling in *China* eat foreign food!"

"That's why in Shanghai anything that's foreign will cost you more," said Mrs. Yu. "Years back, I used to like foreign goods, too, but now that I'm getting on in years, I'm not so concerned with being fashionable. The clothes I wear now are all made from Chinese materials." When they arrived at this point in their conversation, a positively exultant Xichun came beaming into the dining car. Mrs. Yu caught sight of her long before she got to the table and gave her a meaningful glance.

Xichun sat down next to Ziyun and, having overheard the older woman's last remark, said to Mrs. Yu, "What are you looking at *me* for? *I'm* not wearing anything foreign."

Mrs. Yu smiled and said, "Actually, someone as young as you *ought* to wear fashionable clothes."

Xichun smiled and said, "Well, I suppose you have something there because young people like myself are bound to become *wang-guo-nu* at some point in the future. Might as well start practicing up now!"

Mrs. Yu smiled and said, "How is it that you two, hus-

2. "Slaves [*nu*] of a fallen country [*wang-guo*]" was so common a phrase during the 1930s that I use the transliteration of the Chinese.

band and wife, say exactly the same thing? Goes to show that *one bed quilt will not cover two different kinds of lover.*" Hearing her say this, Xichun knocked her knee against Ziyun's leg. He smiled.

"What do you mean?" Xichun asked. "What were you two talking about just now?"

"We were talking about how they sell Western meals in the dining car and how the menus are written only in English, and we both felt that this is an omen of *wang-guo-nu,*" Ziyun answered.

"If you think that's bad, just wait till you get to Shanghai," said Xichun. "If you spend your time complaining about that sort of thing in *Shanghai,* you won't have time to do anything else, believe me." As she spoke, she picked up the menu. Her eyes scanned the English words, but her mouth spoke nothing but standard Chinese. "Noodle soup, deep-fried salmon, simmered ox tongue, braised chicken, pudding, and coffee." The manner in which she said this did not indicate in any way that she was translating for Ziyun's benefit—but he knew that was, in fact, the case.

"And that's all they'll give us for a dollar and a half?" asked Ziyun.

Mrs. Yu laughed and replied, "Judging from the steward's tone, the Chinese food is simply inedible. I'll bet the Western dishes are well prepared. If we make any substitutions, we're not likely to get anything good. I think we'd better stick to what they have on hand if we want to get anything tasty."

"Good idea," approved Ziyun.

"Okay," said Xichun, "let's do as Mrs. Yu suggests."

After they had ordered, the steward asked, "Any carbonated drinks?"

"Order us two bottles," answered Ziyun. Xichun immediately kneed his leg a couple of times under the table while looking straight ahead as though this was of no concern to her. "On second thought," said Ziyun, "what's the point in drinking carbonated stuff on a cold day? Would it be all right if we ordered something alcoholic, Mrs. Yu?"

It was a suggestion that seemed to evoke no small enthusiasm from Mrs. Yu, who now looked Xichun full in the face. Xichun laughed and said, "Mrs. Yu looks to me like someone who enjoys a drink. Since she's treating us to a meal, let's treat her to something to drink. How about a little brandy?"

Mrs. Yu waved the suggestion aside. "Brandy on a train! It would take a Peipinger to come up with an idea like that. You take a beating when you order liquor on a train, you know."

"How many chances do we have to get together like this?" Xichun countered before Ziyun had a chance to say anything. "So what if it is a little on the high side? Anyway, I'll bet it's not going to be any more than ten dollars a bottle. Steward, steward! A bottle of brandy, please."

The steward walked over and suggested with a smile, "Why don't you order three glasses. We also sell it by the glass."

Xichun's almond eyes rounded into a glare, and her face took on a very stern cast. "Do you think that the three of us can't *afford* a whole bottle?" She took out a ten-dollar bill and threw it on the table. "First take the money, and then bring us a bottle of brandy. I assume that order of events is permissible, is it not?" she asked with a cold smile. Ziyun saw quite clearly that at this point he had no choice but to go along with her. Before long, the steward came back, set down a glass before each of them, and filled the three glasses with brandy.

Mrs. Yu picked up her glass and downed more than half of it in a single gulp. She smiled at Xichun and asked, "And how about you, Mrs. Hu?"

"I'm not much of a drinker, but since you are our guest,

Mrs. Yu, I'll drink *half* a glass with you," Xichun replied.

"What's this half-a-glass business? You ought to join me in one *full* one at least," objected the older woman.

Rather than answering her, Xichun looked at Ziyun and asked, "What do *you* think?"

"Since Mrs. Yu knows that I'm not much of a drinker either, how about doing it this way?" Ziyun suggested. "Xichun and I will share a whole glass and keep you company that way."

"The two of you cooperate? If that's what you had in mind, what was the point in ordering a whole bottle in the first place?"

"Well, fortunately, we *are* on a train ride with nothing that has to get done," replied Xichun. "If we get *tipsy,* we go to sleep, and if we *don't* get tipsy, we do exactly the same thing. Okay, then, I'll join you in a whole glass."

"Now that's more like it," said Mrs. Yu. "Let me begin by finishing off the rest of this glass." With another large gulp, she finished off the second half of her glass.

"It's been years since I last had an opportunity to admire Mrs. Yu's capacity for drinking," said Ziyun. "Hasn't declined a bit! Well, in that case, I'll join you in a whole glass as well, but I'll have to take it slowly."

The Western meal arrived, and the three of them put aside their drinks in order to eat. It must be confessed, however, that even the Western menu wasn't really up to snuff: the soup looked like thinned out paste with seven or eight tiny noodles in it; the salmon had a bad smell; and the only thing the ox tongue had to recommend it was a nice, tomato-red color, but the tongue itself had a strange taste. They were also given a cabbage soup, but the cabbage was tough as wood. Later, when the pan-braised chicken arrived, it, at least, lived up to the "pan-braised" part of its name— it was easily as hard as the pan it had been braised in.

There was a loud clatter of knives and forks on the plates,

but the food was certainly not of a quality to inspire any-one's interest in drinking—anyone, that is, with the exception of Mrs. Yu, who continued to put it away until she had polished off three glasses or so. Xichun's glass was still more than half full, a circumstance that inspired Mrs. Yu to comment, "I'd say you didn't live up to your word. You promised to join me for at least one glass, and you still have half of it sitting right there in front of you."

"Well, there's always dinner. Why don't I keep it for dinner?"

"No way!" said Mrs. Yu. "If you can't finish it, then let your husband step in and help you out."

"You know what a low capacity he has; why force the poor man to get drunk?"

"Wouldn't make any difference even if he did," said Mrs. Yu. "He's got a wife to look after him, doesn't he? Don't think I'm gonna let you two get off the hook as easily as all that. *One* of you is going to drink with me. If Mrs. Hu is all that concerned with her husband's welfare, then she ought to be the one to drink."

"Well, all right then," said Xichun, "I'll force it down." But, as she picked up the glass, she looked beseechingly at Ziyun.

Ziyun immediately took the glass out of her hand and said, "Get a load of this." He stretched out his neck and emptied the glass down his throat like pouring water down a sink.

Mrs. Yu looked all around and then said in a low voice, "The wife looks out for the husband, and the husband looks out for the wife. You two are really something else."

Ziyun laughed and said, "Mrs. Yu must have tied one on because now she's talking wine talk." Still smiling, he was the first to leave the dining car.

Xichun took the brandy back with her soon afterward and said to Ziyun, "We'll save this until supper, and then we'll get her good and high. I would never have guessed that she liked to drink so much."

After all the brandy he had drunk, Ziyun wasn't quite himself. There was a stinging sensation in his flushed cheeks, and his head was going round and round. "You mean we're going to keep this nonsense up in the evening, too?" he asked as he flopped down on the lower bunk. "At this rate, you're going to get plastered, too. It was really amusing how, whenever Mrs. Yu addressed you, it was always Mrs. Hu this and Mrs. Hu that."

Xichun sat down next to him, took his hand in hers, and asked, "Did that rub you the wrong way a little?"

"Why do you always take whatever I say and turn it around the other way?" Ziyun asked with a smile.

Xichun ran her fingers over his face. "You really are a bit drunk. Why don't I peel a couple of oranges for you?"

"Good idea," said Ziyun, "but I don't deserve such special treatment."

Xichun looked at him and said, "You deserve many, many things. Why do you have to be so self-effacing?"

Ziyun smiled at her words. Xichun climbed up to the area just below the baggage rack, took some oranges out of a sack, leaned down, and put them on the tea table. Then she climbed back down and sat as close as she could to Ziyun while she peeled the oranges. She even picked out the little white fibers between the sections before putting them one by one into Ziyun's mouth. By the time she had finished feeding him two of them, Ziyun had dropped off to sleep, feeling very relaxed and comfortable.

Although she didn't sleep, Xichun did remain by his side. She looked at a train schedule and seemed to be muttering to herself as though figuring out times between stations. After a while—we don't know how long—the train came to a stop at another station. Xichun happened to look up and saw two carrying poles on the platform, the kind used to carry sweetened rice porridge. Anyone used to traveling the route between Tientsin and Shanghai would know at a glance that this was Bengboo in Anhui Province because that's the only platform where you'd find sweetened rice porridge for sale.

Xichun decided to go down to the platform and have a look around. Unexpectedly, however, just as she stood up, she saw that the young man with the dog was already out on the platform letting his dog relieve himself. Clenching her teeth in anger and disappointment, she stared out the train window. Then, talking to herself as much as anyone else, she said, "That SOB is something else. Gets off at every last stop. Wonder if he stays up all night so he won't miss any." Just as she was thinking this, she turned her head and saw a shadow by the door—Mrs. Yu.

Mrs. Yu put her hand on the door, stuck her head inside, looked around, and asked in a low voice, "Is he really drunk?" Xichun pursed her lips in Ziyun's direction. Mrs. Yu raised her voice and said, "Mrs. Hu, why don't you come out for a stroll?"

"We only stop for ten minutes at this station. Not much point in getting off the train. If we take a stroll and the train leaves without us, what will we do then?"

"Okay then," said Mrs. Yu, "let's go to the dining car and have some sort of carbonated drink. You don't taboo cold things, do you?"

"I don't taboo anything," answered Xichun with a smile. She took Mrs. Yu by the hand as she spoke, walked out into the corridor, and gently pulled the door to.

Ziyun had himself quite a nap and, not seeing Xichun when he woke up, decided that she must have gone down to third class to see her former schoolmate. "No matter what point of view you consider her from," he thought to himself, "this young woman is a truly tender and loving human being. And to think that that young husband of hers shouldn't be blessed with the good fortune to enjoy such a wife! Strange when you think of it—and yet not really strange either since everything depends on fate. Wonder what lucky star was shining down on me that I should have run into such a lovable young woman on the train?" Having reached this point in his thinking, he couldn't help but chuckle to himself.

The feeling he had now was well worth savoring, and so he sat up, lit a cigarette, and contentedly thought about his situation in detail. While doing so, he noticed that her little suitcase was lying unlocked at the head of the lower berth. He began to rummage through it. As he pushed aside some negligees, a stack of bills appeared. They were all ten spots, and he estimated that there must be at least two or three hundred dollars there.

He hefted the stack once or twice in his hand and then returned it to its original place. "This young woman is far, far too careless leaving her money around like this," he thought. "Luckily, she ran into a rich man like myself who wouldn't think of helping himself to a single penny of it, but suppose she ran into one of those lotharios who make their living taking advantage of young women? A man like that would probably seduce her and make off with her cash in the bargain. She's really got to learn to be more careful with her money. I guess it's up to me to give her some advice on that score. Young people like her always need someone who's experienced in the ways of the world to show them how things ought to be done." It goes without saying that Ziyun considered himself as one who was "experienced in the ways of the world." But was he really? We'll have to await further developments to prove that one way or the other.

11

While Crossing the River at Pookow

In Hu Ziyun's compartment, besides the addition of a woman, there was now the further addition of a bottle of brandy. On a long and lonely journey, the company of either a woman or a bottle of brandy is enough to keep a man pleasantly stimulated. And now, having *both* these forms of stimulation available, Ziyun, of course, was no longer the least bit lonely. After they passed Bengboo, he was palpably tipsy and went to sleep.

By the time he had slept it off and woke up again, the electric lights in his compartment had long since come on. Xichun was sitting at an angle on the chair by the window. She had one elbow on her thigh and was supporting her head in the same hand. Her eyelids were drawn partially together as though she were thinking about something. Though she didn't know it, Ziyun had been observing her for quite some time. "I'll bet whatever you're thinking about has something to do with your home life," he said with a smile. "Forget it. Soon as we get to Shanghai, we'll have some *real* fun."

She confirmed that his guess was correct, then sighed and said, "Whenever I'm with you, talking and laughing like this, I actually do forget about everything that's bothering me. When I sit here by myself, though, it all comes back to haunt me. But what can I do?" Following her question with a long sigh, Xichun reached over, picked up the brandy bottle from the tea table, and pulled out the cork. She took a teacup and was about to pour when Ziyun scrambled up from the berth and grabbed her by the wrist. "What kind of nonsense is this! I'll bet you don't have much of a capacity to begin with, and drinking on an empty stomach like this, you'll get plastered in no time. What's the point?"

Xichun held tight to the bottle and said, "No, you can't have it! I'm going to have a drink, and that's that!"

"All right, fine, *have* a drink. But at least wait till after supper. Then, you can take the bottle to the dining car and ask Mrs. Yu to join you."

Still clinging to the bottle, Xichun answered, "I just thought of something we *could* do. When the Shanghai Express gets to Pookow, they have to ferry the whole train across the river, and that's a complicated business—takes hours. While all that's going on, I can get off the train, take a pedestrian ferry across, buy some saltwater duck, and then get back on at Hsiakuan.[1] With saltwater duck for a wine downer, we can drink away the whole night! Then when we pull into Shanghai in the morning, we can go check into a room at the Park[2] and spend a comfortable day sleeping it off."

1. Hsiakuan (pinyin: Xiaguan) is right across the river from Pookow on the southern bank of the Yangtze. It lies within the northwest area of greater Nanking close to the southern terminus of the double-deck Yangtze River Bridge *(Changjiang daqiao)*, which was completed in 1968 and is often heralded as an accomplishment of the Great Proletarian Cultural Revolution (1966–1976); the upper deck of the bridge accommodates vehicular traffic, the lower deck trains.

2. Known in Chinese as the Guoji Fandian (The international) and in English as the Park, this hotel had just been completed in the year in which this novel is set (1935) and thus would have been one of the most glamorous places in Shanghai in which one could stay.

"I don't get it," said Ziyun. "Won't you still have to go on living with the same problems the day *after* tomorrow?"

"Of course I will. That's not the point. It's just that there's no telling what I'm going to find in the family when I get to Shanghai. But, in the meantime, I want to taste at least *some* happiness. Do you have the heart to deny me just one single day of happiness?" Her final question was a powerful one.

Ziyun smiled and said, "Well, since you put it that way. Go ahead and have yourself a drink. But what's the point of the Hsiakuan side trip just to buy saltwater duck?"

"I've got to pick up some cash at a silk store there anyway. Actually, I wrote the store an express letter long before making this trip. I asked them to have somebody come to the Pookow station with the money. But I've found that it's only people who want to *borrow* from you who are willing to do things according to your agenda; people who are paying you back aren't about to do things the way you'd like to have them done. I think it quite likely that when I get to the Pookow station they won't even show up. So I'm going to go to their shop in Hsiakuan and demand payment there. You'll have to go to the dining car for supper by yourself. I won't be able to join you."

"In that case, I'll be here waiting for you. Bring back some nice fresh bread while you're at it."

Xichun laughed and said, "We'll do it just the way I suggested then—drink away the night! In that case, I might as well save this brandy to see which one of us can put away the most when I get back." She put the cork back into the bottle even as she spoke and put it to one side.

"Well now, since you're going to take my advice with regard to the wine after all," said Ziyun with a broad smile, "I'm going to love you all the more." He sat up straight on the berth, clapped his hands together, and then slowly spread them wide, as though preparing to give someone a good hug. Sure enough, Xichun immediately walked into his waiting embrace, nestled her head on his shoulder, and gracefully pirouetted around so as to come down next to him on the berth.

On a long trip such as this, Ziyun had craved some sort of stimulation, and Xichun had amply provided it. When you come right down to it, however, nobody really *needs* that sort of exhilaration, for that which has been stimulated will eventually grow numb. The excitement that Xichun had initially provided just by her very presence was more than ample to begin with. Now, magnified by the brandy, it went from ample to out of sight! In short, Ziyun barely knew which way was up.

Suddenly, however, he was jolted into an awareness that the train had stopped: carrying luggage and packages of all manner and description, people seemed to be bailing out right and left. He raised the window shade and looked outside. They were stopped next to a platform awash in bright light. Xichun let out an *Oh-oh!* stood up, and said, "Oh my gosh! Pookow already, and I didn't even know it." Quickly straightening her hair, she dove into her overcoat, snatched up her purse, clasped it under one arm, and dashed off toward the platform with Ziyun in her wake.

"You really are going to Hsiakuan, then? What happens if you don't make it back to the train in time?"

Already on the platform, Xichun turned back toward him, raised her hand, and said, "Don't get off the train; you might catch cold." Then she continued walking while shouting back over her shoulder, "I'm sure I'll be able to make it back in time. On the off chance that I don't, just take my suitcase, and meet me at the Park." By the time she reached the last word of her instructions, she was already a good ways down the platform. Ziyun leaned out of the car and observed her departing figure.

He was unable to suppress a chuckle as he commented to

himself, "Acts just like a kid." Though one could detect a note of criticism in his words, Ziyun actually liked that kiddishness of hers more than a little. Beaming with pleasure, he returned to the compartment. He saw that her things were strewn haphazardly around the berth. The suitcase of which she had just spoken lay there with one latch closed and one latch open. "Really does trust me," he thought. "Suitcase left open like that. Doesn't worry that I might get into her money."

Sitting on the edge of the lower berth, he lit a cigar and looked out the window when who should he see but Li Chengfu pacing back and forth on the platform. Ziyun tapped against the window and called Chengfu's name. The latter, noticing that Ziyun was alone in the compartment, decided to go in and visit. Ziyun invited him to sit down and said, "People are few and far between out there on the platform. Must be cold. There aren't too many passengers on the train right now either."

"Well, there's a reason behind that. On this particular Shanghai Express, they don't take passes or half-fare tickets. Most passengers who are headed down to Nanking from the north are connected to the government one way or another. People like that can usually finagle a pass or a half fare. Why would they take a train like the Shanghai Express where their passes and half fares are no good? As a banker who's well versed in economics, you must be aware that these days everything has an economic reason behind it somewhere or other. Well, this train does, too. Everyone on it had to pay a full fare. That's why when we pulled into Pookow there weren't all that many people on it." As he spoke, Chengfu noticed that there was a lady's scarf on the berth and asked, "Did Miss Liu get off?"

"She's a fascinating young woman. Took all the trouble to go to Hsiakuan just so she could buy saltwater duck."

"Must be someone who's *used* to riding the Shanghai

Express. The way they've got of taking the whole train across the river saves passengers from having to get *off* the train, *onto* a boat, and then *back* onto the train on the Nanking side. But it *does* take forever. A good four hours or so. That's why passengers who come down to Nanking from the north—even though they can cross the river without ever getting off the train—like to get off at Pookow and take the pedestrian ferry across. That way they get into Nanking three hours before the train does." As the two men chatted, the train started to roll with a bump-bang and a clang. But then after only five minutes it came to a stop again.

Ziyun stuck his head out the window and saw that the train had come to a switch. "Why are we stopped again?" he asked.

"We've been backed out of Pookow Station," explained Chengfu, "and put onto a siding that leads down to the river. The engine will back a third of the train onto the ferry, unhook, wait for it to come back, then back another third on, and so on. On the last trip, the engine itself will go across. Of course, that means that there has to be a switch engine on the other side to pull the first two loads off onto a siding before the engine joins them on that last crossing. Once the Express is all reassembled over there, it will proceed to Hsiakuan Station. You just watch, this old train is going to stop-start and start-stop a whole bunch of times.

"No wonder Miss Liu wanted to go to Hsiakuan for a change of scene," said Ziyun.

"Yes," said Chengfu, "as I was saying before, experienced travelers on the Shanghai Express always get right off the train when it hits Pookow. They can take a passenger ferry across to Hsiakuan, wash up in a bathhouse, go to a restaurant for a proper meal, and *still* have plenty of time to make it back to the train. No trouble at all. That's especially true of the people in third class. While they're on the train, they eat whatever odds and ends the various stations afford. But

Pookow is a terminus, and that creates a problem—hardly any snack stands on the platform. And so the third-class passengers are much better off taking a passenger ferry across to Hsiakuan and eating in one of the little restaurants there."

"Makes sense to me," said Ziyun, "but who looks after their luggage while they're doing this?"

"Hadn't thought of that," said Chengfu. "I'll bet it's only people *without* luggage who can do it that way. But that doesn't make sense either. What would passengers *without* luggage be doing on a long trip in the first place?"

"People who spend the most money are the most comfortable," noted Ziyun complacently. "I'll bet it's the first- and second-class passengers who do what you're talking about."

"Sorry I didn't get off at Pookow, too!" lamented Chengfu. "If I had, right now I could be relaxing in a nice hot bath. There are really quite a few nice bathhouses over there on the southern bank of the Yangtze, you know." The train was under way as the two men conversed, but now it stopped again. "We're probably at the bank of the river," Chengfu noted. "I'm going back to my compartment and put on something warm so I can get off the train as we cross the river and enjoy the scenery." He left the compartment, but before long he came back, laughing as he walked in. "Can't get back to my car because it isn't there! Second class consists of two coaches, and the one that I was on has already been loaded onto the train ferry."

"I've got some brandy. If you're bothered by the cold, have a cup."

Chengfu looked at the bottle on the tea table and asked with a smile, "Is that yours? I'll bet it's brandy that Miss Liu is saving to go with that saltwater duck."

"Yes, but she's not much of a drinker. People with money aren't concerned with such trifles anyway. She really bought it just for the hell of it to begin with."

"She's a most interesting young woman—so very sophisticated and yet kiddish at the same time."

"What do you really think of her after all?" As he asked the question, Ziyun crossed his left leg over his right and swung it gently back and forth. His cigar was partially supported between two fingers and partially supported by his lips, which were parted slightly in a smile.

Sitting on the sofa chair at the corner of the tea table, Chengfu observed the expression on Ziyun's face and was also aware of the faint scent of cosmetics that Xichun had left behind. In the light of all this, he had a fairly good idea of the lay of the land. He smiled and answered, "Well, she is very nice, of course. . . . "

Continuing to swing his leg, Ziyun pressed his friend with a further question: "Do you think she's a *clever* person?"

"Well, that's hard to say because intelligence has so many different levels to it. For instance, some people are very clever but nonetheless open and honest as well, while some other people are—"

Holding his cigar fast between his teeth, Ziyun clapped his hands in delight and said, "You couldn't be more right if you tried! Although Xichun *is* quite intelligent, she treats everyone with a fundamental openness and honesty. Basically, what you have there is a woman to be pitied, a woman just waiting for someone to come along and offer some assistance. I've decided that when we get to Shanghai, I'm going to help her find a way out of her present situation."

"Well, with somebody as powerful and prestigious as you behind her, how can the outcome be in doubt? If *you're* willing to come to her rescue, she's as good as saved."

Ziyun had originally intended to say something, but now he held it back and simply smiled. After they had sat in silence for a while, the car they were in started moving again. Ever so slowly, it rolled from the wharf onto the ferry.

"Nanking has had this ferry for two years now," said Ziyun, "but this is the first time I've taken it, first time I've crossed the river on a train! I'm going to go down on deck and check it out." He put on his overcoat as he spoke. Chengfu accompanied him.

Three parallel rows of tracks with cars on them took up almost the entire deck, leaving a walkway of two feet or so between the outside cars and the ship's railing. The deckhouse was at the bow of the ferry, and as Ziyun looked up in that direction, by the flickering lights on the bridge, he could make out several people directing the operation of the ship. After a prolonged wooh-wooh of the ship's whistle, the reverberating chung-chung-chung of its engines could be heard as the ferry began to move through the water. Their departure from shore was confirmed by a biting cold wind off the river. Ziyun and Chengfu stood side by side, looking out over the water. Chengfu's nose contracted and drew back before the wind. Despite himself, he began to shudder. "More than I bargained for," he said. "Better go get my overcoat."

First class was on the starboard side, while second class was on the port. That meant that Chengfu couldn't walk straight across the ferry's deck but rather had to take a more roundabout route from where they were standing up to the bow and then around to the port side. This took a bit of time. As Chengfu walked, he spotted Mrs. Yu, who was, of course, also riding in the second-class coach. Clad in an overcoat, she kept her gaze on the deck and hurried along as though attending to some urgent piece of business.

When he boarded the second-class coach and arrived at his compartment, Chengfu found his three compartment mates engaged in a round of complaints. One said, "When the train was rolling station to station through the plains, it wasn't a bad ride. But then they had to go and start screwing around with all that stop-start crap in Pookow, and after a couple of hours of that—there we were still in Pookow. That was a little much if you ask me!"

"If we were able to sleep through it all," said the second one, "that would be fine. But as soon as they separated the cars, they also separated our steam lines. Cold enough to freeze your butt off!"

"Even if we did have heat," said the third, "wouldn't be able to sleep anyway. Run a while, stop a while; stop a while, run a while—like to know how you're gonna settle your nerves enough to sleep with all *that* going on?" Rather than contributing his own opinion to this little discussion, Chengfu picked up his overcoat from the berth, put it on, and made his way down the corridor.

He went through the coach door and found that second class was still coupled to third. As he walked through third class, Chengfu noticed that more than half the passengers had gotten off the train back at Pookow. The ones who had remained were heavily bundled against the cold. Most just sat there leaning back against their seats looking thoroughly bored. A few, unwilling to content themselves with such passive resistance, sought whatever warmth was to be had by smoking cigarettes for all they were worth; a few others paced up and down the aisle between the seats as though in training for some sort of walking race.

He heard one passenger complain, "When are we ever gonna get across this damned river? I'm gonna freeze to death right here in my seat." And then another said, "When they came up with this way of taking the whole train across the river by ferry, they had our comfort and convenience in mind. Now people are complaining about it. Folks just don't know when someone's doing them a favor."

But someone else countered that by saying, "I remember before they had the train ferry, you had to get off at Pookow, take a pedestrian ferry across, and then get on another train at Hsiakuan. From getting off the one train at Pookow to getting on the other at Hsiakuan, it only took two or three hours tops. But now that you enjoy the so-called convenience of not having to change trains, it takes you four whole hours! Four! And to think of all the money the Ministry of Railroads must have had to pay for a steam ferry that could carry trains across. . . . "

Stepping from third class down onto the deck, Chengfu was still turning the pros and cons of the train ferry over in his own mind. As he walked slowly along, he noticed two people standing by the steps leading up to the ferry's ladies' room. He heard a woman say in a low voice, "There's probably no problem now. It'll either be Wusih or Soochow. Just wait for the call." He recognized the voice as belonging to Mrs. Yu. Although it was not a secret conversation they were having, still Chengfu felt that it was improper to listen in on the talk of two women who had drawn aside for a private chat. He detoured around them and made his way back to join Ziyun in savoring the river scenery.

Looking up through a thin layer of fog that lent a poetic tone to the river scene, one could see a crescent moon off to one side of the sky as well as a sparse scattering of stars. As one lowered one's eyes and looked over in the direction of Hsiakuan, the fog, of course, presented a much thicker aspect. The result was that the lights of people's dwellings down by the riverside as well as those at various irregular levels higher on up were only faintly visible. They were strong enough, however, to provide a soft radiance that framed Hsiakuan in a dreamscape most pleasing to the eye.

Chengfu shook his head in surprised admiration and observed, "Seen in the fog like this, the river scenery is truly marvelous. I can't find words to do it justice."

"The world is really evolving," said Ziyun. "Things that we wouldn't even have dreamed of when we were kids have all come to pass. Just think, here we are enjoying a river scene from a train right smack dab in the middle of the river! If we'd heard of such a thing when we were kids, we'd have surely thought it was a fairy tale." Just as they reached this point in their conversation, the ferry made a turn so that lights were now visible from both shores.

"Wonderful!" exclaimed Chengfu. "Now I can't tell for sure which side's Hsiakuan and which side's Pookow."

"What a shame Miss Liu isn't here," said Ziyun. "If she were here, what with all her literary training, she'd be sure to have a lot to say. Inspired by a view like this one, think of all the lofty and noble things she'd be able to come up with!"

Chengfu almost burst out laughing at that one, but he contained himself and decided to have some fun teasing Ziyun along. "Miss Liu," he suggested, "has a certain elite and scholarly air to her; she has a literary view of life and the world. Who else but a person like that would get off the train and take a pedestrian ferry to Hsiakuan just to buy saltwater duck for a wine downer?"

Ziyun clapped his hands in gleeful agreement, "Right, right! Beautiful girls aren't hard to come by, but how often do you find a beautiful girl who's also free from all trace of vulgarity? I'd rather have a wife like that than be emperor!"

"Well, you've got a good eye for sizing people up to begin with, and after one whole day and a night of observing the young woman, how can you possibly go wrong?"

"No, not just one day and a night. I've heard about that young woman for a long time now. Comes from an excellent family, and she's married into a family of high-class people as well. But for some reason or other she and that husband of hers can't seem to hit it off."

"How can an upper-class woman like Miss Liu endure such a situation?" Chengfu asked.

"Can't. Why do you think she's running back and forth from north to south on the train? When we get to Shanghai, though, I think that this time she's bound to find some way out of that mess."

"This wind on the river is really too much," said Chengfu. "Let's get back on the train."

"Well, in that case, let's go sit in my compartment. We've been standing out here so long we could really use some brandy to shake off the cold."

"You go on by yourself," said Chengfu. "I want to go back to my compartment and get something warm to put on."

When he heard this, Ziyun began to worry a bit. After all, he wasn't in all that great shape himself and ought to try to keep warm, too. He rushed back to his compartment, sat down without taking his overcoat off, and poured himself half a teacup of brandy, which he proceeded to slowly drink down. As soon as the brandy was in his mouth, sure enough, it did seem to perk him up a bit, and he was soon conscious of a warmth that traveled clear down to his midsection.

He looked out the window and discovered that the electric lights were bright as day. The ferry had already arrived at Hsiakuan. The ferry's great engines continued to hung-dung hung-dung for the longest time before the boat was finally in position next to the wharf. "Chengfu probably won't come," he thought. "Why not lie down for a while? Just sitting here like this is as boring as it gets." He piled pillows under his head and, still wearing his overcoat, lay down on his side on the lower berth. He closed his eyes as ever so many thoughts coursed through his brain. At first, everything was dead quiet, and the train remained motionless. And then, as it was put back together again, the Shanghai Express returned to that same stop-go stop-go mode with which he had become depressingly familiar back in Pookow. Ziyun felt that he had just about all of that that he could take. Forcing himself to stay calm, however, he finally managed to go to sleep.

When he awoke, he was conscious of nothing but absolute silence. This startled him, for this was the way it was whenever the train stopped out in the middle of nowhere. That must be it. They must have left Nanking a long time back! He immediately rolled over, sat up, and looked out the window. A long platform greeted his eyes. A large black sign hung from two concrete posts over it, and on the sign there were written two Chinese characters: *Hsia* and *Kuan.* There were no passengers on the platform, and the powerful lights above it served to make it look all the more deserted. From somewhere came the drawn-out calls of hawkers: "Five-spice dried bean curd!" and "Tea-leaf eggs!"[3] These calls told the passengers that they were already on the south side of the Yangtze River.

Ziyun pulled out his watch—11:45 P.M., only ten minutes before departure time. He opened the compartment door and called out to the porter, "Has Miss Liu come back yet?"

"Not yet," answered the porter, "and if she doesn't come back pretty soon, she's going to miss the train."

Ziyun frowned and said, "What am I going to do? There's no phone number I can call to get her either." He sat down on the berth, pulled out a cigar, and began to smoke. "Judging from how deserted the platform looks," he thought, "it appears that Nanking people don't take this train to Shanghai, and that means they're not going to hold it a second beyond the scheduled departure time. She may not make it. If she doesn't, I wonder if she really will go to the Park and look me up when she gets to Shanghai?" Just as he reached this point in his thoughts, he heard the electric bell that announced the train's imminent departure from the station. So Xichun really *had* missed the train after all! Ziyun was quite depressed.

3. Boiled eggs with cracked shells marinated in tea leaves.

12

Wine, Women, and Song

In the past, no matter whether you traveled by boat or by bus, if a passenger had something important to take care of before boarding and was a bit late in getting there, they'd simply wait for that passenger. But nowadays, when it comes to steamboats or trains, you're dealing with very large numbers of people, and they're not going to be held up for just one or two passengers. As far as Hu Ziyun was concerned, however, it would by no means be excessive if this *particular* train waited a whole hour for this *particular* passenger—Miss Liu. Nonetheless, when departure time arrived, the train left the station not a single second behind schedule.

And so it was that Xichun was left in Nanking while her suitcase accompanied Ziyun to Shanghai. But he still hadn't given up all hope. Perhaps she was chasing the train even now but hadn't gotten on board yet. He opened the window, leaned out as far as he could, and looked up and down the platform. The train, however, was already rapidly picking up speed so that even if she had made it to the platform there was no way she could run *that* fast. Closing the window, Ziyun said to himself, "When you come right down to it, young folks just aren't as prudent as they should be." He took his cigar up from the ashtray and began smoking again. Keenly aware of the fragrance of her clothing and cosmetics, he gazed at her open suitcase. Before long, he began to experience a disappointment that knew no bounds, a disappointment that accelerated right along with the train.

The station lights slowly faded into the distance. Ziyun was devastated. Just then, he heard a voice outside the compartment door: "Ticket check!" The tones were quite feminine, and you could have cut the Shanghai accent with a knife. The knocking grew louder. "The railroad is really going in for male-female equality these days," he thought. "Used to be they employed women only as ticket sellers in the stations. Now it looks as though they're taking them on as conductors as well!" As he opened the door, that same voice broke into loud laughter. One look, and Ziyun was beside himself with joy. There stood Xichun, her arms laden down with paper bags and rush sacks of varying shapes and sizes.

As she stood at the compartment door, she was so amused at her own joke that her eyes were squinted almost shut with glee. Ziyun immediately stood up, reached out with both hands, took all the packages out of her arms, and arranged them on the floor. "How in the world," he asked with a broad smile, "did you ever manage to get on the train after it was already moving so fast? You know, you had me worried to death."

Xichun stepped into the compartment, drew the door shut behind her, and immediately rested her head at an angle against Ziyun's shoulder. "Were you really worried about me?" she asked coyly.

Ziyun patted her comfortingly on the back and replied, "If you want to see just *how* worried I was, just reach inside and feel my shorts—they're soaking wet."

Xichun made a little fist and hammered it lightly against him. "Don't be disgusting," she said.

"I'm not being in the least disgusting," he objected. "I'm just telling you that I was so worried that my whole body broke into a sweat."

"With this compartment as hot as it is and you in a leather overcoat, I'd say it'd be a wonder if you *didn't* break into a sweat!"

Ziyun roared with laughter. "I'll be damned! How scatterbrained can a man get? But the thing *is,* I was so worried about you that I completely *forgot* about taking off my coat."

She undid the buttons on his overcoat and then snuggled in as close to him as she could possibly get. She lowered her head and said, "So you really do love me, after all. Looks as though I'm a pretty good judge of character at that. Later on, I'm going to thank you for your love like you've never been thanked before!"

"Like I've never been thanked before? What does *that* mean?"

"Now, do you really have to ask?" She hung his overcoat on the coat hook as she spoke and then lightly smoothed the wrinkles from it. Ziyun took her hands in his, sat on the lower bunk, and pulled her down next to him.

"I love the way you treat me—makes me feel so relaxed and comfortable. But at the same time I feel I don't deserve such happiness."

"Why must you be so deferential about what you deserve and what you don't? You'll start coming across as a tad hypocritical if you don't watch it. Still haven't had your dinner, right? Let me take out all the stuff I bought, and we'll have ourselves a nice meal." Xichun moved everything off the tea table and spread a piece of paper over it for a tablecloth. She put all the bags and sacks on the floor and began to open them. The first contained imitation ivory chopsticks as well as two knives. She set two places, complete with knives, on either side of the tea table, making it look somewhat as though they were preparing to have a Western meal.

"You think of everything," said Ziyun. "Chopsticks and knives as well! Well, what are we having?"

Xichun answered only with a smile and continued to take things out of the bags on the floor and put them on the table: saltwater duck, ham, five-spice beef marinated in soy sauce, canned dried-meat floss, canned asparagus, and more. She cut everything into small pieces and arranged it all neatly around the table. Besides everything else, it turned out that she had brought two large wineglasses as well, clean and polished so that they glittered.

Ziyun couldn't help but laugh at the glasses. "Have you got anything else to bring out? It's a banquet we're holding, am I right?"

"Well, I'm not planning on sleeping tonight, you know." She pointed at the brandy bottle and said, "I'll not be satisfied until every last drop of that brandy is gone."

"It just won't do to go without sleep," objected Ziyun. "When we pull into Shanghai at seven something in the morning, you'll need your energy to get things done."

Ignoring him, Xichun collected all the debris from the floor and scrunched it up into a large ball, which she put out in the corridor. She pulled the door shut and sat on the sofa chair on one side of the tea table. She pointed to the lower berth across the table and said, "You sit over there."

"Must we drink sitting across from each other?"

"I am the host here," she replied. "It's your place to play the well-behaved guest and sit where I tell you to. Frivolity's not allowed."

"Do we have to be as refined as all that? Let's at least play a drinking game."

Xichun pulled the glass set in front of him over to her side of the table and filled it with brandy. Then she filled her own to the brim as well and put the brandy away. "Anybody who tries to cheat gets fined one glass. Let's play the finger-guessing game."[1]

"What do I do if I lose?" asked Ziyun.

"What do you mean, what do you do if you lose? It's the finger-guessing game, right? If you lose, then, of course, you take a drink just as always."

"No!" Ziyun objected. "If *I* lose, then you give me a *kiss*. But if *you* lose, then I give you a kiss."[2]

Xichun put the tips of her index fingers against the meaty parts of her thumbs, reached across the table, and gently filliped them on both sides of Ziyun's face. "Think you're too smart for me, huh? That way, you'd always win, and I'd always lose. Why don't we do it like this? If *I* lose, you get your kiss. But if *you* lose, then you have to take a drink. How about it? It's a good deal for you."

Ziyun turned that over in his mind and decided that it was indeed a good deal. And so it came about that Xichun and Ziyun sat across from each other and in hushed tones played the finger-guessing game.

Alcohol can indeed be a very wicked thing. If you have a few genteel drinks when alone, you may become somewhat intoxicated, but then you simply lie down and go to sleep. But if you play the finger-guessing game with a friend, you're much more likely to drink more than you ought to—perhaps even two or three times your own capacity—without being aware of it. Ziyun's present situation was made worse by the fact that Xichun had prepared some very tasty

1. There are several versions of this game. A common one requires that you and your opponent make fists and then simultaneously throw them out toward each other with some of the fingers extended, at the same time shouting out your guess as to the total number of fingers being extended. The shouts are usually quite loud, but, given the late hour and the likelihood that other people are asleep, Xichun and Ziyun must guess the totals in hushed voices.

2. In both instances, the word kiss is given in English.

things to go with the brandy. The result of all this was that Ziyun, who couldn't drink much to begin with, polished off a large glass of brandy down to the very last drop.

At night it gets very quiet aboard the Shanghai Express. Furthermore, since the train pulls out of Nanking at midnight, by the time it passes through the various stations on the way to Shanghai, even they have become quiet and lonely places, though during the day every last one of them was a loud and lively center of bustling activity.

By the time Ziyun had finished that glass of brandy, the Shanghai Express was stopped at a large station. Ziyun looked out the window and saw that the two Chinese characters written on the platform sign were *Chin* and *Kiang*. "We must have been drinking up a storm," he said to Xichun. "Where has the time gone? Here we are at Chinkiang already! I'll bet it's two or three in the morning. Don't you think we ought to go to sleep now?"

"What a weaky-bone!" teased Xichun with a smile as she rubbed her index finger against her own cheek in a shame-on-you gesture. "We've only been finger guessing for a little while, and here you are making plans for your escape after one measly glass of brandy. I, on the other hand, despite my many losses, have hung in there like a champ with no thought of trying to weasel out of so much as a single kiss. More than that, I've even kept you company in your drinking and have polished off a whole glass!"

"No, you didn't. You still have more than half a glass left."

"You shouldn't be drunk after the little you've had," chided Xichun, "but it looks as though the brandy has gone to your head. You didn't even notice that I finished my *first* glass a while back. This is my second."

"Really? I honestly hadn't noticed. I really did think it was your first."

"If you think back to how long I held the glass to my lips

each time I took a drink, you'll have some idea of how quickly I finished my first glass." As she spoke, she reached over, took his glass, and poured it over half full of brandy. She placed it back in front of him and said, "If you'd like to show a little respect for my feelings, drink it down, but if you don't care about the way I feel, then forget it."

He smiled, then studied her face, and said, "From the expression on your face, I can tell you're going to be angry if I don't."

"Me? Angry?" asked Xichun in a pout. "I wouldn't dare. It's just that you shouldn't take advantage of me. Here I've been winning most of the time, and I've already drunk one large glass and am well into my second, while you—the one who's been doing all the losing—you by comparison have had only a little." With just the right touch of petulance, she turned her shoulders away from him as she spoke.

"All right! I'll drink it. But when I'm done, you're not to try and get me to drink any more. I'm gonna lie down and rest for a bit after I've finished it, too. I don't want to go to sleep drunk and end up with a head as big as all outdoors."

"You don't have to worry about that," said Xichun. "If you finish off what I poured you, I promise not to bug you again."

"In that case, your loyal servant cannot but obey your imperial highness' order. All right, here I go." He picked up the glass in both hands as he spoke, stretched out his neck, downed it in a few continuous gulps, and then saluted her with the upside-down glass.

Xichun nodded her head approvingly. "Thank you very much, good sir. You were willing to show me some respect after all."

Gulping it down as he did, Ziyun felt as though some-one had set his throat on fire. After a cup of cool tea, how-ever, his throat, at least, was somewhat more comfortable. "Boy, now I really do feel a bit tipsy. Give me a couple of oranges out of the basket, and maybe I can stave off the worst effects."

Xichun looked at him sternly and said, "Come on, now, you're no kid. You ought to know how to take care of yourself better than that. Late as it is, how can you even *think* of eating anything raw or cold?" Having said this, to her own surprise, she tittered.

Although Ziyun thought that he wouldn't feel better until he ate something nice and cool, given Xichun's objection, he gave up the idea of eating oranges. Instead, he smiled and said, "Well, I'm still thirsty. Hot tea ought to be all right, shouldn't it?—Oh no! Oh no!" He bent over and threw up all over the spittoon.

"Oh dear! If I had known what bad shape you were in, I would never, ever have forced you to drink that last half glass." Xichun immediately came over to his side of the table and gently eased him back onto the berth. "Just lie down for a bit while I get the porter to bring us some hot water." Once she had him in a comfortable position, Xichun took a handkerchief out of her pocket and carefully wiped his face and lips clean. Having tidied him up, she had the porter bring some hot water and make them a pot of tea. By the time it was steeped, however, Ziyun was fast asleep and snoring quite loudly. She filled a cup for herself and held its warmth between her palms while staring intently at Ziyun. She nodded her head and put the cup back down on the tea table.

She looked at her watch, then took the train schedule out of her suitcase and began leafing through it. Outside the window, the violent hong-dong hong-dong of steel wheels slamming against steel track clearly indicated that the Shanghai Express was tearing toward Shanghai for all it was worth. Sitting on the little sofa chair, her upper teeth clasped down on her lower lip, Xichun continued to stare steadily at the man on the lower berth. After quite some time had passed, she stood up decisively and turned off the compartment lights.

All evil in this world has its beginnings in darkness. Of course, that is by no means to say that you can't find evil in the absence of darkness, but if evil does occur, one will, without fail, find that it had its beginnings in darkness. Now, why was it that Miss Xichun had hit it off so readily with Mr. Hu Ziyun in the first place? Why had she so easily accommodated him at every turn? It was precisely because she wanted to commit a most wicked and villainous act, the very kind of iniquity most conveniently perpetrated in the dark.

After the Shanghai Express left Chinkiang, the next big station was Changchow, and it wasn't until the wee hours of the morning that the train arrived there. Very few people got on or off. The passengers you'd ordinarily find at a train station simply weren't there. Dimly silhouetted by the dreary electric lights on the platform, only a few quirky souls who craved the peace and quiet of a night train had come down to board the Shanghai Express at that silent hour of the night. Very quietly, they climbed onto the train.

The lights in Ziyun's compartment were on now. Still wearing her down-lined Mandarin dress, Xichun apparently hadn't slept. She thrust her head out the compartment door and looked up and down the corridor. What a coincidence that Mrs. Yu should choose this time of night to come up to the first-class sleeper for a visit. The two women smiled and held each other by the hand as Xichun stepped out into the corridor.

"Is Mr. Hu asleep?" asked Mrs. Yu in a low tone.

"On a tipsy romp through dreamland," replied Xichun with a smile.

Now it so happened that while the women were thus engaged in conversation, the sleeping-car porter on duty was standing fairly close to them. "I've arranged for a relative to meet me at the station in Wusih," said Mrs. Yu. "Haven't been able to get a good night's sleep because I was afraid of sleeping right through the stop and missing her. Your Mr. Hu said he had some books he wanted to give her and asked me to deliver them for him. Do you know where they are?"

Xichun turned around and looked back inside the compartment. Ziyun was snoring. She went in, reached under the berth, and took out a paper package, which she handed to Mrs. Yu. Mrs. Yu took it in both hands, hefted it once or twice, and smiled. "Are they all in this package?" Mrs. Yu asked.

"Every last one," responded Xichun in a low voice.

"Well, you don't have to worry about them with me," assured Mrs. Yu. "I won't lose them."

"Raggedy old books. Doesn't matter if you do. See you tomorrow morning, then." As Xichun spoke, she stepped back into the compartment and drew the door closed behind her. The train was already pulling out of Changchow. Xichun sat on the sofa chair looking somewhat as though she were in a trance, her face turning dark and pale by turns. Trying her darnedest not to let her inner turmoil show on the outside, she forced herself to stay calm. She took up a cigar and slowly smoked it. Ziyun started to toss and turn on the lower bunk as though about to wake up.

Xichun immediately put the cigar down, quickly perched herself on the edge of Ziyun's berth, and gently covered him with a blanket. "Would you like a drink of hot water?" she asked in a low voice.

Eyes still closed tight, Ziyun raised one hand, draped it around the back of her neck, and mumbled, "Why is it you —why is it you still aren't sleeping?"

Treating him for all the world like a child, Xichun patted him lightly on the shoulder and said in a gentle voice, "I'm going to sleep right now." Ziyun continued to mumble for a bit and then began to snore again. Although she had been eminently successful in gently escorting this tipsy man back into dreamland, her own heart was beating a mile a minute. Her spirits had been somewhat tranquilized by the brandy, but her heart was not at all so and continued to thump wildly. Ziyun had gone to sleep with one of his hands pinned beneath him. Xichun gently pulled it out and placed it at his side. Sitting there on the edge of the berth, she now seemed deep in thought, as though working something out.

She took her own small suitcase down from the baggage rack, opened it, and checked to see whether she had a fresh change of clothes. She took out all the cash that was so randomly scattered about inside and stuffed the bills into her coat pocket. She stared at her suitcase for a while and then smiled. Without bothering to close it, she lifted it up and placed it on the upper berth. Then she sat down again and began collecting her thoughts. What's more, she did so in a very composed manner, as though she hadn't a care in the world.

Xichun smiled, put out the lights, and lay down. Whether she had drifted off to sleep even she couldn't have told you, but at any rate, when the train came to a stop at the next large station, she sat up straight. She didn't turn on the lights. Precisely because the compartment was in darkness, she could see everything outside the train quite clearly. There were several vendors there on the platform selling snacks of various kinds and a few dozen passengers milling around as well. Among them was a woman in a coat with a fur collar following behind a man carrying a trunk on his shoulder; both were quietly working their way out of the station.

The platform was protected from the elements by a broad, awning-like structure that continued on down to the ground at the back; in the middle of it was a gate leading out of the station. Xichun could tell without looking at the sign over the platform that they had arrived at Wusih. When she saw Mrs. Yu calmly debark from the train, it was as though someone had given her a shot of tranquilizer: her heart slowed to a much more regular pace. She felt for Hu Ziyun and found that he was comfortably curled up on the lower berth, still sleeping quite soundly. As he exhaled, one was aware of the heavy scent of brandy. Judging from the depth of his drunkenness, by the time the train reached Shanghai, he probably still wouldn't come to.

At this point, Xichun was unable to suppress a wild and gleeful laugh, a laugh that made her entire body tremble and disturbed the sleeper on the lower berth so that he began to mumble: "The train—the train's stopped. In Chinkiang, are we?"

Xichun laughed and answered, "Passed Chinkiang a while back."

Ziyun mumbled some more: "When we get to Chang—Changchow, let me know. Gonna buy—buy some combs there."

"Okay," promised Xichun. "I'll be sure to call you when we get there. Don't worry. Just go back to sleep. Get your energy back 'cause you're going to need it when we hit Shanghai tomorrow. We'll paint the town red."

Ziyun grunted and went back to sleep. After they passed Wusih, she no longer felt like lying down. She sat up again and began to smoke. We don't know what was going through her mind, but, at any rate, she fished cigarettes out from the round tin and smoked them one after the other as the train continued down the track.

From Wusih to Soochow is a trip of a little over an hour. When she heard the train whistle blow—wu-wu-wu—announcing their imminent arrival in Soochow, Xichun became very excited. She turned on the lights and reached up to the upper berth and pulled her suitcase over to the edge. But no sooner had her hand reached it than she suddenly pushed it back again. It was as though she were thinking to herself, "There's really nothing in there. What do I want with it, anyway?" At the same time, her eyes shifted to the person sleeping on the lower berth. The train began to slow down now, and, lit by bright lights from tall electric poles, a wooden balustrade appeared in the window. She remembered that this was Soochow Station. Just as she opened the compartment door, she caught sight of the porter on duty. Rubbing his eyes and yawning for all he was worth, he walked over to the compartment door to see if anything was wanted. "Have we gotten to Soochow yet?" she asked.

"Yes, madam," he answered. "Still awake at this hour?"

"No, not *still* awake. Just woke up. Feel a bit hungry. I know that Soochow Station is famous for New Year's rice cakes and thought I'd get off and buy a couple of slices."

"Okay, then. I'll go with you."

"Are you allowed to leave the train?"

"Well, come to think of it, madam, you should be able to take care of it yourself. The train will stop here for a good fifteen minutes."

"I take this train several times a month. I know the routine. I'll have plenty of time to buy some and get back on the train," Xichun assured him. As she spoke, she went back to the compartment and got her purse.

The porter stood at the door to the compartment and said with a smile, "This late at night it gets pretty cold out there. Better put something on." She picked up her coat, draped it over one arm, and drew the door shut behind her, oh so quietly. Though Ziyun was deep in a drunken stupor, she was still very solicitous of his welfare in that she didn't want any untoward noise to wake him.

It was now four in the morning, just the time on a cold winter's night when you'd find people wrapped in warm comforters dreaming sweet dreams, a time when you'd find no one up except those with urgent concerns or those people who normally worked at night. And so, as was the case with those stations west of Soochow, the only passengers quietly boarding the train consisted of that tiny minority of people in love with the peace and quiet afforded by night-time travel.

And yet, even now, when there were so very few passengers in the station, sure enough, vendors were there selling snacks. On portable flat griddles, they fried strips of glutinous rice into New Year's cakes while hawking their wares in voices so low as to be almost inaudible. "Soochow New Year's cakes with powdered sugar. New Year's cakes with powdered sugar." If you were to look around Soochow Station at that particular time, you could readily spot vendors selling their cakes, but you would look in vain for a Miss Liu buying them.

Fifteen minutes go by very quickly. The train had already pulled out. Now, the night-shift porter in first class has an additional duty; besides helping passengers on and off the train, he is to be vigilant to make sure that no pickpockets sneak aboard. Hence, while the train is stopped, he has to remain very alert. He had seen Xichun get off to buy New Year's cakes, but he hadn't seen her get back on again.

How in the world could he lose track of a female passenger at Soochow in the middle of the night? Ridiculous. Perhaps she had returned to the compartment without his having noticed her. He gently pulled the door open a crack and peeked inside. The lights were on, but there was no wife to be seen, only the husband. Since he had clearly seen the woman off the train, he felt at least partially responsible for her.

"Mr. Hu, hurry up and get up. Your companion got off at Soochow and didn't get back on again," said the porter. But his voice was very low, not nearly loud enough to wake Hu Ziyun, who was sound asleep.

13

—

So, She Was a Crook!

—

—

—

During his night of wine, women, and song, Hu Ziyun fulfilled his wanderlust while lying in a comfortable berth—
surely one of the most felicitous experiences that life can
offer. It was a pleasure he would be able to enjoy all the way
from Nanking to Shanghai. As happy as a man can be, he
completely forgot his surroundings and drifted off into a
restful and pleasurable sleep. At precisely this moment,
however, the porter came in and roused him from his slumber with the shocking news that Miss Liu had gotten off the
train in Soochow! He sat up, rubbed his eyes, and looked
around the compartment. Sure enough—no Miss Liu! After
he had time to collect himself, he asked the porter, "How
come she got off the train?"

"Said something about being hungry and wanting to buy
some sweet rice cakes," replied the porter. "She was about to
get off the train without her coat until I reminded her that
it'd be cold out there on the platform. Then she threw her
coat over her shoulders and left the train. I saw her get off,
but I didn't see her get back on."

Hu Ziyun laughed and explained, "Nothing to worry
about. She's just up to one of her pranks again. Back at Hsiakuan, she got on the train long before it started rolling but

didn't come back to the compartment even after the train had pulled out of the station. It was only when I was worried half to death that she'd missed the train and had broken into a good sweat that she finally showed up. She'd been in second class all that time! Bet that's where she is now—holed up in second class. In Mrs. Yu's compartment, no doubt."

"Do you mean that same Mrs. Yu who came to your compartment several times before we crossed the Yangtze? She got off the train at Wusih. But long before that, back when the train pulled into Changchow, she came here to your compartment. Miss Liu gave her a couple of parcels. Said they contained old books that you wanted the old lady to give to a friend of yours in Wusih."

A restful slumber had, to a good degree, dispelled the lingering effects of the brandy, and the shocking news that the porter brought had served to sober him up all the more. He still thought that Xichun was up to one of her pranks but felt that *this* time she had gone too far. Despite himself, his heart began to race out of control. He lowered his feet to the floor, thrust them into his slippers, and, glassy-eyed, looked at the porter. "Did Mrs. Yu *really* get off at Wusih?"

"Now, why would I joke around about something like that? I saw her get off with my own two eyes." As the porter spoke, Ziyun's face changed from red to a pale white; his eyes slowly froze into a straight-ahead stare and no longer seemed capable of turning in either direction. "As a Southerner, Miss Liu is familiar with all the stops down here," the porter added. "She knows if she misses this train, she can always take the morning one." Apparently incapable of further conversation, Ziyun merely nodded his head. Sensing that Ziyun had a lot on his mind, the porter saw no point in remaining in the compartment and quietly withdrew.

Ziyun raised his arm and looked at his wristwatch: 4:45 A.M. This prank was not in the same class as her Nanking escapade. Back then, the train was just pulling out of the station, and she was visiting in another car. No big thing. But *now*—now it was in the wee hours of the morning. No one was up, and there'd be no place on the train where she *could* hole up even if she wanted to. He pulled Xichun's suitcase over next to him and opened it. Her clothes were still there, but the letters were gone, and there wasn't a single bill left of the money that had previously been so carelessly strewn about. He couldn't help but be somewhat suspicious.

Recalling that she also had a small traveling case in the baggage rack just under the ceiling of the car, it occurred to him that he might find some clue to her disappearance there. When he stood and reached up to get it, however, he caught sight of his briefcase and noted that it had been shifted from its original position. Didn't seem to be shut tight either, for he could see a tiny crack between the cover and the main body of the case. *He* would never have left it like that. Who had been messing around with it? Ziyun hurriedly took it down and put it on the lower berth. He opened it and looked inside. From the top of his head clear down to his toes, his entire body was seized with a violent shudder. Cash, stocks, bonds—gone! All gone! He had been cleaned out! "Shit! Shit! Oh shit!!"

Since he was alone in the compartment, there was no one to *see* what color his face was at this point. The thing that Ziyun himself was aware of was that his clothes were soaking wet. He was even conscious of sweat beading up on his forehead and then tumbling down in a waterfall over his face. He reached into his kimono pocket, pulled out a handkerchief, and wiped at the cascading perspiration. As he stood there, he attempted to steady himself with the other hand against the closed top of his briefcase. From briefcase to shoulder, however, his entire arm trembled.

In the compartments to either side of him, people were

sound asleep. Though he ached to tell someone what had happened, he didn't dare disturb anyone. Leaning back against the compartment wall, once again Ziyun slowly froze into immobility. After quite some time, he raised his head and sighed. He sat up, filled his pipe, and, with a tranquillity surprising under the circumstances, smoked it. His calm exterior, however, was belied by the violent pounding of his heart. Ziyun's capacity for tobacco today went far beyond normal. He smoked one pipeful after another, and, in the end, all that tobacco actually *did* seem to help him collect his thoughts, for he now called the porter in and told him: "Go fetch Mr. Li Chengfu from second class. I don't care whether he's sleeping; just get him. Tell him I have some urgent business to discuss."

Wake a paying passenger in the middle of the night? The porter was in a tough spot. He stood there in a daze not knowing what to do. Ziyun raised his head and glared at him. "*You're* partially responsible for what happened here tonight too! Listen, and listen good: I have just lost a *huge* sum of money! I've just lost tens of thousands of dollars! Why are you just standing there? Go!" The porter stepped back in shock. Then he looked at Ziyun again and noticed that a deathly pallor had crept across his face. Pipe clasped between his teeth, Ziyun slowly added, "Actually, once things have come to this pass, there's no point in my blaming you. Just hurry up, and fetch Mr. Li."

Since a major felony had just occurred on the train, the porter had no choice but to carry out Ziyun's order and scurry off as fast as his legs would carry him in search of Li Chengfu. As soon as Ziyun caught sight of his old friend, he smiled bitterly and said, "Chengfu, I've just made a total ass of myself. What am I to do?"

"The porter said you'd lost a large sum of money. The first thing is to get in touch with the authorities on the train." As Chengfu spoke, he glanced at the upper berth and asked, "Where's Miss Liu?" Seeing that the porter was standing outside the compartment, Ziyun drew the door shut. Then he pulled Chengfu toward the lower berth, and the two men sat down side by side.

"A damned mess! No, an absolute disaster. I was taken in by a swindler, hook, line, and sinker! Fell for it like a ton of bricks!"

"What in the world happened?"

"Miss Liu got me drunk and then got off the train in Soochow. I was completely out of it. Didn't know anything about what had happened until the porter woke me just now and told me. And then, when he told me that Mrs. Yu had gotten off the train at Wusih with a couple of parcels from this compartment, I thought that something was really amiss. When I opened my briefcase, I found that a big pack of government bonds along with some stocks were all gone! Lost some cash as well, but I didn't care as much about that—only four or five hundred. But, just in government bonds, there must have been over $120,000!"

"Wow! Now *that's* no small sum. Do you have the serial numbers recorded somewhere?"

"Probably. But what good does that do? All she's got to do is hand them over to some foreigner, and she's home free. She can get the money, and the whole transaction will be seen as open and aboveboard. Even if she doesn't do that, I've no way to track those two women down anyway. Boy, that Xichun really knew how to pull a scam! Brought Mrs. Yu in on the deal because she knew I was acquainted with her."

Chengfu sat there and, stroking his chin, mulled it over for a while. Finally, he said, "But you're close to the family Miss Liu was running away from, right?"

Ziyun shook his head and then—strangely—burst into a loud, raucous laugh. "I feel like getting mad and laughing at the same time. She wasn't *really* related to my friend's family. She must have been an imposter, pure and simple. And I was way too careless. If I'd only questioned her closely about my friend's family, I could have determined that she was a scam artist right at the beginning. That was no small sum she made off with! I *can't* just let it go, but I'm so mixed up that I can't think of how to get it back either. You've got to help me think of some way out of this mess."

Chengfu reached up and ran his fingers through his hair. He shook his head. "That's no easy task."

Ziyun took the tin of cigarettes that Xichun had smoked from and passed what was left over to Chengfu. "Have a smoke, and take your time."

Chengfu thought of the history of this tin of cigarettes over the past two days and nights. He lit up, hesitated for a bit, and then asked, "Do you mean to tell me that *before* this you didn't know this Miss Liu at all?"

"Met her for the very first time when you and I ran into her in the dining car. You *know* the complete history of our relationship after that. Why ask?"

"But if you didn't know her, then why? . . . " He suddenly stopped on that *why* and, suppressing the rest of his question, continued smoking.

Ziyun blushed and said, "She turned me on. It's as simple as that. And here I thought she was the prim and proper young matron." As he spoke, he held his pipe in his left hand and gave his own head a frustrated slap with his right. "I can't bear to think about what followed without being absolutely furious with myself!" he said, stomping his foot lightly against the floor. "And I've got no one to blame but myself. *I'm* the one who did it!" He slapped his own thigh several times in disgust.

"It's all water over the dam now," said Chengfu. "Regret doesn't help. Now the question is whether you're willing to have this widely known?"

Before Ziyun's initial blush had time to recede, his face began to contort with a new worry. "Why," he asked with a forced smile, "would I ever want something like this spread around? I'm a highly respected man in society, am I not?"

"All right then," said Chengfu. "If you *don't* want it known, that means we can't report it to the railroad police. But if we *don't* report it to the railroad police, how are we ever going to find the culprits? And if we don't catch *them,* how are we to recover the large sum that's been lost?"

Having been subjected to a cold dose of reality by his friend, Ziyun said nothing. He simply sat so totally engrossed in puffing on his pipe that one would have thought he didn't have a care in the world. At this point, it seemed that the train was negotiating a switch, for it rolled, swayed, and banged around so much that two teacups side by side on the little table began to knock into each other with a loud clink-clank clink-clank.

Noting that Ziyun's bearing was now very natural, Chengfu smiled and said, "I am very impressed with your ability to remain calm in the face of such adversity. Quite admirable of you."

"And what would I do if I weren't calm?" asked Ziyun. "Everyone on the train is sound asleep. Can I jump up and down, scream, pound the table, and wake everybody up? Besides, by now my money is miles and miles away. What good would all my pounding and screaming do? Would that make my money come flying home to roost?"

"You've thought your way through it all right, but that doesn't bring us any closer to a solution to your problem. I think we still ought to notify the authorities on the train so they can send a telegram to the Soochow Station."

"I thought about that possibility right off," said Ziyun. "Trouble is, the people in charge at the station have control over only what goes on *inside* the station. Anything beyond the confines of the station is outside their jurisdiction. The only thing a telegram would accomplish would be to make me a laughingstock."

"This way won't do, that way won't do—anything I *suggest* won't do. Does that mean you're prepared to take the stocks, bonds, and money and just kiss them all good-bye?"

Pipe hanging from his mouth, Ziyun seemed lost in thought. Then he put his pipe down on the table, folded his arms across his chest, and stared at the hanging light under the ceiling. Having finished the cigarette he was smoking, Chengfu took another from the tin and lit it. "I seem to detect the hint of a smile," he said. "I'll bet you've come up with a plan after all."

Ziyun suddenly sat up straight, slapped both hands against his thighs, and said, "Yes, I have it! She has two friends down in third class. If Mrs. Yu from second class was hooked up with her, it would seem very unlikely that those two in third class should be above suspicion. I'll go question them. Good idea?"

"Yes, it's worth a shot, I'll grant you. But you've got to remember that running into friends on a train is a very common occurrence. If you want to say that everyone Xichun ran into is suspect—that might be pushing it a bit."

"I know that as well as you do," said Ziyun. "Nonetheless, let's go down to third class and sound them out. Let's see what they have to say for themselves, and then we'll have enough to go on so that we won't insult people out of hand." As the two men talked, they forgot about what time it was, and their voices grew ever louder.

At this juncture, there were two light knocks at the compartment door. When Ziyun opened it, the porter handed him a calling card on which was printed a family name followed by a surname: Qi Youming. When the porter saw that Hu Ziyun was puzzled, he explained: "This is Master Qi from the compartment next door. When he heard that

Mr. Hu had lost some money, he expressed an interest in coming over and having a chat."

"Fine," said Chengfu. "Show him in." The words were no sooner out of his mouth than in crowded a young man in a colorful pair of pajamas. At a glance, Ziyun recognized him as the young fellow whom he had so often seen walking his dog. Ziyun had been very annoyed with this young man because he always stared at Xichun. Now that she had absconded with a small fortune, however, it occurred to Ziyun that the man might have had good reason for looking at her the way he did. Ziyun stood up, and the two men shook hands.

Qi Youming put his hands in the pockets of his pajamas and rolled his shoulders once or twice. Eyebrows raised high, he looked at Ziyun and said with a smile, "Mr. Hu, I know very well who you are. Manager of the Kongyou Bank, if I'm not mistaken. Your humble servant has long done his banking at your honored establishment. My father is Cabinet Minister Qi." Ziyun acknowledged this with an "Oh," and the three men sat down to chat.

Youming looked at Ziyun and said, "When I saw Mr. Hu bring that female into his compartment, I thought of telling him what I knew of her, but since it was none of my business, I didn't think it was my place to come out and defame her. Besides, I thought that, at the most, she'd try to bilk you out of only a thousand or so. Never occurred to me that she'd attempt a scam on such a *massive* scale!"

"Judging from the way you talk," noted Chengfu, "you must know the lady rather well."

Youming crossed his legs and swayed back and forth with a rather self-satisfied air. He was obviously quite pleased with himself. "Rogues and rascals can never hope to escape these experienced eyes of mine. She's a well-known female con artist. There's no counting the number of people she's taken in. I'm surprised that someone as at home in high society as Manager Hu hasn't heard about her."

Ziyun's face turned purple. Meditatively, he scratched his cheek with his index finger, then shook his head and said, "I tend to be too open with people. She said she was a divorced daughter-in-law from the household of old friends of my family. Wanted me to help her find some way out of domestic difficulties she was having. I took her at her word. Does Mr. Qi happen to know her name?"

Youming laughed and replied, "I'm afraid only *she* knows that. Not only is her name not known, but she's always kept her address a well-guarded secret as well. That's why, after she pulls a scam, it's not easy to track her down. And even if you did, you wouldn't be able to find out where she'd hidden the money." Chengfu wanted to know why. Youming's only answer was first to look at Ziyun and then to look back at Chengfu and smile.

Chengfu still didn't get it and asked, "Do you mean she'd risk her life rather than tell?"

Youming shrugged and replied, "Whenever anything in society is tied in with sex, there are bound to be secrets that people don't want known. If she didn't take advantage of that fact, how could she have become as successful as she has? Once people are caught in her scam, they usually stick corks in their mouths about the whole business, and *she's* home free." That made Ziyun feel even worse. He began stroking his chin between his thumb and first two fingers while sighing over and over again.

Chengfu said, "Back to square one. *This* way won't do, *that* way won't do. Do you mean to say we just throw it all up for grabs and let her go scot free?"

Youming took another cigarette, crossed his feet, and seemed engrossed in rocking his knees back and forth, first toward each other and then away again. "If you're going to have any hopes of getting the money back," he observed, "then you have to get your hands on a weapon you can use against her. She's afraid of me because I'm not intimidated by her and she knows I'll blow her cover wherever and whenever I run into her. Since I've got her little game down pat and she knows it, there's no way she'd dare mess with me. Cause if she did, I'd have her locked up."

"I don't get it, Mr. Qi, " said Chengfu. "Didn't you just say a moment ago that she plays the sex scam because anyone she takes in won't dare blow her cover? And now you say you've got her game down pat. That's got to mean one thing: you've been taken in by her sex scam just like all the others. In that case, then, how is it that you have no compunctions about standing out and blowing her cover when everyone else is afraid of doing so?"

Youming pointed at himself with both hands and asked, "What does someone like me have to worry about? I'm not some government bureaucrat hanging onto my rice bowl for dear life. Nor am I some glittering celebrity in the social world either. Suppose she *does* go around telling people that I paid her for sex? Be my guest. No problem. I'll freely admit it. What's she gonna do? Take me to court for consorting with prostitutes? Big deal."

"Besides," he explained, "on the *northern* end, the scam she runs has got to be connected with Peiping or Tientsin. And in those cities I've got connections like you wouldn't believe with *both* the army *and* the police. All I have to do is give them a few pictures of her to circulate, and her business goes belly up. Come to think of it, though, I have to take some of that back because *now* she's made enough money on this caper alone to last her a good half lifetime. Who knows? Maybe she'll give up the business. Then it won't do any good even if I *do* ask them to keep an eye out for her."

Another thought seemed to have occurred to Youming, for he quickly cupped one fist inside the other hand and respectfully saluted Ziyun. "I hope you don't suspect *me* as well," he said with a gentle laugh. "I assure you, I am in no way hooked up with that young woman. In order to allay any misgivings that you might have in that direction, it probably won't do any harm to share my own experiences with her.

"It all began last winter when a friend of mine and I were on our way to Tientsin for a little vacation. She and an old woman in her fifties were both on the same train. Well, we were all sitting in the parlor car, and in the beginning we didn't pay any attention to each other. But then she started making eyes at my friend, and before you knew it she had him hooked. In Tientsin, my friend and I were putting up at the National. Turned out *she* was staying at the same place. One night, when my friend and I went to the ball-room for some dancing, she tagged along. In the days that followed, you can pretty well guess how things developed without my having to spell it out.

"My friend often did business with a bank there in Tientsin, and he'd brought along several checks to draw on that bank for whatever money he might need on vacation. To make a long story short, while he was asleep one night, she stole a check for two thousand dollars, stamped it with his personal chop, and succeeded in cashing it before my friend knew what was going on. Took a diamond ring right off his finger and made off with that as well! The three of us had hung around together for maybe a week, but in that time, if you throw in the ring plus whatever he'd spent on her, she had managed to do him out of seven or eight thousand dollars. Luckily, my friend was situated so that he didn't have to care about an amount like that, and so he just let the whole thing go. But, at any rate, I thank my lucky stars that I didn't get involved with her, though I did have an opportunity to see firsthand how she operates. That's why, Mr. Hu, she always seemed afraid whenever she saw me. Why wouldn't she be? If she ever tries to mess with me, I kid you not, she'll get some of her own medicine—a double dose!" His laugh was loud and confident.

"In that case," said Ziyun, "if she ran into you, Mr. Qi, *you* could easily handle her."

Youming thrust out his fist with thumb held high and proclaimed, "You better believe it! Trouble is, there's no way to find her."

Ziyun threw back his head, puffed his pipe a bit, and then offered somewhat hesitantly, "There *might* be. She's got two fellow students in third class. Perhaps they know her address."

Youming shook his head. "Fellow students, is it? I daresay even her mom and dad haven't the foggiest notion as to where she lives. In sum, if you tangle with *her,* the result's a foregone conclusion: she disappears, and so does anything you have that's worth taking."

As Youming spoke, he looked out the window and saw nothing but blackness. Now and then in that long stretch of night, a few lights would fly by, and beyond them one could make out quivering black shadows—a copse of wild bamboo close to a village. "Just the kind of scenery," commented Youming, "that lets you know we're south of the Yangtze now."

"We must be almost to Kunshan," said Chengfu. "If we're going to do anything, now's the time to make our move. Otherwise, we'll have to wait till we're in Shanghai." He stared intently at Ziyun.

"Send a telegram to Soochow, and see if we can get to the bottom of all this? Nothing would please me more. But each of us has his own unique situation to consider. If this gets spread around, think of the great harm it will do to the trust and confidence I've built up in the business community over the years—and in high society as well, for that matter. What am I to do? Damn it all, what *can* I do?" He

◄ 215 ►

let out a very audible sigh and simultaneously stomped one foot heavily on the floor.

As they were talking, the muzzle of a dog introduced itself through the crack where the compartment door had not been quite pulled shut. Youming clapped his hands and called, "Buck," whereupon the dog managed to work the door open far enough with his nose to come in. He immediately jumped up on his master, who, in turn, threw his arms around the dog's neck and planted a couple of kisses on top of its head. Gently rubbing the dog's back, Youming commented, "Everyone says I make too much of this dog, but I don't agree in the least. To be sure, the dog doesn't do any work for me, but on the other hand he'll never do me any harm either. I may not be able to raise a benefactor on dog food, but then I won't raise an enemy either." He laughed loudly at his own humor. "But I go too far. How can one compare dogs with human beings?"

Ziyun said nothing. He calmly filled his pipe with tobacco and seemed to give himself over entirely to the pleasures of smoking. Youming smiled at him and said, "Now, that's what I call a banker! Loses all that money, and acts as though he doesn't have a care in the world."

"Ah," sighed Ziyun. "The money's not going to come back, so what's the point in vilifying Miss Liu?" Having said this much, once again he seemed to calm down and concentrate on his smoking. Truth known, however, he was sitting there thinking to himself, "When Mr. Qi came barging in, volunteering his services, I thought he'd probably be of at least some help, but all his jabbering only makes me feel worse." And so Ziyun simply stopped talking to him.

Youming, on the other hand, didn't seem to mind at all. "In times like these," he said, "you run into all kinds. Men will trade their lives for money, and women, of course, will swap their bodies for the same thing. Sooner or later, the day always comes when Mr. Moneybags runs into Miss

Swapbody. Might as well run into a Shanghai hoodlum down some dark alley. She'll skin him alive, skin him as clean as a pig or a chicken. Poor old Moneybags really takes a screwing on that one. Spends his good money on the broad, gets robbed of all he has in the bargain, and then *he's* the one who's seen as some sort of animal."

Chengfu thought it somewhat odd that a person like Youming should have a fairly refined appearance yet also have such a vulgar way of expressing himself. Chengfu smiled, stood up, and said, "With all our jabbering, all we've done is confuse Ziyun to the point where he can't think of anything to do. It's like the old saw about finding an address: *Ask everyone on the road and your progress will be slowed.* Why don't we all leave and give him a little peace and quiet?"

"Don't think about it anymore, Mr. Hu," advised Youming. "The more you think, the more it's going to bother you. With all our talking, we'll be in Shanghai before we know it. Believe you me, a dazzling metropolis like Shanghai will make you forget everything!"

Now Youming was beginning to get on Chengfu's nerves. He pulled on the sleeve of his pajamas and said, "When somebody loses a huge sum of money, he's bound to feel a little out of sorts. How do you expect even Shanghai to cheer him up?"

Youming turned around and observed Ziyun. His head was hanging down, he said nothing, and he really did look quite dejected. Even Youming got the message. He reached out and patted Ziyun on the back. "Doesn't amount to a hill of beans, old man. Just pretend you took a loss on government bonds." Smiling, he tugged on his dog's leash and left the compartment.

Deep in thought, Ziyun held his pipe in one hand and propped up his head with the other. While he was thus occupied, the wheels of the train, neither accelerating nor decelerating, sped down the tracks with a steady roar, reminding people that the Shanghai Express was still hurtling through the night. Ziyun suddenly roused himself: if he was going to act, it would have to be now. If he hesitated any longer, the train would pull into Shanghai, the passengers would scatter, and even the administrative personnel aboard the train would disappear. At that point, there would be no way to hunt her down even if he wanted to.

"And to think that Mrs. Yu—an actual acquaintance of mine—would hook up with her to do me in! And what about that couple in third class? Seemed to be friends who hadn't seen her in a long time. Bet they were in on the scam, too! No matter what the case, it wouldn't do any harm to go down and talk to them. Besides, without Xichun around to get me all befuddled, my mind will be clear. I'll know how to talk to people again, too. All right then, I'll play the whole thing by ear when I get there." As he was thinking all this, one of his thoughts spilled out into open speech: "Let's go then." He stood up and started to move his feet even as he spoke. He drew open the door and stepped out into the corridor. Will this little expedition to third class turn up any trace of Xichun? Well, that would depend on how he handled the whole thing.

14

Soochow Again

It goes without saying that at this late hour the third-class passengers had long since dropped off to sleep. Even those among them who had, with aching backs, managed to sit up until this hour had finally reached the end of their ropes. The seats themselves were wrapped in a soporific fog of dim yellow light emanating in weak golden rays from a few round bulbs inside nipple-shaped glass covers set into the high ceiling of the car. Bareheaded, Ziyun had not changed into his pajamas back at Hsiakuan. Hence, he was still wearing the same silk robe he had worn all day. As he walked toward third class, he was closely followed by a porter. When he had to cross over the exposed metal platform that covered the couplings that held one car to the next, a fierce wind ripped in from a ninety-degree angle to the train and wound his silk gown tightly around his frame. His body could not help but shudder in the cold air; his mind, however, was so totally concentrated on the $120,000 he had lost in stocks and bonds that he barely noticed the wind. Finally, he arrived at third class.

Zhu Jinqing and his wife were in the second coach of the third-class section. When Ziyun opened the door to the first coach, a blast of cold wind woke two passengers who were curled up on seats near the door, and they sat up. As soon as the door was closed again, however, the wind stopped, and they curled back up and went to sleep again. Ziyun saw that in the whole car there couldn't have been more than a dozen people scattered about. Except for two passengers who were leaning back against their seats and smoking, the others were all flopped this way and that, sleeping. Among them were two women of about the age of the young woman whom he had seen Xichun wave to back in Tientsin, but even in the dim yellow light he could see that neither of them was in an outfit that you'd call modern.

Ziyun continued on to the second coach of the third-class section. His sudden arrival in the depth of night startled the porter awake as though he had been some monster. He stood up and silently followed along behind Ziyun and the first-class porter. When he saw Ziyun looking all around, he asked, "Which car are you coming from, sir?"

"I'm from first class, but it's imperative that I find a friend in third class with whom I have some urgent business."

"And what's your friend's name?"

That stumped him for a moment. Then he replied, "I'll know him when I see him."

At this point, the first-class porter explained the whole thing to the third-class porter, who said, "That's right, a woman from first class came down to visit a couple in this car twice during the daytime. That was the couple she came to see right over there." He pointed to a couple close by who were sleeping—in fetal position—on seats opposite each other. All Ziyun could do was stand there and stare at them, for he was embarrassed to disturb either of two young people whose snores announced that they were comfortably asleep. Not knowing what their relationship was, the third-class porter bent down and shook Zhu Jinqing awake.

"Mr. Zhu, there's a friend here looking for you."

Zhu Jinqing sat bolt upright and asked, "Are we in

Shanghai yet?" He rubbed his eyes, focused them, and was surprised to find that there were three people standing before him.

"Mr. Hu here from first class," the third-class porter explained, "has come looking for you."

Jinqing stood up and quickly surveyed Ziyun. "The face isn't at all familiar."

"Come barging into third class in the middle of the night and wake someone up who doesn't even recognize me—doesn't make a hell of a lot of a sense," thought Ziyun to himself. Smiling, he nodded his head and explained, "I have some urgent business I'd like to ask your advice on." Still at a loss, Jinqing simply continued to stare at him. "Remember when the train was stopped in Tientsin," Ziyun continued bravely, "how a certain Miss Liu and I walked past your window. Miss Liu waved to your wife in greeting and. . . . "

"Oh, oh, oh—now I have it," said Jinqing. "Yes, that's right. I met your wife in Tientsin."

"She wasn't my wife."

"Wasn't your wife? How can that be? She even said she was your wife."

At this point, Ziyun lowered his voice and spoke in ever more serious tones, with the obvious intention of intimidating the young man. "She was *not* on the up-and-up. As a matter of fact, she was a female con artist!"

Jinqing, however, was not a young man to be intimidated. Putting on an equally severe expression himself, he looked at Ziyun and said, "Let's see, someone I don't even know comes here and wakes me up in the middle of the night for the sole purpose of letting me know that someone *else* is a con artist. Do I have it right?"

Of late, Ziyun always seemed to end up on the *un*reasonable side of things. This was no exception, and his initial arrogance quickly evaporated as he answered, "Well, naturally, I wouldn't come and wake you up to ask your advice unless I had some reason to do so. In the middle of the night, Miss Liu made off with a substantial part of my money. Got off the train at Soochow, and disappeared. According to what she told me, she and your wife were fellow students, knew each. . . . "

"What? *We're* suspects now as well? That's right, she and my wife were fellow students. So what? You're in first class. We're in third. You mind your business, and we mind ours! She stole your money? What the hell has that got to do with us? Do you even know what kind of people you're dealing with here?"

He threw out his chest and stepped menacingly toward Ziyun. Fearing that a fight was about to break out, the third-class porter crowded in between them and said to Zhu Jinqing, "I think you may misunderstand the situation. It's like this. Mr. Hu here has lost a lot of money and hasn't the foggiest notion of where he can find that Miss Liu. He remembered that she'd come back here a couple of times to talk with friends of hers and thought it might be a good idea to come down here and see if either of you knew where he can find her."

Having been awakened by this time, Zhang Yuqing was straightening her hair and until this point had listened to them in silence. Now she said, "The two of us were fellow students a while back, but we hadn't seen each other in quite a while. She told me she was Mr. Hu's wife and was staying in a first-class compartment with him. How can it be that Mr. Hu doesn't even know where she lives?"

This little storm in a teacup had awakened everyone in the coach, and now they were all standing around enjoying this bit of unexpected entertainment. Hu Ziyun was a man who had always been concerned with the image he presented in society, with always putting his best foot forward. He had never before been the cynosure of *any* crowd. Now, he was not only center stage, but center stage in a most sala-cious play. What was he to say?

At this juncture, someone in the crowd said, "First class is not like third. Up there, they've all got their own private sleeping rooms. Once they're inside, all they've got to do is latch the door. How could that woman possibly get in to steal anything?"

"But she was staying in Mr. Hu's compartment to begin with," explained the first-class porter.

"In that case," said Zhu Jinqing, fixing Ziyun with a glare, "she *was* your wife after all. When your wife runs away in the middle of the night, what the devil are you doing coming down to *third* class to look for her?" Everyone laughed heartily at Jinqing's question.

"No, no, no," replied Ziyun. "That's not the way it was."

"Then exactly how was it?" asked Jinqing. "A woman sleeps in *your* compartment, and *you* lose a pile of money—what does that have to do with us?" Everyone laughed again.

Ziyun found the whole situation increasingly embarrass-ing. "I'll explain it some other time," he said, "some other time. . . ." He turned around on that second *some other time* and walked away. When he got back to first class, he was far angrier than when he had left, for not only had he totally failed to learn anything about Xichun, but he had gotten his own nose rubbed in the dirt in the process! He sat down and thought disconsolately, "Can this mean that I take over $100,000 and just kiss it all good-bye?" As he continued to think such bleak thoughts, unconsciously, he began to tap his foot against the floor. "That fellow in third class had it right!" he thought. "A woman sleeps in my compartment, and I lose a pile of money. What right does that give me to go barging down to third class to ask questions? Good idea to steer clear of women in the first place! Especially a woman I've never met before! Over $100,000 isn't easy to come by. And I traded the whole amount for one, single, solitary bottle of brandy!" Thinking in this vein, he caught sight of the brandy bottle on the little tea table. He picked it up, took it out into the corridor, opened a window, and hurled it down toward the tracks.

No small sum, $120,000! How he longed to take this stinking-skin-sack of a body of his and send it into oblivion along with that bottle! All that money down the drain, and he wasn't even able to come right out in the open and talk about it freely so there would be at least some hope of recovery. This was unendurable! Unendurable! His spirits had already been dragged down from a night of wine, women, and song, and now they were taxed to the breaking point by this new pain, the pain of not being able to come straight out and discuss his experiences. All that money! All this new pain of not even being able to talk about it! Consciousness receded, and Ziyun collapsed on the corridor floor.

As the train drew closer and closer to Shanghai, the first rays of the rising sun appeared in the east. Shanghai! Political struggles, social turmoil, luxury, extravagance, braggadocio—these were phenomena that Shanghai could show you at any time and in any place. And now into such a place came this Hu Ziyun. After his collapse, he succeeded in reviving himself, gathered his thoughts together, and got off the train. It did not necessarily follow, however, that the sum he had lost would ever be returned to its rightful owner. Nor is this just some off-the-cuff remark—there are facts to support it.

It was something past four in the afternoon on a winter's day who knows how many years later. The Shanghai Express was about to pull out of Shanghai's North Station, headed back to Peiping. The sky was filled with giant dancing snowflakes the size of goose feathers. The snow that had lain thick on the road outside had been turned to mud by the constant stream of traffic in and out of the station. And now one could hear a never-ending ji-ji ja-ja as the wheels of automobiles and the feet of pedestrians sloshed through the mud. Beyond the station entrance, the thickly falling snow blended into a deep white fog through which silver and pale green automobiles slowly probed their ways.

Looking as fresh, tender, and ruddy as polished apples, here and there, the faces of women protruded out from the high collars of fur coats. The snow took nothing from their delicate beauty as they emerged from automobiles and made their way into the station followed by porters carrying suitcases protected from the elements by shiny coats of purple shellac. One could also see those so-called fat cats from Shanghai's Bund.[1] They were wrapped in overcoats so bulky that they could move only with difficulty. Wearing fur hats, cigars hanging from their mouths, paunches thrust forward, the fat cats entered the station in a steady stream. Their leather gloves held walking sticks with which they continually gesticulated as they barked out orders to a cohort of porters carrying baskets and shouldering trunks.

Automobiles were so thick outside the station that it was virtually impossible for pedestrians to maneuver among them. Here and there in the swarm of vehicles one could spot a few rickshas as well. Typically, the passenger being pulled would clasp a suitcase on his lap; a basket would be

---

1. At that time, Shanghai's *waitan* was known in English as "the Bund." The word *bund* comes from Hindi and refers to an embanked thoroughfare along a river. In this case, the thoroughfare was Chungshan Road East, which ran along the Hwangpoo River. At the time of this novel, the Bund was controlled by foreigners and was in effect the Wall Street of China. The men described here were, no doubt, members of the comprador class *maiban jieji,* that group of men who served as a link between their own countrymen and the foreign businessmen whose manners—note, e.g., the walking stick—they often aped.

piled on top of that and rise higher than his head; sand-wiched between his back and the backrest of the rig, a large net basket would bulge out to the sides. All of this, of course, signaled that the passenger was wealthy.

At this time, when all kinds of vehicles were hurrying this way and that like a chaos of insects across the ground, there appeared a rather singular man wearing a lined her-ringbone overcoat. Several places had been rubbed thin and shiny, and the elbows were completely worn through. The hem was so frayed it looked as though the lower part of the garment was nothing but tassels. Since none of the buttons was fastened, you could see through to the grey gown, stained with dirt and grease, he was wearing underneath. His felt hat had originally been dark gray, but it had been exposed to the elements for so long that it was now a black-ish green; its rim drooped down around his head like so many lotus leaves, and the front part hung down so low it hid his eyebrows. His face was covered with a porcupine stubble.

A bedroll was pinched in between his left arm and body, and his right hand held a raggedy canvas bag. Wearing a pair of tattered felt shoes, he threaded his way through the traffic. As he made his way through the muddy water, some of it splashed up onto the hem of his coat.

A blue car with a black license plate passed quite close to him and splashed mud all over the front of his coat. He glared at the driver. The driver in turn stuck his head out the car window and spit at him: "Fuckin' pig!" Before he had time to repay the compliment, the car was well on its way. He changed his strategy and began trudging toward the station behind a vehicle that was slowing down.

"What's the big deal about an automobile?" he asked himself. "Back then, yours truly had so many cars he got sick of riding in them! And only ten years ago at that! Back then, was there anyone who hadn't heard of Hu Ziyun?" Continuing to mumble to himself, he entered the station. This was many, many times more lively than the station at Chengyang Gate in Peiping. From the information desk clear down to the ticket counter for first and second class, every window was crowded. Trembling a bit, Hu Ziyun put down his canvas bag and fished four dollars out of his cotton robe. Then, following the crowd, he made his way to the counter for third class.

After he had received his change and had stepped away from the counter, it was difficult for him to put his ticket away because of the canvas bag in his right hand and the bedding tucked under his left arm. Hu Ziyun stopped dead in his tracks and put the canvas bag down on the floor. Someone behind him who had just bought a ticket and was now heading away from the counter lost patience with him and kicked his canvas bag to one side. "An old bumpkin who doesn't know which way is up, and he has the gall to come to Shanghai!" When Ziyun turned around and saw that it was a soldier in a gray uniform, he didn't dare respond in kind. He hurriedly put the ticket away, rushed to his bag, picked it up, and walked away.

As you approached the platform, there were several narrow gates in the iron railing that separated it from the station. First- and second-class passengers, wearing all sorts of fashionable clothing, went through the first. Mixing in with them, and right under the nose of the ticket taker, Hu Ziyun went through that gate as well.

Outside the station, the snow was falling more and more thickly now. Although the passengers on the platform were protected overhead by a roof, that didn't prevent snow from blowing in from the sides. The passengers varied greatly in what they wore. Some were clad in heavy winter clothing, while others wore costumes more appropriate to summer.

However they may have differed in clothing, the vapor coming from their noses was identical, and its whiteness announced in no uncertain terms the intensity of the cold.

The lined, foreign-style, raggedy overcoat that Ziyun wore was not nearly as good as a Chinese-style padded robe would have been for keeping out the cold. Well, how about the cotton gown he wore underneath the overcoat? Wouldn't that help? Perhaps. But, like Ziyun himself, that cotton gown had been round the block once too often, and the cotton wadding inside was no longer full and thick, as it had been when the gown was new, but was now so worn and flattened down that it no longer provided any real protection from the frigid air. Ziyun shivered constantly.

When he saw men in heavy fur coats and caps pass him by with large, self-assured steps, their chests thrust forward, he thought to himself, "Don't be so damned pleased with yourselves. Sooner or later, the day will come when you'll be as I am now. I once wore a coat and cap like that myself, but what does it all amount to now? If a man doesn't heed the advice of his friends, if a man is impetuous and gets confused, it doesn't matter how much money he has; the day will come when he'll be as down and out as I am today. Dressed as warmly as you are, how can you even imagine the suffering of a man who can no longer afford warm clothing?" Conscious of nothing but his own thoughts, Ziyun continued to walk along the train platform. When he happened to raise his head and look up, he discovered he was at first class! He scrutinized the car. "First class?" he thought. "Soft sofas, steam pipes so hot that you're uncomfortable in a padded cotton gown and think of nothing but taking off as many clothes as you can. Yet the poor people outside the train don't have any clothes warm enough to keep out the cold."

As he stood there observing the first-class car, someone inside shouted, "This is *first* class! What the hell are you looking at? Third class is up there. You must have walked right past it. Hurry up, and go back where you belong!" Ziyun glared at him for a moment but then had no choice but to lower his head, turn around, and go back from whence he came. After passing a few cars, he came to third class and was just about to get on board when he caught sight of an old man whose beard and hair had both turned gray. Wearing a tattered old padded jacket, and shouldering a battered bamboo trunk, he was doggedly making his way along the platform. His head was almost lost in a cloud of white vapor emanating from his mouth and nostrils as he huffed and puffed under the load.

Ziyun put his own things down on the platform, rushed over to the old fellow, and took the trunk from his shoulder. He smiled at the man and said, "Better let me help you with that, old codger. You look as though you can't manage it all that well. Your hands and feet must be numb with the cold."

Having been relieved of the load, the old man stood still and gave Ziyun the once-over. "You're no youngster, yourself. What do you want to help me for?"

"Don't worry about it, and don't be misled by this beard of mine; it's just that I'm so poor I haven't been able to afford a shave in a while. Actually, I'm not all that old."

"Well, toting that heavy trunk had its advantages, too, you know. Made me sweat, and that made me feel warm. Where you headed anyway?"

"I'd like to go back to Peiping," Ziyun replied. "Trouble is, I don't have enough money for the fare. So right now I'm going to Nanking first and try and borrow money from some friends. I'll take it from there after that."

Ziyun was able to carry his canvas bag with the same arm that pinched his bedding against his side and still manage to lug the old man's trunk along with the free hand. Still chatting, the two men boarded the train. In the third-class coaches at the Shanghai end of the Express, things are different than they are north of the Yangtze. In third class down at the southern end of the route, you'll find quite a few well-dressed people. Hence, when these two old men in threadbare clothes boarded, everyone stared at them. Noticing that there was at least one passenger on every one of the double seats, Ziyun turned to the old fellow and said, "Looks like we'll have to split up if we want to find any place to sit."

As he spoke, he spotted a double seat nearby with only one person on it, a young man in a silk gown. He put down the bamboo trunk and was just about to sit down when the young fellow, with a very serious air, picked his feet off the floor and deliberately swung his legs across the empty seat. "This one's taken," he announced. Ziyun noted that the young fellow's shiny hair had been plastered down with an expensive pomade and his complexion had been worked smooth by a generous application of cold cream. A sharp-looking youngster like that, of course, would never be willing to sit next to a beat-up looking old man.

On the double seat across the aisle, there sat a chubby, middle-aged fellow in a fur coat that had seen better days. "It just doesn't do to go third class," the man mumbled to himself as much as to anyone else. "Freezing day like this, and they don't even give us any steam to keep a body warm. What are they tryin' do, kill us?" "No point in talking to him," Ziyun decided. "With all the complaints he has, there's no way he's going to tolerate a bedraggled-looking fellow like myself for a seat mate."

And so Ziyun continued pacing up and down the aisle with his canvas bag and bedroll. Then he began to think, "These people are something else. Just because they have a bit more money than I do, they think they're too good for me. Well, I bought a ticket just like anyone else, and a ticket entitles me to a seat whether they like it or not." With that last thought in mind, he plopped down heavily beside another passenger and threw his canvas bag and bedroll down by his feet. His seat mate was not, apparently, going to raise any objection. So! He had a seat!

His seat mate, however, took out a handkerchief and, holding it across his mouth and nose, walked off and found himself another seat. Ziyun was still pleased with himself nonetheless, for now he had both spaces on the double seat all to himself. He picked up his canvas bag and bedroll and arranged them on the seat next to him. He gave his shabby coat a couple of tugs in the right places and leaned back quite comfortably against the back of the seat. He fished around in the breast pocket of his coat for a bit before retrieving a cardboard pack of cigarettes.

He got his thumb and first two fingers into the pack and groped around for quite some time before managing to pull out a flattened, bent, and somewhat torn cigarette. He took a couple of red-headed matches out of his pocket, scratched one of them against the seat, and lit up. As he looked out the window and saw poor people in short jackets walking this way and that on the platform, he thought that even though he was only in third class, he was much warmer than they were with their shoulders drawn up high, heads pulled down between them, and hands thrust under the fronts of their jackets for warmth. When he thought back to the miserable existence he had led while bumming around the Shanghai streets, it was more than he could bear.

Now, however, he took comfort in the fact that he was leaving Shanghai, a city that was a wretched place for anyone who had fallen into poverty. *Leaving*—it was a thought that rapidly improved his mood. He couldn't tell, of course, what the future might hold, but at least the interior was more accepting of someone whose clothes were a bit on the ragged side. Once away from Shanghai, at least, he wouldn't be subject to that Shanghai curse, *Zilu!* at every turn.[2] As if intent on fostering Ziyun's leave-taking mood along, the train blew its whistle and began to roll toward the west. As Ziyun watched Shanghai's skyscrapers disappear one by one behind him, it was as though the extravagant and glorious dreamland of the first half of his life was rapidly receding as well. At this juncture, a northwest wind blustered through a crack in the window and struck him like a speeding arrow, its cold penetrating far deeper than would have been the case had he encountered it out in the open.

Off in the distance, the skyscrapers had disappeared entirely by now; and, closer by, the straw shacks along the railroad tracks put up by Northerners who had migrated into greater Shanghai were no longer to be seen either. The mirage that was Shanghai was now truly ended. Outside the window, the only dwellings to be seen now were farmers' homes. Although the snow was falling thick and fast over the countryside, beyond the humble farmhouses, copses of emerald green bamboo appeared. Small ponds of various sizes and shapes could be seen beyond the verdant bamboo. Set off by the reflected light of the snow, the water in them appeared black. Here and there, a white goose or two could be seen swimming in a pond. How enviable! Human beings couldn't compare to those marvelous geese: on a freezing cold day like this, there they were out in great nature swimming back and forth without a care in the world.

And *he* was a man who had once possessed a million-dollar fortune. Gold bars! Women! All vanished into thin air! He once had a home where he could seek refuge, he once

2. *Zilu* (filthy pig) is a term of contempt specific to Shanghai; in Mandarin, it would be pronounced *zhuluo*.

had—"Ticket!" Just as he was getting lost in his own thoughts, the word penetrated his ears. Ziyun looked up and saw the conductor accompanied by two other men in uniform standing by his seat. He reached into his overcoat. But even after he had rummaged through every pocket in his overcoat as well as those in the gown beneath it, he was unable to produce a ticket. Where was it? At first he had gone through his pockets sitting down, but then as he became more excited he stood up; at first he had searched with one hand, but then as he became more desperate he used both.

The conductor fixed him with an angry stare and said, "Well, do you have a ticket, or don't you? I have an entire coach to check. I can't afford to waste my time on one person."

"But I *have* a ticket," insisted Ziyun. "If I didn't, how could I have gotten into the station in the first place?"

"Keep looking for it, then. If you can't find it, then I'll have to fine you according to railroad regulations." As he spoke, he moved away to check on the rest of the passengers. Ziyun was close to panic. He took off his tattered overcoat and went through every nook and cranny of it. "If you buy the ticket on the train," he thought, "then you're fined three times the cost of the original!" He knew the regulation. "I certainly don't have that kind of money. Even if they threaten to throw me off the train at Kunshan, I still can't come up with money like that. Wonder if they might let me go anyway without paying the fine?" Now he was so beside himself with anxiety that he broke into a sweat. That turned out to be a sort of blessing in disguise, for even though there were no steam pipes in the car, his sweat was warm, and he no longer felt cold.

After a frantic search through all his clothing, he sat down quietly and began to think. Where had he lost the ticket? He carefully went over that interval from the time he had his ticket punched to get onto the platform down to the time when he had boarded the train. He remembered quite clearly that during that entire period he had the ticket in his pocket. How could he *possibly* have lost it? Before he had finished thinking it through, the conductor was at his side again. "Found your ticket yet?"

Standing up, Ziyun smiled at him and said, "I honestly *did* buy a ticket, but. . . . "

The conductor bent down, picked up a third-class ticket from the floor next to the foot of the seat, and thrust it toward Ziyun. "This yours?"

"Yes, yes! That's it!"

The conductor gave a hollow laugh and said, "Well, go on and take it, *Zilu!*" He threw the ticket at Ziyun and left. All things considered, Ziyun can be counted as having received a gracious pardon through the kindness of his highness, the conductor. And even though it had cost him being called *Zilu!* yet one last time, he didn't seem to mind in the least.

Once the train was past Kunshan, the snow scenes became ever more magnificent. Everywhere you looked, you saw a vast sheet of such thick and lush white that it was no longer possible to distinguish earth from sky. No one in third class, however, was interested in appreciating the beauties of the snow. They were all trying to keep warm: some curled up into balls and squished themselves up into the corners of their seats; some sat with their feet engaged in furious little dances on the floor; while others walked up and down the aisle as fast as their legs would carry them. When Ziyun stopped sweating, he began to feel cold, too. He picked up his overcoat from the seat next to him and put it back on. Much to his surprise, the sweat that had initially kept him warm now began to cool on his body, and before long it soaked through his undergarments and stuck clammily to his skin.

At just this time, a third-class porter passed by carrying a large pot of hot water. Several passengers grabbed at him as he went and asked, "How is it that there's no steam pipes in here? In this snowstorm, the cold is more than any of us can take."

"Pipes are broken," he replied.

"Well then, they oughta be fixed right away," said another passenger.

"How are we supposed to repair them while the train's in motion?" asked the porter.

"What kind of talk is that!" Ziyun put in his own two cents worth. "Do you mean to say if the steam pipes up in first class went on the blink you wouldn't fix them—motion or no motion?"

"Easy for you to say since you'll never ride first class. Anyhow, I'll bet it's a lot more comfortable here than that little rat's nest you were probably holed up in back in Shanghai!"

As the porter walked away, it was all Ziyun could do to keep himself from running after the man and giving him a couple of good rights. But, dressed as seedily as he was, he wouldn't have had the nerve to call the man to accounts anyway. Nevertheless, the porter's remarks moved another passenger to remark, "In this life, you can *afford* to die, but you can't *afford* to be poor. On a train, you'll always find *most* of the passengers in *third* class, but who are the ones who get all the special treatment? First and second class, that's who. We really ought to let those first-class passengers come down here and get a good taste of what it's like to ride third, if you ask me!"

Listening to this, Hu Ziyun lowered his head and remained silent. He thought back to something that had happened many years ago, to a time when *he* had ridden first class and objected because the heating pipes were *too* hot! "Now here I am in third," he thought, "complaining that there's not enough heat, and the porter acts as though I don't know my place in the world. If you look back on how I acted back then from my present situation, then killing would have been too good for me!"

As he was thinking these thoughts on this short winter's day, the sky had already turned dark, and the ceiling lights came on. Only three of the dim third-class bulbs were working. "A measly three lights to light a coach as big as this one!" he thought. The car was so dark that it brought to mind the third-class car he had visited on that last trip when he had come down from first trying to find some trace of Liu Xichun. Then it had been a little after five in the morning; now it was a little after five in the afternoon. Then the train had been somewhere between Soochow and Kunshan, just as it was now. He remembered how he had suspected Liu Xichun's friends of being in on the scam merely because as a first-class passenger he thought everyone in third was open to suspicion. Could it be that people now suspected him of this or that merely because he was a third-class passenger?

While he was engaged in such musings, the train pulled into Soochow. On this snowy day, very few people got on or off. Although there were some people walking around under the electric lights on the platform, on the whole the place seemed deserted, lacking that busy hubbub one associates with a train station. Even so, the intermittent cries of peddlers rang crisp though the cold air: "New Year's cakes with powdered sugar! Cakes with powdered sugar!"

Ziyun grabbed the sides of the window, pushed his face tight against the cold glass, and looked outside. Among the passengers scattered here and there on the platform was a foreigner with a dog on a leash strolling up and down by the train. There was also a young woman in a fur coat carrying a burgundy overnight case in one hand. Ziyun immediately leaped from his seat and yelled, "Catch her! Hurry up and get her, she's a con artist and a thief!" As he spoke, he ran toward the door of third class.

The porter stopped him. "Hey, hey, what the hell are you doing?"

"Why are you stopping me? She stole $120,000 from me! I've got to catch her! I've *got* to!" He broke away and continued toward the door.

The other passengers all had a good laugh. "No money to buy decent clothes with, but he's got over $100,000 for somebody to make off with? He's gone round the bend for sure!" said one of them in a loud voice. Ignoring all of that, Ziyun rushed down to the platform. He nailed every woman he met with a fierce glare as though he would like either to beat her or to curl back his lips, bare his teeth, and tear the flesh from her body. Trouble was, every one of them had a man following along behind. One young woman in her twenties particularly caught his attention. She had a suitcase in each hand and seemed to be having difficulty carrying them. She put them down and stood still for a while.

Along came a mustached man of about forty or so. He was dressed in a Western suit, parts of which were visible under his fur coat. Definitely a fat cat from the Shanghai Bund, decided Ziyun. The young woman smiled at the man and said, "Excuse me, good sir, could you tell me which way I go to get to the first-class coach for Peiping?"

"What a coincidence, *I'm* going first class to Peiping, too. Let me show you the way," he answered, picking up her suitcases and heading down the platform.

"Hey there," shouted Ziyun at the man. "Aren't you afraid of being taken in? You'd better watch out!" In this old world of ours, however, men who are going to be taken in by pretty young women will—come what may—be taken in by them; and men in pursuit of the fairer sex will expend every last ounce of their energy in pursuing them.

With a blast of its whistle, the train began to roll away, leaving behind on the platform a man who had taken leave of his senses. Large snowflakes danced through the sky. In the wind that roared across the platform, Ziyun continued shouting his warning in the direction of the departing train.

Translator's Afterword

◄ | ►

Redeeming social value—
It has none;
But everybody reads it
And it's fun.

On hearing the name Zhang Henshui, most Chinese will make the immediate association "Mandarin Duck and Butterfly School" or perhaps *"Saturday* School." Both tags referred to popular literature of the kind scorned by serious writers of the period. The "Mandarin Duck and Butterfly School" was so called because some popular writers of the 1910s larded their works with these traditional symbols of pairs of romantic lovers. The *"Saturday* School" was named after the magazine *Saturday (Libai liu),* which appeared on the newsstands every Saturday morning "for one hundred weeks beginning in June 1914, then halted publication, only to be revived for another hundred weeks beginning in March 1921."[1]

"Serious" writers of modern twentieth-century Chinese

literature were, on the whole, better educated than their "popular" counterparts. Had the civil service examination system not been abolished in 1905, most of them would have sat for the exams; if successful, they would have gone on to become high officials charged with the political and moral health of the realm. But the exams were abolished, and then in 1911 the country changed from empire to republic, a political metamorphosis followed in 1919 by the cultural upheaval usually known as the "May Fourth Movement." Sparked by the transfer to Japan of rights in Shandong Province previously held by Germany, a transfer effected at the Versailles Peace Conference that ended World War I, what began as a political student protest soon became a cultural movement that rejected traditional Chinese culture and embraced all that was Westernized and modern.[2] Ironically, the leaders of the May Fourth Movement were the same young people who a century earlier would have preserved for future generations the very culture they were now out to destroy.

As it was, many of these young May Fourth intellectuals turned to the writing of fiction as a tool for modernizing the country, the same fiction that had been so disdained in traditional China as "small talk." In an essay titled "On the Relationship between Fiction and the Government of the People," Liang Qichao (1873–1929) had suggested that intellectuals do precisely that. He faulted traditional fiction for propagating outmoded beliefs that held the country back. Writing in 1902, he suggested that intellectuals take over the production of fiction and use it for the social good:

> Alas! Fiction has entrapped and drowned the masses to such a deplorable extent! The thousands of words of the great sages and philosophers fail to instruct the masses. But one or two books by frivolous scholars and marketplace merchants are more than enough to destroy our entire society. The more fiction is discounted by elegant gentlemen as not

worth mentioning, the more fully it will be controlled by frivolous scholars and marketplace merchants. As the nature and position of fiction in society are comparable to the air and food indispensable to life, frivolous scholars and marketplace merchants in fact possess the power to control the entire nation. Alas! If this situation is allowed to continue, there is no question that the future of our nation is doomed! Therefore, the reformation of the government of the people must begin with a revolution in fiction, and renovation of the people must begin with the renovation of fiction.[3]

Fiction is still disdained, but it is not beyond salvation, if only intellectuals will write it and use it for the social good —exactly what happened almost two decades later when May Fourth intellectuals took up fiction as a tool for exposing the evils of society or propagating the various isms that they espoused. In doing so, of course, they created a gap between *serious* fiction and the *popular* variety.

Several features of the "serious" literature that these young intellectuals wrote are worth noting. It provided food for thought (popular works served up intellectual snacks). It often required interpretation (with popular literature, what you saw is what you got). It was presented in language that called attention to itself and was often Westernized in both content and syntax (popular fiction stuck to more traditional syntax and situations). It demanded the active participation of the reader (in popular works, the reader could remain fairly passive). It emphasized reason (in everything from love stories to military novels, popular literature tended to emphasize emotion). Its authors fancied themselves as intellectual leaders (popular writers were content to be part of the audience to whom they sought to sell their wares). It tended to be global in concept (popular works delighted in close, personal observation of minute events). It sought to instruct (popular literature sought to entertain).

Can one use such a list of general features as a yardstick

to determine whether a particular piece of May Fourth fiction is popular or serious? Probably not—at least if one sees the choice as either-or. The list can be useful, however, if viewed as identifying the opposite ends of a literary continuum along which to situate particular writers. In any event, serious literature demanded serious and well-educated readers, a very small part of the population at best.

Lu Xun (1881–1936) was certainly one of the most serious of the May Fourth writers. And it is likely that his minimally educated mother found her own son's works difficult if not downright incomprehensible. She could, however, understand a popular writer like the author of *Shanghai Express*. Lu Xun even bought Zhang's novels for her. Lu Xun died in 1936, but Zhang was still alive when the new government of the People's Republic of China was making commemorative museums of Lu Xun's ancestral home and the various places he had lived as an adult. In decorating the rooms that his mother had occupied back in Shaoxing and later on in Peking, it was decided that, in order to make the ambience more authentic, the works of Zhang Henshui, whom she so loved to read, should be prominently displayed. Zhang was asked if he could supply the two museums with copies of his novels for this purpose. He refused, saying that he did not want to elevate his own position by association with someone else, especially, one would imagine, a literary giant like Lu Xun.[4]

In the preface to his *Jinfen shijia* (Lovely women of a noble family), Zhang tells us of his own attitude toward writing:

> When I wrote *Jinfen shijia,* I was initially concerned with how to present it so that people would *want* to read this novel of mine. Then I took another step in my thinking and wondered how I ought to write it so that my readers would *benefit* from having read it.

Now, however, I don't see much point in worrying about such things. All that I ask is that my readers pick up this novel of mine and use it to while away the time—perhaps after a hard day's work, or after tea or wine, or when they're feeling bored, or whenever the mood happens to hit them. All that I require of my works is that they do not lure people into the trap of wrongdoing.

I dare not speak of isms or artistic elegance. My fiction will have fulfilled its purpose if I can get people to read it and forget that it is fiction.[5]

Zhang goes on to say that he realizes that there are people who criticize his work as superficial and pointless; he freely admits that this may be true but points out on his own behalf that it is difficult to avoid doing that if you want to write a popular *(tongsu)* work.

When Zhang says he is not very good at isms, one is reminded of one of his contemporaries who was not very good at them either—Lao She (1899–1966). Lao She is usually considered a part of the serious contingent of May Fourth authors. Yet, when, for example, in his short stories he appears in his favorite guise as first-person narrator, he is quite clearly not above his readers, inculcating isms, but one with them, a stance taken by many popular writers of the period. Again, it is a matter of degree. Lao She also wrote fiction that by any measure would fall toward the serious end of the continuum, novels like *Luotuo xiangzi* (Rickshaw) and *Lihun* (Divorce). And occasionally he wrote stories—like "Kaishi daji" (The grand opening)—with little redeeming social value, largely just for the fun of it.

The afterword to *Chunming waishi* (Romance of the imperial city), one of Zhang Henshui's best-known novels, affords us another glimpse of his attitude toward his writing:

Now that I've finished this work, I'll be more than satisfied if my contemporaries read it, like it, and consider me their friend—whether they've ever met me or not. And after I am dead, after the trees have grown tall round my grave, after my skull has turned to mud, if this novel has the good fortune to live on so that readers of *another* generation come to like it and even feel close to its moldering author, then I'll be doubly satisfied. What pleasure can human existence possibly afford greater than this: that I who lived a hundred years earlier will make friends with men and women, both young and old, who live a hundred years later?[6]

Zhang Henshui was easy to read, and his style was never "intimidatingly Western" (Sally Borthwick's apt phrase), as was often the case with the serious novelists of the 1920s and 1930s. Explaining the popularity of *Tixiao yinyuan* (Fate in tears and laughter), his best-known work, Borthwick has pointed out that its "most common vocabulary amounts to only a few hundred characters. That the result is a natural, unfettered if rather matter-of-fact style and not a kind of Basic Chinese is a tribute to the author's mastery of his medium."[7]

In discussing differences between serious and popular literature, I have yet to deal with the question of quality. It is well to remember that writing serious literature did not necessarily a good author make, nor did writing popular literature guarantee a bad one. Zhang Henshui, a quintessentially popular writer, was also a highly talented, articulate novelist who wrote works that were often of greater artistic merit than those of most of the serious writers of the period—*and* more fun to read.

◄ || ►

An actor and a druggist too—
Making money? Hadn't a clue!
The object of much local mirth,
Was "Zhang the Afterbirth"!

Zhang Henshui was born in Jiangxi Province in 1895. Nothing unusual there—but there was. The family came from Qianshan County in Anhui Province. They did not belong in neighboring Jiangxi. Way back when, the Zhang family had been in the noodle business, and they did very well at it. To protect themselves in times of chaos, however, they had taken up the military arts and were quite proficient in that line as well. When Zhang Henshui's grandfather was only fourteen, he became something of a local celebrity owing to his remarkable physical strength. At the time of the Taiping Rebellion (1851–1864), this same grandfather fought so well against the rebels that he attracted the attention of the government forces, and they promptly enlisted him. When it was all over, he ended up in Jiangxi Province, where he rose to the rank of brigade commander (*xiezhen*), a position that at that time combined both military and civil functions. Zhang's father received a quasi-military training, did not sit for the traditional civil service examinations, and ended up serving grandfather as an administrative secretary (*shiye*). And so it was that Zhang Henshui came to be born in the women's apartments of a brigade commander's *yamen* in Jiangxi Province.[8]

The future writer grew rapidly into a chubby, somewhat lethargic lad who liked to sleep so much that his mother was fond of calling him her "moron." Zhang Henshui showed an early and abiding interest in fiction, so much so that his father tagged him "the novel nut." What was truly remarkable about him, however, was his voracious appetite for books, magazines, and newspapers of *all* kinds. In addition to fiction, he loved poetry, memorized a great deal of it, and at an early age began to compose some himself. This was to prove a lifelong love.

Zhang Henshui's early education was a desultory mix of teachers and schools. Then, in 1912, his father died suddenly, leaving behind a large family (Zhang had five brothers and sisters). The grandfather having died in 1901, the family was without income and had no choice but to move back to their ancestral Qianshan in Anhui Province, where the young author-to-be kept on reading fiction and writing poetry.

While on the subject of poetry, it might be well to explain Zhang's pen name—Henshui.[9] Many young men of his generation aspiring to distinguish themselves in literature took literary names. Zhang's pen name calls to mind *chouhua henshui sheng* (he who bemoans the passage of beauty and time), which he may have derived from a line in one of his favorite *ci* (traditional lyrics) by Li Yu (937–978), last ruler of the Southern Tang. A romantic—sometimes considered "decadent"—poet like Li Yu was an entirely appropriate source for the pen name of a writer who would later become famous for his romances.

As the country moved away from the Manchu monarchy that had been established in 1644 and rushed headlong toward the Republican Revolution of 1911, Zhang Henshui began to come in contact with the "new culture," at first through the translations of Lin Shu (1865–1924) that appeared in the *Short Story Monthly*. He "was especially impressed by Western methods of characterization and uses of nature to advance the narrative."[10] As we have seen, the young Zhang was also an avid reader of Chinese literature as well, traditional linked-chapter novels *(zhanghui xiaoshuo)* in particular.[11] As a mature author, his own style of fiction was to reflect this: it would be based on the traditional Chinese novel, influenced by Western literary techniques. His fiction would be new in another sense as well: it would reach his readers through modern newspapers and magazines, a circumstance that made it possible for him to attract a very large reading public, one composed primarily of the urban petty bourgeoisie.

At the end of 1914, a cousin came through Qianshan who was passionately interested in modern plays. He suggested that Henshui go off with him to join a drama group. This traveling troupe was managed by two leading lights in the development of modern Chinese drama, Chen Dabei and Li Junpan. They presented what was known as *wenming xi* (enlightened drama) to distinguish it from traditional local opera and such. Zhang was taken on by the troupe to write advertisements and playbills; when occasion demanded, he also acted. It is likely that his ability to write page-turners through the dramatization of characters and plot had much to do with his early love of the theater.

Zhang's year with the traveling troupe (1914–1915) afforded him a wonderful opportunity to travel and to observe a large cross-section of Chinese society. The downside of all this was that the pay was irregular and ticket sales eventually plummeted so low that he was reduced to sending home for money. Finally, when he could not subsist any longer, he went home. The family was unhappy with him for depleting family funds without having made anything of himself in the process, and the locals thought him so useless that they gave him the nickname, "Afterbirth."

After several months of this depressing life at home, a cousin got into a scrape in Shanghai. Reasoning that Henshui had been to Shanghai and was familiar with things there, the family provided traveling money and sent him to help the cousin out. After Zhang had accomplished this familial duty, he had money left over and decided to take a trip to Suzhou. While there, he ran into Li Junpan, Xu Zhuodai (the well-known writer of popular humorous fiction), Qian Huafo (a well-known opera clown), Huang Qiushi, and others who had organized a new drama group and were performing in Suzhou. They invited Zhang to join them. He stayed with them a few months, but with the same result: he couldn't make enough to live on. Deciding that he'd had enough of the theater, he returned once again to Qianshan.

It was now 1917, and Henshui was twenty-two with still no career in sight. At this juncture, he received a letter from an acquaintance, Hao Gengren, suggesting that Henshui join him in a combination business and travel venture, emulating the protagonist of *Lao Can Youji* (The travels of Lao Can),[12] an itinerant medical man, by traveling around China and buying and selling medicine to cover expenses. The two set out, saw many famous sights, and met many famous people, but did not find the business end of their venture as easy as they anticipated. At one point, broke and exhausted, they came across an old lady in ragged clothing selling tea by the roadside who not only let them have water for free but gave them boiled soybeans to boot. It was a small incident, perhaps, but Zhang Henshui remembered it to the end of his days, often telling the young people in his family, "When people are down on their luck, you'll find that the most generous are often the poorest"—folk wisdom reflected in much of his writing, especially *Shanghai Express*. Eventually, they sold their remaining medicines and went to Shanghai, where Zhang stayed with a relative and did a lot of writing, some of which was even published. But, on returning to Qianshan yet again, after a year and a half he was still fully deserving of the nickname "Afterbirth."

When the modern press arose,
Zhang joined the corps;
Honed his writing skills, then penned
novels galore.

Following the collapse of his dream of seeing the country as a peripatetic druggist, Hao Gengren returned to Wuhu (in Anhui Province) as editor-in-chief of the *Wanjiang ribao* (Wanjiang daily). He soon took a job in Hunan Province, however, and wrote Zhang Henshui suggesting that he replace him at the *Daily*. Zhang agreed, was approved by the management, and took over the editorship of this small paper at a salary of eight yuan per month. For the next three decades, the newspaper business would be an important—if not the most important—part of Zhang's life.[13]

As a small paper, the *Daily* depended largely on outside sources for its news. But, in addition to his editing responsibilities, Zhang was expected to write two daily essays on current affairs. And he decided that he would also write some fiction. He serialized the vernacular novel *Nanguo xiangsi pu* (Southern love) in the literary supplement to the paper; at the same time, he began to serialize two other novels in the Shanghai *Minguo ribao* (Republican daily). At this point Zhang's life had finally taken shape as a journalist and a popular novelist.

The next year, 1919, marked another turning point in Zhang Henshui's life—it was the year he moved to Peking. While in Shanghai on business, Zhang ran into an old friend from Peking who hinted that it was possible to get into Peking University without having to take the regular entrance exams. Zhang returned to Wuhu, resigned his position at the *Daily*, and moved to Peking. Whatever his intentions on setting out for the capital, however, his first priority was to find work. His first job was with the *Shishi xinbao* (China times), contributing four articles per day for a salary of ten yuan. It was a spartan existence, but it was Peking!

It was love at first sight. Everything about the capital intrigued him. Quickly and eagerly, he became well versed in the ways of his adopted city, where he was to live until the outbreak of war with Japan in 1937. This was so much the case that he would later be recalled as being "more Peking than the native Pekingers."[14] It was here in Peking that Zhang would write some of his best-known works, including *Shanghai Express*, which was serialized in the Shanghai magazine *Lüxing zazhi* (Travel magazine) from January to December 1935. He would continue to work as a journalist during this period and also wrote short stories, poetry, and essays.

Zhang Henshui never lost the talent of fashioning his work to his audience. *Shanghai Express* is a case in point. It is, first and foremost, a story.[15] But it is also a travelogue, honed to the particular interests of the readers of a travel magazine. What's it like to take the express from Peking to Shanghai? What's the route? How many stops does it make along the way? Is there time to get out and stretch my legs? What's for sale at the various stations? Can third-class passengers use the dining car? Is it expensive? Does it make sense to go third class if you can afford second? Dare I even consider first class? And so on.

Since relations between the sexes so often provide material for Zhang Henshui's fiction—*Shanghai Express* is again a case in point—one may well wonder what his own love life was like. Like so many others of his generation, he was subjected in late 1913 to an arranged marriage. The young woman, Xu Wenshu, was from an official family that had fallen on hard times. Zhang Henshui left her as soon as possible after the wedding, although he always supported her financially, even bringing Wenshu and his mother to Peking as soon as he was able. In 1937, on the eve of war with Japan, he sent them both back to the countryside, where Wenshu served his mother until her death. Wenshu herself died of a stroke in 1958.

In 1926, he picked out a second wife at a sort of crafts school for girls (*xiyisuo*) in the poor section of Peking.[16] Once the girls in the school reached a marriageable age, their photographs were posted on the wall outside so that men could select a "picture wife." Zhang chose Hu Qiuxia. She was originally from Sichuan, where her father had been an unskilled laborer. She had been lured from her native province and then sold as a maid (*yatou*) to a household in Peking, where she was so maltreated that she finally ran away to the protective atmosphere of the crafts school. She was a simple, honest, straightforward person with little education. She bore Zhang a son and a daughter. After her marriage, she taught herself to read well enough to cope with books and magazines. It is unlikely, however, that she and Zhang had much in common, and, after the establishment of the People's Republic in 1949, she went to live with her son, Xiaoshui, surviving until 1982.

By 1931, Zhang was already famous as the author of the enormously popular romance *Tixiao yinyuan* (Fate in tears and laughter). At the time, his sister happened to be teaching at the Chunming Girls' Middle School. One of her students, Zhou Shuyun, had become a devoted reader of *Tixiao yinyuan*. A meeting was arranged, and before long Miss Zhou became Zhang Henshui's third wife. She was seventeen at the time, he thirty-six. Unlike his first two wives, Shuyun was well educated and highly cultivated: she sang well, knew and liked Peking opera, was a good cook, and knew how to entertain his friends. Zhang and his third wife (he later gave her the name Zhou Nan) had four sons and two daughters,[17] bringing his total number of offspring up to eight. Even in the mid-1930s, when he had only four children, he was hard pressed to support his family. In 1935, when he wrote *Shanghai Express*, he was working on at least half a dozen novels simultaneously.

◀ IV ▶

Spends the War of Resistance,
In the Nationalist camp.
But chats with Premier and Chairman
Lend him a kosher stamp.

On 7 July 1937, Japan launched a full-scale invasion of China, and, in January 1938, Zhang Henshui moved to Chungking, wartime capital of Nationalist China (the wartime capital of Communist China lay to the north in Yenan). In March, he became an executive member of the All China Association of Writers and Artists against the Aggression, which was under the leadership of Lao She. Zhang remained in Chungking throughout the war, doing newspaper work and writing fiction. For the duration of the war, the Nationalists and the Communists were more or less united against a common enemy, but, when the war ended in 1945, a bloody civil war ensued, the Communists emerging victorious in 1949 and establishing the People's Republic of China. As someone who had spent the war years in Chungking rather than Yenan, Zhang was open to suspicion, but two works that he wrote while in Chungking stood him in good stead with the new government.[18]

In 1939, he began to serialize *Bashiyi meng* (Eighty-one dreams) in the *Xinminbao* (New people's paper). The "dreams" were really satires strongly critical of the corruption, greed, and opportunism rampant in wartime Chungking. Despite its title, the book contained *fourteen* dreams, each lying somewhere between an essay and a short story. Throughout the work, Zhang put forward *qijie* (moral integrity) as an antidote to the depravity he saw all around him. In an epilogue, he claimed to have taken the title of the work from a saying popular in Chungking at the time: *Jiujiu bashiyi qiongren meifan chi* (Nine times nine equals eighty one, a poor man's food equals none).[19] Published serially through April 1941 and appearing later as a single volume, *Bashiyi meng* was so popular that it was republished in Yenan. When Zhou Enlai visited Chungking in the fall of 1942 to brief the press on the status of Chungking's Communist allies, he praised the book for the role it had played in exposing the reactionary forces in Chungking. Actually, Zhang's was more of a loyalist critique; nevertheless, the fact that he had written it put him in good standing in Yenan circles.

Then, from February 1940 to December 1941, he serialized *Shuihu xinzhuan* (New water margin), his third historical novel. The traditional Chinese novel from which it was developed, *Shuihu zhuan* (Water margin), was immensely popular. Presented in the traditional linked-chapter format and dating from the early sixteenth century, *Shuihu zhuan* describes a large-scale rebellion that occurred in Shandong Province in the twelfth century. Taking off from the original, Zhang's new version of the story describes how the various heroes of the original novel managed to put aside their differences and join together to resist the barbarian Jurchen invaders from the north. The parallels to the Japanese invasion of 1937 are obvious. The original *Water Margin* was already a favorite of Mao's Zedong's (he saw its protagonist, Song Jiang, as an early and highly admirable peasant).[20] Mao now praised Zhang's *New Water Margin* as well. When the chairman was in Chungking for peace talks with Chiang Kai-shek in 1945, he made it a point to meet with the press and talked one on one with Zhang for almost two hours. After the establishment of the People's Republic, Zhang may have been criticized, but he was never subjected to the harsher treatment meted out to many other May Fourth writers, surely a result of having made friends in high places. Furthermore, he was neither a Communist nor a Nationalist. He felt that a newspaperman had to remain neutral if he hoped to retain any credibility with his readers; if a newspaperman was to represent anyone, he was to represent the people in keeping a check on government.

◀ V ▶

Workers, soldiers, peasants as well?
Too much to learn that's new!
But Zhang can tales of old retell,
Keep travel diaries too.

Zhang was opposed to the civil war that broke out at the end of World War II. Uncharacteristically abandoning the journalist's neutrality, he held that, while it was right for Chinese to resist an invading enemy, there could be no justification for Chinese fighting Chinese. However, when the Communist troops occupied Peking in February 1949 and soldiers were garrisoned at Zhang's home, he accorded them an enthusiastic welcome. Nevertheless, one month later, he lost his job at the *Xinmin bao* (New people's daily), and, over the next three days, the paper published a seven-part article accusing him of being a Nationalist agent. Zhang was deeply hurt, but fortunately no further political action was taken against him. Unfortunately, he suffered a cerebral hemorrhage in June, which left him partially paralyzed and his speech impaired.[21]

In July, the Representative Assembly of All Literary and Artistic Workers was convened in Peking and was addressed by no lesser lights than Mao Zedong, Zhou Enlai, and Zhu De. Zhang had been invited but could not attend because of his failing health. Hearing of his condition, Zhou Enlai sent someone to see him, to bring him the documents of the meeting, and to invite him to serve as an adviser to the Ministry of Culture. He was also invited to join the Writer's Union the same month and promptly did so. All this provided the ailing Zhang with economic security at a time when he was slipping into poverty.

By 1953, Zhang was well enough to complete the draft of a novel based on an old popular legend, *Liang Shanbo and Zhu Yingtai.* In 1954, he was invited to write an account of his impressions of Peking after liberation. The next year he traveled south and kept a diary recording still more postliberation impressions. And he continued writing essays and travel sketches. He also wrote on how to write popular literature and on the history of the traditional *zhanghui* novel. In fact, after 1949, despite his failing health, he wrote some twelve novels, most reinterpretations of traditional tales, before succumbing to another cerebral hemorrhage.

Several years before his death, Zhang noted that someone estimated that, over his creative lifetime, he had written something on the order of thirty million words! In explaining how this was possible, he quoted from the preface to his *Chunming waishi,* in which he had described Chongming Island at the mouth of the Yangtze River. Chongming Island, he noted, is almost fifty miles long and ten miles wide, yet it had not existed in high antiquity. It was brought into being over the centuries by the gradual accumulation of alluvial soil and debris at the mouth of the great Yangtze, eventually resulting in a very large island replete with towns: "'Gradual accumulation' is also the explanation for my having been able to write so many books. Since many of them were first published in newspapers, I was pressed into writing six hundred, seven hundred, or even a thousand words per day.[22] Thus, I developed the habit of writing to a schedule. What's more, I was able to immerse myself in the writing of novels even in the chaotic and noisy environment of an editorial office. And I wrote that way for decades."[23]

Zhang Mingming remembers her father's own self-image as he presented it to the family: "Father often told us that his profession was that of reporter and editor. He wrote novels because, given that profession, he had to supply filler for the papers and also because he needed the money to keep his family in food and clothing. If he *didn't* write novels and were to depend entirely on his newspaper salary, he wouldn't have enough to live on. And so, father used to say, he was an amateur novelist."[24] Despite his humility and practical attitude, he was such a popular writer that, in order to increase their sales, other novelists signed his name to their works. In fact, when the Catholic church in China put together a list of fifteen hundred modern Chinese novels and plays to guide the reading of the faithful, Zhang Henshui himself looked over the listing of his own books and disavowed twenty-three of the fifty-five novels attributed to him.[25] During his lifetime, Zhang Henshui wrote something on the order of between sixty to ninety-one novels.[26]

Notes to the Afterword

1. See Perry Link, *Mandarin Ducks and Butterflies* (Berkeley and Los Angeles: University of California Press, 1981), 7, 253. According to Zhou Shoujuan, one of *Saturday*'s most faithful contributors, the magazine was named after the American *Saturday Evening Post*.

2. In what follows, *May Fourth* is used (admittedly imprecisely) to denote this "new" Chinese culture of the 1920s and 1930s.

3. Liang Qichao, "On the Relationship between Fiction and the Government of the People," trans. Gek Nai Cheng, in *Modern Chinese Literary Thought: Writings on Literature, 1893–1945,* ed. Kirk A. Denton (Stanford, Calif.: Stanford University Press, 1996), 80–81.

4. Yuan Jin, *Xiaoshuo qicai—Zhang Henshui* (Biography of a remarkable novelistic talent—Zhang Henshui) (Taibei: Yeqiang chubanshe, 1992), 212.

5. Zhang Henshui, *Jinfen shijia* (He Fei: Anhui wenyi chubanshe, 1985). *Jinfen shijia* was originally serialized over the six-year period 1926–1932 in the literary supplement to the Peking *Shijie ribao* (World daily news). It was subsequently issued as an independent book (published in Shanghai by Shijie shuju in 1932), the edition for which the preface was written.

6. Yuan, *Xiaoshuo qicai—Zhang Henshui,* 262. *Chunming waishi* was serialized in *Yeguang* (Evening light), the literary supplement to *Shijie wanbao* (World evening news), between 12 April 1924 and 24 January 1929 (Hsiao-wei Wang Rupprecht, *Departure and Return: Chang Henshui and the Chinese Narrative Tradition* [Hong Kong: Joint Publishing Co., 1987], 14).

7. Sally Borthwick, translator's preface in *Chinese Middlebrow Fiction from the Ch'ing and Early Republican Eras,* ed. Liu Ts'un-yan and John Minford (Hong Kong: Chinese University of Hong Kong, 1984), 261. In addition to an informative introduction to Zhang's works, Borthwick also provides good, eminently readable translations of several chapters of *Tixiao yinyuan* (Fate in tears and laughter) (see pp. 264–287).

8. The account in this section is drawn largely from Yuan, *Xiaoshuo qicai—Zhang Henshui,* 5–8, 15–19, 40, 42–45; Rupprecht, *Departure and Return,* 2–6, 9; and Zhang Zhanguo and Wei Shouzhong, *Zhang Henshui yanjiu ziliao* (Materials for the study of Zhang Henshui) (Tianjin: Tianjin renmin chubanshe, 1986), 188–193 (this useful volume contains the only—and rather incomplete—*nianpu* [chronology] of Zhang's life that I have seen [see pp. 188–228]).

9. His given name was Fangsong, although family members preferred to call him Xinyuan, his courtesy name.

10. Rupprecht, *Departure and Return,* 4.

11. The traditional linked-chapter novel linked the beginning of the new chapter with the end of the last, often leaving the hero in a cliff-hanging sit-

uation to be resolved at the beginning of the next chapter. Traditional novels also used epigraphs (sometimes rhymed) suggesting the content of the chapter, a practice that Zhang frequently imitated (*Shanghai Express* is an example).

12. *Lao Can Youji*, by Liu E (1857–1909), is available in an excellent English translation by Harold Shaddick, *The Travels of Lao Ts'an* (Ithaca, N.Y.: Cornell University Press, 1952).

13. The account in this section is drawn largely from Rupprecht, *Departure and Return*, 12–13, 19; Yuan, *Xiaoshuo qicai—Zhang Henshui*, 31–36, 47, 59–60, 73–78; and Zhang and Wei, *Zhang Henshui yanjiu ziliao*, 194, 197, 202.

14. This is reported by Zhang's daughter, Zhang Mingming, in her *Huiyi wode fuqin, Zhang Henshui* (Remembering my father, Zhang Henshui) (Tianjin: Baihua wenyi chubanshe, 1984), 62.

15. An able analysis of the novel may be found in Rey Chow's *Woman and Chinese Modernity* (Minneapolis: University of Minnesota Press, 1991), 76–83.

16. The *xiyisuo* was a social services agency that provided training for the orphaned and homeless; it may even have served as a reform school as well, for the revised American edition of *Mathews' Chinese-English Dictionary* (Cambridge, Mass.: Harvard University Press, 1966) defines it as an "industrial school or reformatory."

17. Zhang Mingming, who later wrote reminiscences of her father's life, was a daughter of this union.

18. The account in this section is drawn largely from Rupprecht, *Departure and Return*, 22; Yuan, *Xiaoshuo qicai—Zhang Henshui*, 184–186, 191–195, 209, 211; Zhang and Wei, *Zhang Henshui yanjiu ziliao*, 211–215, 514; and Zhang Mingming, *Huiyi wode fuqin*, 118–123, 134. I have followed Zhang and Wei for publication dates.

19. The multiplication table was also called the *jiujiu biao* (nine-nine chart); therefore, "nine times nine" means "as big as it gets," and the title could reasonably be transiated as *Dreams of Things as Bad as They Get*.

20. See C. T. Hsia, *The Classic Chinese Novel* (New York: Columbia University Press, 1968), 35, n. 34.

21. The account in this section is drawn largely from Rupprecht, *Departure and Return*, 27–29; Yuan, *Xiaoshuo qicai—Zhang Henshui*, 211; and Zhang and Wei, *Zhang Henshui yanjiu ziliao*, 220–221, 223–225, 228, 231.

22. Lao She remembers Zhang as having told him that he wrote three to four thousand words a day (see Rupprecht, *Departure and Return*, 22–23).

23. Zhang and Wei, *Zhang Henshui yanjiu ziliao*, 98.

24. Zhang Mingming, *Huiyi wode fuqin*, 193.

25. Jos. Schyns et al., *1500 Modern Chinese Novels and Plays* (1948) (reprint, Hong Kong: Long Men Bookstore, 1966), 121, entry 13.

26. Rupprecht, p. 201, n. 1.

A Note on the Translation

So as to give the book a 1930s flavor, throughout the translation of *Shanghai Express* I have used common spellings found on English-language maps of the day for place-names. As most readers will be aware, since 1949 the pinyin spelling of Chinese has been standard in the People's Republic of China. For the convenience of readers familiar with the newer form of romanization, pinyin equivalents are provided for all place names on the map at the front of this book. For the given and family names of the various characters in the novel, however, I have used the pinyin spellings. I have also used the older spellings of place-names in the afterword and pinyin renderings of other words. For the sake of simplicity, I have used *Peiping* throughout, although for a while it was known as *Peking,* as noted in the translation.

I should like to thank Jianmei Piao of the Stanford University Libraries for reading the entire translation and checking it against the Chinese. Jianmei caught some howlers, for which I am very grateful. I should also like to thank Eileen Chow, a doctoral candidate in the Department of Comparative Literature at Stanford, for making a final pass through the entire translation and the afterword as well. I am indebted to Joseph H. Brown for his meticulous care and considerable expertise in editing the entire manuscript. And last, but by no means least, I should like to express my heartfelt gratitude to my editor at the University of Hawai'i Press, Sharon Yamamoto, for both her editorial skills and her unflagging support and enthusiasm for this translation.